And They Danced Under The Bridge

And They Danced
Under The Bridge

John Bentley

Dedicated to my children, Alex and Sophie.

Special thanks go to my dear friend John Broughton for his moral, literary and technical assistance. Without him, *'And they danced under the bridge'* would not have been written.

CHAPTER ONE

THE POPE'S PALACE
AVIGNON
early May, 1348 AD

Elysium angels looked down on the sad, afflicted, desperate town of Avignon. Saints Jean, Laurent, Martial and the rest had witnessed wise counsel bestowed from the commanding towers of the Palace go unheeded. Patience tested, consumed. This was their day of atonement. Nemesis in her moment, the Furies' boundless punishment, Hera's loathing of Zeus: all paled set against the apocalyptic pestilence that had devoured the wicked place.

The people with houses not yet shut up stood in line since dawn before the carved stone portal of the Grand Audience. Restless, they awaited the ceremonial opening of its colossal iron-bound doors. In the beginning, the emergency law resulted in congregations increasing tenfold. But the clergy, too, were smitten without mercy and the churches closed, the Audience and the cathedral being the only seats of worship still ministering. Religion played no great part in the citizens' lives but despair had driven them to clutch at any comfort, to hope against hope, to pray for survival. Old and young, men and women, sound and infirm, babes-in-arms composed the ominous procession. They wore neither festive clothes nor fine sandals. Talk, for what it was worth, was barely audible. They had little to say. The most pernicious event that had or would ever bedevil their lives had rendered them incapable of expressing feelings. Pain in every household, Death personified round every corner, they had become callous, cynical, cold-hearted. They scorned human kindness as a weakness, self-preservation demanded strength not sympathy, but to what end pleasantries? Each knew the lot of the other and the demise of any child ravaged one family as it did a neighbour's.

"You...you're from Rue d'Annanelle..." one thought "...the cart fetched out six last night..." It was not said loud. The man from Annanelle looked at the next. "You be the wine merchant...Place Trois Pilats...your wife and three babes only today..." He, neither, voiced what he knew. Communal grief silenced everyone.

The prime bell tolled and they filed with leaden, nervous step into the building constructed of immense, fawn-coloured, sandstone blocks. Draughts of cool air refreshed them, a relief from the balmy, oppressive heat of the streets. From front to rear the floor was paved with smooth, granite slabs. They marvelled at frescoed walls one verge thick. These were interrupted by tall, narrow windows admitting sunlight into the otherwise gloomy hall. A soaring, vaulted, wooden ceiling decorated with fine, vibrantly coloured carvings shrouded the cavernous space above the nave. From the entrance Marius' eye was drawn to the east stone altar draped with pure damask. He admired the heavy brass candlesticks either side of a crucifix, a simplicity that belittled a mystical symbolism so powerful that it turned heads. Peoples' jaws dropped in disbelief at such opulence, the like of which was foreign to their ungodly lives. They looked heavenward where, suspended on a chain attached to a roof member, a pierced brass censer swayed to and fro above the assemblage: the pendulum of a clock of destiny counting down the days. No choice but to inhale the cloying, pungent perfume, tart and acrid to some, ambrosial and intoxicating to others. For many, this was their first experience of attending church, the discovery of an unknown world of the dark, the sensuous, the surreal; of men in strange robes speaking in unfathomable tongues. Moved – awed, but through fear and desperation - they turned to the

Lord. They believed on a whim, yearning clarity for this capricious sphere that was their profound wilderness. As the nights grew darker, an intrinsic optimism for a lighter day rose, but it was hidden under the bushel of seeds they had planted. There was no solace, no abatement. Without salve or physic for cure, their vital flames extinguished and putrefying around them, they were drowning in hellish burial pits like unblessed food for worms.

Marius Nerval ushered his wife, Dominique and their young son Fabien, asleep in her arms, to find a vacant place. One of the rough wooden benches lined in rows towards the back of the Audience served. More of their neighbours appeared. The cushioned pews to the front were reserved for the great and good. But, soon, all the seats were taken.

A tall, blond-haired, invincible man of some twenty-four summers, Marius worked hard to provide for his wife and child. There was honest employ unloading trading boats and in the warehouses of the port downstream of the Dominique gate and he joked his wife was responsible for its name. Wages could be supplemented mixing mortar and carting stone blocks for the masons building the new town walls. Marius and his young family moved south to Avignon from Carpentras when the grape harvest failed there and pickers on the vineyards were not required. His understanding of the reasons for his own father leaving the native Limoges was not clear. Whenever the boy had asked the question there was avoidance or, at most, a vague allusion to a feud. He knew no more than this. Both father and mother passed on before he had further explanation. Dominique inched closer to her husband, heedful of the stranger sitting on their other side. He sensed her unease and, putting an arm around her shoulder, said, reassuringly,

"No need to fear him, woman, if he was infected he would be dead like the rest."

Then he realised,

"I know him though, he works at the port" and he leaned across,

"Hail, Charles! How are you?"

The man looked up but they did not shake hands as was the custom. The reply came,

"Marius, I am sick of heart, if not yet of body, but it won't be thus much longer…"

"How do your wife…and daughter?"

"Taken! Taken…both…these seven days. I would be with them…why…why should *I* be spared!"

Marius offered no answer. The man continued,

"A priest came to the house but…no use to man nor beast…priests, witches, devils, conjurors…the same! All useless! My family were one day healthy, the next…taken! The watchman said I could wash off the cross from my door now they be gone and it be after these fourteen days with no marks on me…but why not me! Why!"

The man shed tears of misery. The plague was indiscriminate: it purged the good, it slaughtered the bad. Nobody was immune.

Still the censer swung, giving forth its bitter scent. A man on the bench behind touched Marius' shoulder, who turned round,

"Guy! The carter! My neighbour, what is it has you come here? Tell."

"Nothing to lose, Marius…cannot make anything worse…"

"You mean…?"

"Aye! All my household…wife, children, father, e'en the lodger…but me left breathing. Used my own cart to carry bodies to churchyard," The wretched man paused to collect his thoughts, 'it's been a devil of a time, Marius…and the burier made off with the bedding to fire…didn't have windings for 'em and…" It was too painful for the man to continue. He bowed his head in tortured silence.

Marius looked further along the row. There was his friend, Luc, with wife, Marianne; Lacroix and Breton, fellow workers on the New Palace; Marcel the innkeeper; Martin the farrier. So many ordinary folk assembled through a shared calamity. In the front pews he saw the Magistrate and his runner boy. A strong man, broad of shoulder and girth, sitting back straight with chin thrust forward, determined to be recognised for the greatness of his title. He wore a green velour cap, his badge of office. It was customary when entering hallowed premises for men to doff their headwear, the women remove scarves, but he, the Magistrate, kept on his cap until the last moment before the minister's appearance. He believed only the Holy Father exercised more power. Occupying a position of prominence, this was the only ranked personage Marius registered apart from two wool merchants, the Pagnol brothers. They ran a lucrative business, since Avignon had become a significant river trading port. They resided in a large dwelling in the town, if Marius recalled correctly.

"I know none of these people", Dominique whispered to her husband, so as not to wake the child who still slept. "Maybe not", Marius answered, "but, rest assured, they will know you. The women gossip and the men listen. I've a name since I work within the palace, then on the walls and at the port it's hard not to be known". She was not sure whether Marius was boasting but she accepted his word and regained her quiet, as was a wife's obligation.

Some moments passed while they watched the congregation grow when Marius nudged his wife.

"Dominique... over there... in the corner... well, I'll be... that fellow, head buried into his coat collar, trying his best not to be spotted..."

She strained her eyes then spoke up,

"Yes! How could I not know that one! Carel Rostand! *He* is the last man I'd have thought to find in here... he begs at the Saint-Roch gate, doesn't he?" Dominique was adept at assessing personalities but Marius just scoffed,

"He does that! And the Magnanen and the La Ligne gates and... and all the others! He scrounges like another man does an honourable job! The sergeant moves him on so he waits a half hour before choosing his next corner to start again. He thinks nobody notices him in that dark spot, well I do, for one! What's he doing, then?"

"Marius, the same as us all, praying for a blessing from the good Lord above, a light to guide us out of this misery, safety and healing for our children. He's here as we are."

"Umm! You could be right", Marius said, "but I don't trust *him*, never have done."

Yet deeper, in a shadowy recess of the Audience, sat a man Marius could not identify. A figure whose keen regard locked on them through the service, he made mental notes, squinting in the gloom. When someone blocked his line of sight he moved his head sharply so as to not lose them. His attire was more tasteful and less threadbare than the rest. He remained unnoticed, so carefully had he chosen his vantage point. Marius would later know this mysterious character as one of Clément's spies: the Pontiff's eyes and ears to inform him of the coming and going of the townsfolk he viewed with persistent distrust.

As the cantors in the choir rose and their incantations grew louder, the front pews stood, the benches copied. Their chants soared to meet the void above, the censer exuded yet stranger scents - camphor, sandalwood, honeysuckle and lavender – while all but obscuring the altar, screen and vestry. A bell tolled, slow, hard, menacing, then faster and more strident. All eyes strained through the half-light, gazes fixed on the door. The cacophony of noise ceased, then a shocking silence. Clément's silhouette appeared, at first featureless in the doorway. Would deliverance enter by this door they had not realised was open to them? The congregation held its breath.

CHAPTER TWO

LIMOGES
1304 AD

Pierre Roger and Edmond were inseparable, childhood friends. With parentages of contrasting wealth and standing, they were equal in their puerile games, pranks and mischief. They stole apples from orchards, played hide and seek, dared each other for bold but harmless challenges, and teased the girls. They shared a passion for hunting and fishing, taking any opportunity to accompany adults on their trips, observing and learning the skills to become proficient in the sport. Years before their less adventurous peers, Edmond and Pierre Roger were adept at setting rabbit traps and following wild boar tracks. The former wore a woollen tunic, coarse to the skin and tied at the waist with a cord, while the latter's costume was worsted, finer and of superior quality. He had a leather belt with brass buckle.

Pierre Roger's father was a lord, enjoying a modest estate in the woodland north of Limoges. His hunting parties often took refreshment in the tavern kept by Edmond's family. While the innkeeper's ambitions for his son were little greater than to take over running the inn, the lord wished his offspring to enter the priesthood. He held influence over the monks of the Bénédictine abbey Saint Martial of Limoges, due to financial donations, so the boy was reserved a place as a scholar.

"I dare you to bring down an egg from the nest atop that tree, and unbroken," Edmond said to his friend.

"Are you serious?" Pierre Roger's expression darkened. The oak was fifteen verges high and while its lower boughs were sturdy, the upper branches were flimsy and liable to snap under any weight.

"Sure I'm serious! A dare's a dare, you should know that! So, are you a coward? It's up to you."

"Have I ever refused a challenge... have I?"

"You have not, that's true, not yet anyway! This is a *real* challenge for you, though." And Edmond's voice trailed off as he waited for a decision, aware that one game above all others frightened his friend, climbing. He was prone to severe vertigo.

"I accept, then!" Pierre Roger blurted, trying hard to sound confident.

"And you'll not back down? No changing your mind... "

"I said, I will! But I have to... "

"Hey!' Edmond interrupted, 'no excuses! You'll do it this instant!"

His heart sank as his gaze moved up to the bird's-nest, but a speck in the heavens. Edmond was right, a mother bird's head protruded out of the nest, so she would be hatching eggs.

"Go on! What are you waiting for?" Edmond asked, in a sardonic tone. Their bond was strong but as they grew, so did a distinct element of rivalry.

Pierre Roger stood at the base of the tree and tightened the cord around his waist. He reached tentatively for the first branch, then the next. After four verges he hesitated. Panic surged through his veins. *'Will I get back down safely? The vertigo will spin my head, I know, and my legs will turn numb and leaden. I won't look down! Anything but that! But will I lose control of my arms... until I get to the ground again... then I will breathe and my mind will clear... and... '*

The climb took time until he was within touching distance of the nest. Holding on tight with one hand, he removed an egg with the other. The mother flew away noisily with fright, feathers fluttering through the air. He held the egg gently between his lips and made his descent, slowly.

Back on terra firma he swallowed hard then handed his trophy to Edmond, who was amazed but disappointed by the event.

"Well done! I doubted you'd do *that* dare."

"You should not underestimate me, my friend." Pierre Roger retorted, satisfied with his achievement, "but now I must return to the house, father has chores for me. Meet you here tomorrow? I've got a good challenge in mind for you!"

"Yes, till then." Walking back down the track to the tavern, Edmond was preoccupied, wondering what awaited him.

Early the next day, the boys met as arranged.

"Hey, Edmond!" the other greeted, slapping him on his shoulder, "are you ready?"

Edmond feigned incomprehension. "For what?"

"Stupid! Your dare! It's your turn today and I've been thinking on it for a while and… but no, follow me." And he led Edmond towards the river. They came to a still ox-bow lake, familiar through their fishing of pike and perch, but Pierre Roger walked them on further downstream. Round a bend and enormous weeping willows protected both banks where the channel narrowed and descended to surge violently over a span of boulders worn to a silken sheen. Between the run and the cascade a maelstrom of white water relentlessly beat the stones.

Pierre Roger halted to watch the normally ruddy complexion of his friend turn sombre. There was no need to explain the dare. Edmond had a deep-rooted fear of water. Fishing from the safety of the bank did not pose a problem, but immersed in it was another matter. He could not swim.

"Your dare…" and the challenger paused, taking evident pleasure in the boy's increasing unease, "is to cross the river there and back. You must use the rocks. So, do you accept?"

Edmond, silent, mortified, stared at the rapids but he had no choice. To refuse was cowardice, and his disgraced name would be around the town. He could not live with the shame.

"I'll do it!" Edmond replied without hesitation. He undid his sandals, shed his robe and, naked, placed a first step into the raging torrent. The vicious, icy cataracts lashed his bare limbs and he struggled to retain balance. His hands could not grip the velvet-smooth boulders but, bent double, he lurched from one stone to another. Finally, and exhausted, he reached the far bank, gulping air and shaking his arms in an attempt to restore lost circulation the cold had induced.

Looking back to Pierre Roger, he felt a burst of pride for what he had achieved. The return crossing would be easier and, although he came close again to losing his footing, he had overcome the ordeal. The boys had met each other's spiteful trials and both were content. But, as time passed, their wrangles progressed to quarrels, with a jealousy fired by anger.

LIMOGES
1305 AD

On his fourteenth birthday, Pierre Roger entered the Bénédictine abbey Saint Martial, as was planned. His father, the lord, had not given his son any say: he would be trained in Latin, mathematics and science, all disciplines essential to the priesthood. He would board with the monks, returning home infrequently. Learning how to manage a tavern occupied Edmond and so they drifted apart, which rendered a message he received all the more surprising.

"I seek one Edmond Nerval," announced the messenger, knocking on the hostelry door.

"That is I. Show then," Edmond instructed.

"Sire, there is no scroll. Pierre Roger told me to listen closely so I can now relate the word to you."

"That is unusual, but tell me what the... the novice wants of me."

"Pierre Roger will be calling on the lord, his father, fourteen days hence. He requests you join him then for hunting. The last part is...umm...ah, yes, he said it would be for 'old time's sake, and I must take your answer back with me."

"And so you will, fellow, but first may we offer you ale, bread and cheese? You will have a hunger after your journey."

"That, sire, I will not refuse, my thanks."

While the messenger supped and ate, Edmond paced to and fro, uncertain of his friend's motives. There had been no contact for a year and more but, he supposed, it could do no harm. He leaned over the runner.

"On your return, tell him I look forward to renewing our friendship. I will have knives honed and arrows feathered. Can you remember that?"

Surely, sire. Now I must depart."

The day for their reunion dawned fine with clear blue skies, a gentle breeze and moderately warm. Ideal conditions for hunting. Edmond walked towards the tree where they always met, the same his friend had climbed for a dare and Pierre Roger was already waiting. They embraced but exchanged few pleasantries. Edmond handed over a quiver filled with arrows, a longbow and a short sword in its scabbard. Along a familiar trail he led the way deep into the forest where herds of wild boar rutted. As they moved furtively in an awkward silence the creatures, amorously occupied would be least aware of their presence. Shortly, they reached the spot.

"Get down!" Edmond hissed "if they hear or scent us they'll be off. Haven't those monks taught you common sense, if nothing else!"

"There's no call to speak thus, and don't *ever* dishonour the Brothers..."

Before them in a clearing a single family of boar grazed on berries and leaves. A hog, its sow and four piglets, were oblivious to their pending doom. Both men advanced, then crouched, concealed by thick undergrowth.

"I'll take the boar first" Pierre Roger pronounced under his breath.

"No! We need the sow...fatter...she'll carve into a better joint...sells for more," insisted Edmond, trying to give orders while keeping his voice low. Yet, his friend pushed him aside in defiance and drew an arrow from his quiver. Slipping the bowstring into the arrow's notch, he rose and took aim.

"Did you hear me? I said go for the sow...we'll deal with the boar after..."

But, at this point, the hunt was lost. Their voices had startled the beasts that scattered in all directions, escaping, letting out horrendous squeals.

"A pox on you! Damn it! Look what you've done? I don't know what Jesus has been telling you at yonder abbey but it's not how to use your brain!" Edmond shouted.

"What are you saying? I receive wisdom and blessings from Our Lord! I pray, I give thanks, I...but *you*, cur, blaspheme! You take His name in vain! May He punish you and cast you into the bowels of Hell! And be sure, you *will* answer to Him come the Day of Retribution! May He..." Edmond could stand no more of this hostile tirade. He flung down his bow and quiver. In an instant, all became a red mist. A blur of anger, hatred, offence, enmity, a clarion call compelled him to strike Pierre Roger full in the face with clenched fists. He met with no resistance and the man slumped to the ground. *Just the start*, Edmond decided as he rained blow after blow. Not content with the damage thus far inflicted, he kicked and stamped on the man's chest.' *Let that be a lesson for you and your pious kind! You've had it coming to you!'* His countenance was no longer human but hideously swollen, contorted, ruined, bleeding profusely. Edmond finally ceased the attack on the motionless body, gathered himself and calmly left the clearing.

A group of Bénédictine monks, sent out to search for Pierre Roger, chanced upon their apprentice, barely alive, days later. He was nursed back to health by their kind attention. The body was scarred and would heal, his soul was indelibly embittered.

Edmond warmed with wicked satisfaction. '*So, it's done and finished. I'll hear no more of it.*' He was, though, deluded in his assessment of the affair. He left confident he had meted out the punishment Pierre Roger merited: he had settled a score for the pomposity and jibes. What he ignored was the power of recrimination. Whether in his own lifetime or that of his offspring, vengeance would come.

CHAPTER THREE

AVIGNON
1347 AD

Pope Clément passed without a sound along the corridors joining his private rooms to the outside world. Tightening the cord around the waist of a monk's brown habit and, ensuring the hood fully covered his face, he left to greet the morning spring sunlight. The disguise served him well. It was not unusual to see all manner of pilgrims and worshippers dressed in a similar fashion, according to their orders.

Past the papal cathedral lay the wooded Rocher des Doms area marking the northern edge of Avignon. Tall chestnut and strong cork oak trees, planted many centuries before by Roman settlers, protected the town from the destructive mistral wind. *Avenie ventosa, sine vento venenosa, cumvento fastidiosa* – Windy Avignon, pest-ridden when there is no wind, wind-pestered when there is. Folklore tells the mistral has the force to send a man to madness.

Sitting on a fallen bough, alone, profound meditation consumed Clément. '*Deo gratias* – Thanks be to God. *The world is at peace, our cup overflows with His bounty, we are blessed, but we are not worthy – Non sumus digni. The See of Rome lives in fair Avignon and we want for nothing. Deo gratias. I am still in my middle age and I trust my passion and my faith to be resolute, to answer the Lord's bidding, come what may. To study His writing and feel His love flow through my body is the greatest of His gifts. I live a frugal life and I would give rather than receive, but I am not perfect, no mortal is so. It is Thy command to drive out evil thoughts and bear no malice. We must love out neighbour. Lord, I conduct myself and my papacy with humility.'* Clément's thoughts were delusional. His life-style was lavish, his heart consumed by a burning desire for revenge.

Approaching voices interrupted his veneration, two men taking the air. As they neared, he recognised them as priests from the Saint Denis church. They walked by, nodding in taciturn acknowledgment. On several occasions past there had been reason to dispense discipline on the same two for unacceptable behaviour while serving the Lord. *'My excursions, when time permits, inform us on the peoples' behaviour. My colleague, the Magistrate, is efficient in this regard, but my clerics require a particular surveillance. Their comportment needs to be impeccable. They know the standards I demand. But, I set store on Julien, my Cardinal Priest, to report peccadillos among my Curia. Ah...now I remember, those two men were suspected of entertaining whores! They convinced me, however, it was false accusation. I issued only a warning. Further instances and I would be compelled to take more serious action.'* He theorised, sermon-like but quietly, within his thoughts.

'What can you preach to us? If on humility, you yourselves are the proudest of the world, puffed up, pompous and sumptuous in luxuries. If on poverty, you are so covetous that all the benefices of the world are not enough for you. If on charity... but... we will be silent, for only God knows what each man does and how many satisfy lust!' Clément was devout, yet immoderate. The priests carried on their way. Under this masquerade the Pope began a regular early morning walk. His papal duty was to understand, sympathise, counsel, punish, and praise the common folk constituting his flock - and this, whether within the walls surrounding his Avignon see or beyond, in his wider Church. *'I will know them by their toil. I will overhear their gossip and feel their concerns for it is now infrequent they number my congregation. I spread the Word through my personal audiences but this is not sufficient. I must appreciate their lot and admire their efforts, for they are hard-working and honest.'*

He faced the direction of his palace to intone Timothy 2:15. '*Do your best to present yourself to God as one approved, a worker who has no need to be ashamed.*'

Aromatic scents from purple lavender and pale blue rosemary pervaded the weather. Flowering jacanda and magnolia swayed gently, lending colour to the dense shrubbery bordering the woodland.

'*You are indeed beautiful, my Avignon. Laudate Dominum* – Praise the Lord. *I will go through the Roch gate to watch the traders on Saint Bénézet bridge that marries our fair abode with the Kingdom of France. Ah...I see them, and at such an hour...carts laden with sacks of flour, salted sides of beef, vegetables and fruit, logs and vats of wine. What would we become without Bénézet's crossing?*'

Regaining the town and turning into Rue Rempart du Rhône, he peered from under the cowl... '*the baker's shop...shutters already open...such variety of breads... Rue Crillon...the smithy, forge white hot...sparks flying from under his hammer...he has much metal to temper...hunting swords and snares, woodchoppers' axes, steel hoops for the cooper...we are in your debt. Every blow on your anvil is a prayer.* Rue Rempart de l'Oulle... *the Exchange...money dealers and tax collectors...all making a healthy profit, I'll wager...we give thanks for their offices.*'

A young woman, of no more than twenty-three summers, dressed in a woad-blue tunic and woollen shawl, came in his direction. Alice did not realise the identity of the monk ahead and they passed without a word. Clément knew her, though, as she did him. Rue Saint Dominique...'*I have seen this beggar many times...such a sad man in tatters and unwashed...pity him...*' He dropped a livre coin into the mendicant's bowl. 'Take this, my son and be part of our family. Commit to the Lord whatever you do and your plans will succeed.' Carel Rostand mumbled words of thanks. Saint Charles gate... the docks where vast warehouses lined the banks of the river. Square-rigged barges thirty verges long kept the middle channels to catch favourable winds. Fifteen, even twenty, horses moving along the towpath hauled boats joined in trains. Farther downstream, six moored boats, one lashed alongside the next, provided accommodation for those of greater means wishing to escape the warm stench of the *intra muros.* Such condition was rampant during the hot summer months. Clément entered a tavern, placed money on the counter and muttered an order for ale. He sat in a niche of the gloomy place, head always bowed and covered. Tobacco and other herbal fumes floated in dense clouds, rendering the clientele but a dim ghostly outline.

'...I hear strange voices...I would believe them Pentecostal brothers speaking in tongues, but...no, they make vulgar noises like those from the north provinces...I know of a fishmonger who carries cod...does a good business and I've heard say the smell on his person is as putrid as his merchandise...I am sure, there are fellows singing in a tone even of Rome and beyond! Some quarrel in accents of Arab tribes but all bring trade and wealth, so they are welcome here. Laudate Dominum.'

He drained the tankard, rose and made for the door, gesturing a valediction politely to those men, occupied with drinking, back-slapping and cursing, who noticed his presence. Outside, fresh but malodorous air was in stark contrast with that of the tavern. At the archway he paused before a wooden hut attached to one of the warehouses. The sign above the door announced 'Douanes' – 'Customs'. Within, the Magistrate assiduously pored over lists of goods in and out, one of his sundry functions being the collection of taxes due to the lord of Avignon, Charles II of Naples. '*The Magistrate labours for our communal benefit. I am truly fortunate to number him among my servants and friends.*' Returning to the Rocher des Doms he passed street vendors, wine merchants, leather beaters, potters, soothsayers, flower sellers, fruiterers, drinking houses, cheesemakers, lenders, physics, jugglers – merchants and professions of every description, all prospering and profiting adequately. '*You, the common inhabitants and passers-by, may not be overly rich, but you are content and that is a gift from on high. You are clothed as should be: capes to protect from the rain, tunics woollen and, for some, worsted. Your children smile, you assist the crippled elderly* to cross the street. *I pray the Spirit of the Lord enters your lives, as hard work merits.*'

Clément returned to his chambers as he had departed, in secret. The monk's habit replaced by everyday white cassock, he summoned a prelate to bring wine.

"See I am not disturbed this morning. I shall be in prayer" he instructed.

"Of course, Holiness" the prelate understood and retreated.

He must kneel before the Sacrament and thank the Lord for the ordinary, for the normal, the small discounted joys from which true happiness flows. His flock might take them for granted but he, the Pope, may not. On behalf of the dwellers of Avignon, his intercession sought to ensure continued favour from the Almighty. Enveloped in deep thoughts, but not dark, rather hopeful, confident, grateful, pride welled in his heart. Five years had elapsed since the crowning as Pope, a time he viewed with satisfaction. The new palace and chapel buildings progressed well, congregations had increased to a degree. Paying his clergy their *don gratuit* salary posed no difficulty since finances were plenteous and as regarded money he admitted to being 'a sinner among sinners.' He commissioned artists to paint hunting and fishing scenes – recalling childhood memories – on the chapel walls, and fabulous tapestries adorned the cold stone expanses. He recruited the best musicians from Northern France. Performing for Clément was an enviable honour. He often recited from Psalms '*My cup overflows*", *and so it is, O Lord, praise be! Thy largesse is boundless and we are not worthy. Throughout my life I have been blessed with Thy Grace and without Thy Bounty I am nought. Yet, there are many of this earth who have enabled my acquisitions and high repute, if so they be. I owe much to many and I am minded to reward them. Thy gifts, Holy Father, we cannot measure but I would place a consideration on those persons, abbeys and churches that have assisted me, without whom my present glory... no! Forgive me, Father! I mean to say 'Thy Glory'. My life calling is to celebrate Thy name. The good people have, this day, moved me to give thanks, to re-*

spect the value of the simple and virtuous. Thus, I will make donations from my own coffers. But, to what amount? I understand not the mystery of money, I have not had need to deal with such lesser matters.'

"Guard! Enter!"

"Holiness?"

"Send for Julien, tell him to come within the hour."

Julien, Cardinal Priest in the Curia, was almoner among other duties, distributing charity on the Pope's behalf.

"Julien, I would ask your... umm... advice."

"Of course, if it be within my knowledge."

"How much does a lord, whosoever, receive as an annual income?"

"A strange question, for certain... " and he paused before answering, "I would say five hundred gold écus, or thereabouts."

"Good. That is all, Julien."

The priest left and Clément sat at his desk and arranged inkwell and fine calfskin parchment scrolls. Dipping pen into ink he began the first missive, concentrating on the past that had affected the present:

"***CHAISE-DEI, in oblationem venerabili de abbatia*** – *To the Abbot of Chaise-Dieu abbey* – *DONUM FACIMUS 1000 écus* – *our gift* – *IN GRATIAS CANTANTES* – *with gratitude* – *PRUDENTER UTI PECUNIA* – *use this money wisely*"

'*The monks of Chaise-Dieu took me in, anno Domini 1301, as a mere boy. It was in that House of God I first knew the wonder of the Lord. I learned the Scriptures. I was shown abstinence and the power of prayer. There, my vocation to spread the Word began.*'

He trimmed the quill anew to a fine point and, taking a fresh vellum sheet, scribed similar messages.

"***TO THE COLLEGE OF SORBONNE, PARIS*** – *DONUM FACIMUS 1000 écus* – *our gift*"

'*I ministered as Prior at this place, anno Domini 1307. Their library is the envy of the world and only mine now surpasses it. I became a true scholar there, with their guidance and patience. As provisor they consulted me on ecclesiastic and theological affairs. With my doctorate I spent rewarding time teaching the Bible and debating its verses.*'

"**TO THE PRIORY OF SAINT BAUDIL** – *DONUM FACIMUS 500 écus*"

'*My master, Pope John XX11 summoned me to be Prior. The place was close to Chaise-Dieu, it was anno Domini 1324. Such pleasant, honest souls. Their kindness I shall not forget.*'

"**TO THE ABBOT OF FECAMP** – *DONUM FACIMUS 500 écus*"

'*Anno Domini 1326. As Abbot of this fine abbey my mind was opened to Thy truth, O Lord. The Bénédictines also distil a magnificent liqueur, and I confess to partaking, but in moderation.*'

"**AD EPISCOPUS ATREBAS** – *To the Bishop of Arras* – *DONUM FACIMUS 500 écus*"

'*I served as Bishop and royal councillor. A challenging time if I recall correctly. I charged Edward, king of England, to pay homage to our Philip, anno Domini 1328. I received no reply and returned to our country, my mission unaccomplished.*'

"**AD ARCHIEPISCOPUM SENONENSEM** –*To the Archbishop of Sens* – *DONUM FACIMUS 500 écus*"

'*This is a peaceful place and though my time, anno Domini 1329, was short, I prospered from their generous devotion.*'

"**ITAQUE DE ARCHIEPISCOPO ROEN** – *To the Archbishop of Rouen* – *DONUM FACIMUS* – *1000 écus*"

'*Anno Domini 1330. I am thankful to them all in this city. The Word has entered their hearts and homes. Bless them.*'

ANNO DOMINI 1342. '*I am crowned Most Holy Pope Clément V1 with no preliminary politicking, only divine inspiration. Praise be to Heaven.*'

To each scroll was sewn a pendent tag bearing the impression in wax of his signet ring. They were signed "Clémentine V1. Et Sigillum Suum" – "Pope Clément V1 and His Seal". Without this authentication the gift could not be accepted. '*Dear Lord, I perform my labours with love and compassion, and the all-seeing God knows my reasons for making gifts to the deserving. Even so, I implore Thy succour for there is evil within me, a bitterness and resentment I cannot lose. Jesus teaches*

*an unforgiving heart will consume the spirit in the end, and I believe.
Vengeance is the Lord's and He will repay. So, I must leave it to His wrath
and not be overcome by evil, but good. That is the way, I know. Dear Lord,
extinguish the burning in my being. Deo gratias.'*

Papal envoys delivered the vellum letters, each accompanied by a
leather pouch containing his benefit.

CHAPTER FOUR

CARPENTRAS, Vaucluse Department
1347 AD

Marius tugged the hood of his tunic to shield his face from the Mistral wind. Its name meant 'masterly' in Old Occitan dialect, and that December morning, he appreciated why - its bitter wet blast was strong enough to cow the hardiest soul. The cold robbed the day of the dawn chorus, leaching any hint of sonorous brightness from the grey, icy day. There was little light along the steep, rough cart track and he took care not to turn his ankle in the deep ruts. The path skirted the estates of the Cabasse Fils vineyard, a vast 100 arpents of fertile land. The walk of two leagues would have been shorter had he cut straight through the myriad rows of vines but that route was forbidden by the owners. Prejudice led them to believe a catastrophic blight the previous season was brought about by trespassers, and they suspected competitors. Easier to blame them than face reality, the grape destruction due to a venomous, sparkling rain alongside the pestilent, yellow, sap-sucking *phylloxera* aphid.

At the brow of the track, Marius paused to catch his breath. Taking in the endless view of row upon row of trellised vines trained on stakes to offer protection from the wind. This method also provided a leaf canopy to moderate the burning Provencal sun. The walled Cabasse chateau stood proud in the distance. His pace quickened down towards the winery, the heart of wine production housing enormous vats, racks and presses. The foreman was a thick-set, ignorant Cabasse employee charged with hiring, firing and paying labourers on the ter-roir. He performed his duties to the letter. A prominently sited cabin at the gateway gave him authority over whosoever entered or left. As he drew closer, Marius saw there were three men already standing in line in front of the hut. He took his place behind them, waiting for the shutters to open and others soon joined the queue. Work was mainly outside in this season, checking the stakes were secure and the trel-lis ropes properly attached. The fortunate few were assigned indoors, sheltered from the elements at the cooper's orders, banding, rolling and stacking barrels.

'*I pray my luck be in today! God knows we need the money!*' at which point, the foreman's voice boomed –

"Name?"

The man at the head of the queue shuffled forward.

"Renier" he replied. Some moments passed as the official ran a finger over his list.

"In the winery. Go! Three days' work."

"Thank you kindly, sir." The man gave a broad smile at being chosen.

"Next?"

"Gilles." A pause.

"Inside. Go! Two days with the cooper. Next?"

"Bliaud." Another pause.

"Let me see...ah, yes, on the north field. Get orders from the over-seer first." It came to Marius' turn.

"Name?"

"Nerval" he answered with hesitation.

"Nerval..." the foreman repeated, again looking down his list.

"...nothing today for you."

Marius' jaw dropped.

"What? What do you mean, *nothing*?"

"I said *no work*, did you not hear me?" he snapped.

"But you've let those three men..."

"Be off, Nerval, or I'll set the dogs on you!"

'How can this be? He turned me away last week and the week before that! He's giving jobs to others but not to me...'

Looking back over his shoulder as he walked off, he was astonished to see the men who had stood behind him ushered towards the winery. He could not take in the reason for such treatment and his return journey was yet colder, so dejected did he feel. The wind blew more spiteful, the ground harder underfoot from a frost still not lifted.

'I do not understand. They spoke highly of my efforts with last year's harvest. I picked grapes week upon week. I earned a good wage and life treated me well. But, today, that money has been spent and there is little left for us.'

The influential Cabasse Fils vineyard was the only employer of any note in Carpentras. The men either worked with the vine or were laid idle. What Marius would give to turn the sandy, pebbled soil again this year on the gentle, sun-soaked slopes, especially after the blessed winter rain. These conditions, he knew, would hasten growth and plump the grapes. Common folk like himself could only dream about tasting a fine red from the first pressing, but the rougher wine from the second, that was another matter.

Monsieur Cabasse, a third generation wine-grower, was well-liked in Carpentras, using his wealth for the benefit of the town – alms houses and the drinking fountain two of his philanthropic contributions. Few people were aware the Catholic Church was the real owner of the vineyard and accrued its profits. When Clement V, the first of seven Avignon popes, resided in Carpentras, the reputation of Cabasse wines flourished. The clergy were enamoured of the drink, maintaining it was a requirement of the Mass – *vinum theologium*, holy wine. Even to an untrained eye, the volume they ordered far exceeded ecumenical needs. Catholic monks had designed fields of vines and developed wine production. Thus, the Church dominated the entire area, wielding power over those employed and those not.

It was with heavy heart that Marius left the estate that day. His wife, Dominique and baby son, Fabien, depended on him: he was a good husband and father, placing their well-being and happiness before his own. Certain affairs, such as earning a living wage, were beyond his control as that morning had vouched. Other men laughed at him, but he valued his woman's opinion.

The track became a pathway with six cruck cottages to either side, one of them Marius' home. He hesitated to enter. How could he tell Dominique of his failure to find work? Searching for the right words, his eyes passed over the dwelling, the carved timber beams supporting the thatched roof, the walls of wattle and daub, the windows naught but holes. Ashamed at the meanness of the cottage with its curtain covering the doorway since he could not afford a wooden door, how might he explain his inadequacy?

Inside, Dominique sat on a low nursing chair, baby Fabien at her breast. She looked up as her spouse entered in silence, filled a cup with ale from a wooden pin barrel and drew a chair to the table. An expression of anger and despair clouded his face.

"What news, husband?" she asked, though the answer was manifest.

"News?" he barked, "the tidings are black like the night! I can only think the Devil himself is at large!"

"Calm now, calm, Marius. Tell. There is a remedy for any bad fortune."

"Hark, Dominique, the foreman has refused me…again."

"How so?"

"He gave no explanation, just turned me away. I could accept it if the winery needs no hands but, the man behind me was given work! Where is the fairness in that?"

"There is none, but we will find a way, believe me."

Marius thumped the table, his frustration erupting.

"Come, take your son, gentle, he's done feeding and will sleep in your arms." As he cradled Fabien, the child's angelic countenance drove away his melancholy, if only for a moment.

Dominique kissed Marius on the forehead. She understood his moods although she, too, was at a loss. '*Without wherewithal, how will we survive?*'

"Do not despair, my love. The Lord will provide' but she knew her words rang hollow, "I must fetch water now." Outside, she placed the rope handle of two pails onto the ends of a yoke and made her way to the well beyond the last cottage. Meanwhile, Marius laid the boy with care in the crib made with his own hands. Replenishing his cup with ale, he scowled around their home. One room had to suit their needs. The floor was covered with straw that his wife raked up to change whenever a farmer allowed her to take a sheaf or two from his barn. How he appreciated her hard work. She used the same straw to stuff the mattress in the corner. With pride and gratitude, he glanced at the log fire burning in a central pit, two andirons holding a bar from which hung a blackened stew-pot. A small clay oven served to bake bread and a mouth-watering aroma stirred his appetite. They ate at a wooden table to one side of the house, away from the smoke some of which escaped through a hole in the roof. Marius's lip curled as the green logs spluttered and unpleasantly enveloped them in a fug. Thinking about discomfort, his eye passed to the toilet bucket in another corner that he emptied daily into the communal cesspit in a field behind the houses. One blessing was their cow, thank God for the beast that supplied them with milk. Each evening they brought it inside and tethered it to a post for safety: bears and wolves prowled by night.

His stomach rumbled, a waft of soup of cabbage, lentils and onions reached his nostrils to mingle with that of freshly baked bread. Dominique staggered in with two pails of water.

"I'm *not* going to..."

"Quiet, Marius, for you will wake Fabien."

"Sorry" and he resumed in a hushed tone, "I'm not going to give up. They *must* take me on...I've worked there since I was fourteen years old...I shall present myself again tomorrow."

"You're right, my love, and I'm sure you will be employed."

On his bed that night he tossed and turned through worry. At daybreak, he repeated the walk along the track to the chateau and found himself first in line with four other men falling in behind him. The shutters opened for the foreman to cry out,

"Name?"

"Nerval."

"Nerval…uhm…no, nothing for you today. Next!"

Enraged, he moved closer to the window, grabbed the foreman's tunic and readied to punch him in the face but, he pulled away from Marius' grip.

"Off with you! Be gone! My hounds have not yet eaten breakfast!" He normally threatened these animals although nobody had ever seen them. Marius had little choice but to obey. As on the previous morning, the gruff official allowed other men to enter the winery but not him.

'*What to make of this business? There must be something afoot but I know not what…*'

He arrived home to find his wife sitting at the table, weeping and wringing her hands.

"Dominique! What ails you? Is it Fabien?"

"No, he's well, but while you have been away, Cabasse's servant…" She broke down, distraught. He sat, putting a comforting arm around her. On the table lay a sheet of parchment.

"Hush, hush now. A Cabasse servant, you say? We have never had that honour, so what was his purpose?"

"We have to give up our home."

"You are mistaken, that cannot be true!"

"It *is* so, Marius. He said his master has written it, *there*' and she pointed to the sheet, but she hesitated, biting her lip, 'I cannot read…"

The message read:

This day, December 28, anno Domini 1347, Cabasse Fils serve due notice on NERVAL Marius as with his family to quit. The dwelling is in rightful possession. Under tithing arrangement anno Domini 1328 the field beyond the brook falls also to Cabasse Fils in perpetuity. Eviction will be enforced, one month from this day's date. All chattels and livestock equally remaining fall to the same Cabasse Fils.

"I do not understand, husband, what is its meaning?"

"The master of the chateau is throwing us out, they call it *eviction!*"

"And does he have the right?

"Sadly, he does."

"Our house is not ours, then?"

"It is not. I will explain. I have not shared the nature of it with you before, it needed not concern you, but the time has now come."

He rose, went to the barrel and quaffed a cup of ale. Fabien slept throughout, his new-born innocence shielding him from his parents' chagrin.

"You knew not my father, Edmond. In truth, nor did I. He departed this world when I was but an infant. While you were born in Carpentras, my family is from Limoges. Father kept a tavern and he had a good trade, so mother said, but he was drinking away the profits. He preferred *eau de vie*, they also call it *brandy*, which only men of means can afford. She often related he warranted it since a healer, one who spent more time in the inn than tending the sick, boasted *eau de vie* 'prolongs health, dissipates superfluous matters, revives the spirit, and preserves youth.' She was not a woman familiar with the art of medicine. Beatings ensued, with no cause. The hostelry gained a bad name – fighting, gambling and whores – and she threatened to leave him should he not surrender the inn. He agreed, if with reluctance."

"He had heard of the chateau and the Cabasse Fils vineyard that would adopt any farmer's uncultivated field abutting their own properties. With his meagre funds he bought a piece of land and that is how he and my mother happened here. The intention was increase its grape yield so, the farmers would plant vines and live rent-free in the cottages as recompense. It was known as *tithing*. The grapes went to Cabasse Fils. Should the harvest fail or the farmer pass, the cottage reverted – as did the field – to them. My father, due to demon drink, deceased, though mother survived him. Of course, that you know. I see, now, Cabasse was waiting for her demise to serve notice on us. They win and care nothing for the poor or serfs like us."

"I realised nothing of this story, husband. But, if we are to depart, where do we go?"

"Let me think. Take Fabien out for a while, give me time to consider. You said yesterday we will find a way…"

"And so we will," she added, lifting her son from the crib, wrapping him in a shawl and leaving the house.

She returned an hour later and sat at the table waiting in silence for Marius to speak. Fabien drank her milk.

"I have decided what we must do." His wife fixed her gaze on him.

"Tell me, do."

"We *will* leave this place, as they want! Cabasse Fils have power over our very existence: they say when we can work, they say when we cannot. Our voice is not heard in any quarrel so, damn them! A plague on their name and a pox on their women!"

"Wise words, my love, I too curse them."

"At first light' Marius continued 'I will go to Avignon. There I will get honest service. I have been told there is much building for the Pope's chapel and new town walls. Strong, young men will be wanted. Wife, we have watched the river boats, laden to founder with I know not what goods. There are docks and warehouses there so, trust me, I will find employ and we will rent a house to live, worry not. I love you and Fabien from my soul, and I will care for you to the grave."

Tears of emotion and gratitude ran down her cheeks.

AVIGNON
1 December 1347 AD

"Enter!" Clément called sharply. The papal guard pushed open the door to his office. Julien, the Cardinal Priest, accompanied by an assistant Prelate, approached the Holy Father's desk. They stood still, heads bowed in reverence.

"Julien, and my Prelate, I welcome your safe return. All manner of beasts and philistines roam abroad, without the walls. Laudite Dominum."

"Laudite Dominum," they invoked.

"In Limoges, did you chance on the tavern whose name I provided?"

"Excellency,' Julien began, it was not difficult, but... "

Sensing the priest's hesitation, Clément was at once angered. He half rose from his seat, clenched fists showing white knuckles.

"But! But! Do you tell me you did not find Nerval? You are well rewarded and honoured to be among my closest aides and I expect, nay demand, good tidings, not excuses! What have you got to say?"

"The man you seek sold the tavern and moved with his wife to Carpentras. We journeyed to that town and enquired of the baker, the carter, the constable...many folk...but none knew the name Nerval..."

"None! Julien, you have failed me!" Clément interrupted, but the cleric persisted,

"Nonetheless, we spoke with an elderly canon in a church there and...he recalled conducting a burial for a certain Edmond Nerval."

"A burial, you say?"

"Yes."

'Edmond...dead! After all these years! Should I take pleasure from his demise or accept God's will? Called to eternal rest, he has cheated me, there's no mistake!'

"Is that all you know?" he asked Julien, disappointed.

"No, there is more. Nerval's wife attended the funeral, as we might expect, and she had a babe in arms, a son named Marius, if the old canon remembers well."

"A son!" Clément repeated.

"Aye. That's all he knew, but a gold écu jolted his memory. The widow and boy reside in a house tied to the Cabasse Fils vineyard."

'The good Lord indeed moves in mysterious ways, Deo gratias. Our venture in the Carpentras winery is at last rewarding us! I will communicate with Cabasse. The Church must show interest in its investments.'

"Julien and my Prelate, you have fulfilled your mission. For that, my deep appreciation. You may now resume your duties."

Alone in his study, Clément collected his thoughts. *It is an opportune time to discuss ecclesiastical affairs with our brother, the Bishop of Carpentras.*

He took a clean vellum sheet, dipped his quill into ink and wrote.

CARPENTRAS
29 December 1347 AD

"How long will you be away," Dominique asked, concern etched on her brow.

"I cannot say. The journey will take two days. When I reach Avignon, I will first secure employment and accommodation, but the place is unknown to me so I will meet the residents and see how the land lies. I will return to fetch you both as soon as I have made progress. We have yet time before Cabasse turns us out on the streets. Fear not, my dearest, God has arranged our fates and we must believe in Him. It is a new chapter in our lives."

He embraced her and Fabien and set off down the track leading south, away from the vineyard and Carpentras, towards Avignon. In a pouch attached to his waist he had his remaining few écus. Over his shoulder he carried a sack containing bread, cheese and a wineskin.

'Avignon! Fair Avignon! I have heard many good things spoken of you. So, you will be our oyster, my Dominique and Fabien the pearls.'

CHAPTER FIVE

AVIGNON
29 December 1347 AD

Marius did not look back to his wife and son. His focus had to be on the journey ahead, to a town unknown and strange to them that would determine their future. Day had dawned, and if he kept its weak December rays to his left, the route would lead south to the river Rhone. A sturdy oak thumb-stick he had whittled served to beat through the forest undergrowth where shrub hindered progress. It would do as a cudgel, should it be needed. Into a cord round his waist he pushed a well-honed dagger. '*I know not what manner of wild beast I may encounter, so I will be prepared. When we were young, tales of wizards and werewolves frightened us so we never dared venture into the dark wood.*'

It was not far before the track narrowed to a path which, in turn, died away. '*I will reach the river by nightfall, then follow its course till I make Avignon. It's a time of great promise and I trust in the Lord to guide me along the way of righteousness.*' From the position of the sun, Marius estimated it was now midday. He came upon a clearing, from where intruders could be spotted, a suitable place to rest a while. Sitting on a fallen bough, he ate bread and cheese washed down with rough red wine. The trek, so far, had passed without incident, not a soul in sight. Overhead, only a breeze rustling the leaves on the trees and birds singing overhead broke the peace. '*Better you don't relax,*

Marius. What's that sound over in those bushes? An animal, for sure...'
He drew his dagger in haste and crept in its direction. Of a sudden, with a startled squeal, a huge wild boar reared its head. Man and creature froze, neither sure of the other's next move. He gasped seeing its trunk, short but massive, neck thick and muscular. Piercing deep-set eyes fixed Marius, then the mouth opened to reveal razor sharp tusks, the likes of which, he realised, could amputate a man's arm without effort. Motionless at first, the tableau dissolved with a vicious blow of his stick to the feral brute's head. It had the good fortune to sport a winter coat of long coarse bristles that absorbed the full force of the stroke. Yelling in fear, it turned and fled, a strident cry ringing out through the dense forest. *'I only hope this racket is a warning for the rest of his herd! My life is testing enough without fighting boars!'* To his relief, neither the beast nor its sounder emerged.

As daylight faded, the woodland thinned into open meadow. Some leagues on and his objective appeared ahead: the silvery waters of the Rhône, sheer grandeur in nature, turbulent central currents, lethargic eddies and pools at its banks. Marius, though not learned, knew she was a proud old lady who had witnessed all events of any import in the history of France. He remembered his mother – the memory saddened him – relating stories of Charlemagne when he was a boy - the great king might well have travelled on the Rhône. He imagined standing beside his mother on the crowded riverbank, waiting with impatience for Charlemagne to pass by. How his subjects cheered! The barge, under sail, decked in royal blue; the King of the Franks with his full beard and flowing locks, crown encrusted with jewels, a golden mace held high. A tap on the shoulder caused him to spin round, withdrawing the dagger to defend himself against an attacker. To his surprise, a small old man, with wizened face, unkempt hair and clothed in a tattered tunic, appeared as if from nowhere.

"What the...! Who are you?" asked Marius, jolted from his dreaming.

"Who am I? Sire, put away your weapon, I will not harm you."

'He's right there! More a midget than a man!'

"They call me Georges…Old Georges…yes, that might be since I am old…what think ye? And do I know you…?"

"You do *not*, old man! I am Marius, that's all you need," he answered, not trusting the stranger.

"So, Monsieur Marius, what brings you to the river…I'd wager you've not come for the fishing?"

"You're right, I travel to Avignon."

"Ah, La Belle Avignon!"

"The same."

"Though I have no reason to help you, Monsieur Marius, you can go no further tonight…the dark…you'd likely fall in the river and be devoured by the water monster…wouldn't be the first either…no, you need shelter."

"That's true."

"You can sleep in my hut over there." And he pointed downstream to a shack, half-concealed by weeping willows and bulrush, "I have to be elsewhere." He did not explain himself.

"Why such kindness, I wonder, and what is there in it for you?"

"A question you should not ask! Trust in God's love and man's goodness. If I can be of service to my fellows, I will. Simple as that!"

"I do not wish to offend you but I am not accustomed to being treated thus. Now, if you know Avignon, what counsel can you offer, for I seek work and accommodation there."

"Advice? I would tell you to find the Magistrate. He has offices next the Palace and at the port. Be it pope or beggar, at one time or another they will come across the Magistrate, believe me. Do not cross him. If you are out of favour so will be your life, if you get my drift?"

"I do. Thank you kindly."

The bedraggled old man turned and disappeared into the gloom.

'Well I'll be blessed, if that isn't the Good Lord helping me! It augurs well.'

The hut offered a welcome roof for the night. On a pile of straw, he slept through to dawn the next day. The Good Samaritan was nowhere to be seen, and he awoke to find a bowl on the table with apples, cherries, bread and a pitcher of cider. He consumed breakfast with relish. In the earthen floor he scratched, with the tip of the dagger, '*Merci*'. The weather fair, he set off along the riverbank, a spring in his step, and covered a good distance. Soon, the ramparts of Avignon loomed.

'*It has, indeed, the face of a beautiful lady. The walls are tall and strong to repel intruders and gateways well defended by loyal guards. She hosts the Palace of the Church, remarkable towers rising majestically to inform the heavens of the Pope's wisdom. Praise be! The tales of old Avignon will exceed my wildest dreams and, if it please the Lord, may I reside here with my family in peace for the years to come.*'

Calling at the first tavern *intra muros*, he rented a room for the night. The squalid state of the inn hardly caught his attention, so fatigued was he from the day's exertions. He supped on broth, the content of which was not easy to determine, and a tankard of watered ale. The landlord approached to remove his bowl and enquire whether more drink was desired. An obsequious fellow, eyes close-set and yellowed, broken teeth, his apron filthy. He leaned over Marius, exhaling foul breath. He asked -

"Did sire enjoy our humble fare? We are renowned in the town for our…hospitality, should I call it…yes, we offer a warm welcome and even warmer chamber…" The diminutive man paused, stepped back and by his expression expected Marius to comprehend what he meant by 'even warmer chamber', which he did not. The man resumed.

"We have only the nicest…cleanest…shall I say *companions* to ensure sire's satisfaction…" Of a sudden, Marius realised he provided girls, whores by any other name. It was but two days since leaving Dominique and he had no intention of betraying her. '*So, it seems the innocent beauty of this town viewed from without possesses a vulgarity in its heart. No matter, for tonight, I shall sleep alone and surely not frequent his establishment again.*'

"I'll take another ale, though I've drank better from a washing pail! Then bring me a candle. You can sell your 'nicest companions' to some other blockhead, I want none of it!"

"Of course, I did not mean to suggest that…" And deciding discretion would be the best choice, he bowed and disappeared into the cellar to fetch the beer. Marius looked up and was surprised to see every customer in the place staring at him. He stared back. They were pleased with the altercation, as it was rare for anyone to square up to the landlord. They broke into wide smiles, raised their tankards to him and called "well said! And "that's the way!" And "you told him proper!" *'Strange meeting such folk but better get used to it. Before retiring I'll ask about a job.'*

"You," he addressed to the man at the next table, "do you know how I can find work?"

"Ay, find the foreman's hut by the Palace, he always has need of men."

"Thank you." He took the candle holder from the counter and climbed the dark stairs to find the allocated room. Sparsely furnished it was, but he cared not, and sleep overcame seconds after laying his head on the dingy, straw-filled mattress. The following morning, refreshed, he went downstairs. The landlord was sweeping the floor to clear up the previous night's dropped food and ash from pipes. He looked up at Marius's arrival, nodded but said nothing, evidently bashful his inn had not elicited a more favourable reaction the night before.

"There," Marius said, placing a coin on the counter. With no reason to offer any polite valediction, he said only 'good day to you.' Outside, the streets were deserted and clean, fresh air was welcome after the cloying atmosphere of the tavern. The Palace was easy to locate, its dreamy towers rising above the rooftops. As the old man had said, the foreman's office was at the entrance to the stonemason's yard, a hive of industry even at this early hour with men sawing stone blocks, sculptors carving figurines and masons mixing mortar to a consistency that suited their craft. Marius knocked at the office door and waited a response. After a short while, the foreman opened a wooden grille and looked Marius up and down. He had a rounded red face with a benevolent expression in stark contrast to the surly innkeeper.

"If it please you, I come from Carpentras, north of here. My wife and son await my good news so I may then fetch them. I'm seeking work. I am strong, honest, willing, and you will not be disappointed with my efforts."

The boss spat out a twist of tobacco and his brow furrowed as if coming to a decision was a weighty affair.

"We are short of labourers and the new chapel is but half complete. His Holiness reminds me so every day, and that's no lie. Let me see... ah, yes..." After consulting a leather-bound ledger on his desk, he continued, "We can offer you employ as a mason's labourer. Day starts at six and does not end till three in the afternoon, and it be hard toil even for a fine young boy like you to make 'e sweat but it pays well... what say 'e?"

Surprised, and thinking of the difficulties he had experienced on the Cabasse estate, he accepted at once. "My thanks to you. But with my wife and child in Carpentras I cannot begin until..."

"Do not worry, report to me after you've made your arrangements. You're a stranger here, but I know 'em all... Avignon men, that is to say, and they all know me too! I wish you a welcome here."

Leaving the yard, such good chance overwhelmed him. '*The spinning Wheel of Fortune has stopped for me. I cannot believe my luck! Time after time I was turned away from the vineyard and, here, I've been successful at the first time of asking! The Lord is watching over me, for certain.*' He heard most boats loaded and unloaded in the afternoon. *If I am hired at the docks, I will then be ready after the Palace. This could all suit me fine... two jobs! Dominique and Fabien will want for nothing.*'

With handshakes and smiles the overseer gave directions for the port: Rue de la Croix, then Rue Paul Sain. He felt satisfied with the mission so far and optimism prevailed. A stranger, for sure, but he experienced an affinity, an appreciation, even love for this haven. Soft warm pastel colours – the yellow sandstone of the Palace, orange of the houses' pantile roofs, brilliant white of their walls, green of the shutters – dispelled a nip in the December morning air. His aim that day was to obtain work with the barges to supplement money from the stonemason and secure a house for his family. The return journey to Carpentras could be broken overnight in the river man's hut, assuming the former hospitality would be repeated.

Avignon's repose afforded him undisturbed tranquillity to absorb the town's courteous ambiance. Delightful rows of cottages, side by side, followed the street or grouped around secluded courtyards, each with an individual personality. Private precincts kept secret their stories of past inhabitants, sworn never to break a trust. A water-well in the centre, benches shielded from the summer heat by overhanging branches of gnarled old willow trees. The occasional stray cat meowed with a snarl and shake of the head to express its sovereignty and warn him away. A hound dozed at the threshold of its owner's residence, too lazy - even if awake - to acknowledge the trespasser's presence. *A fine guard dog, that one! I could enter, rob and flee unnoticed.* The place gave up a sense of nature, of contentment, an impression of living at ease with the world.

A few streets on, he glanced back at the Palace to admire its commanding spires and crenelated battlements, signs of its military past and religious authority of the present. Cobbled roads flanked by narrow pavements; tables and seats awaiting customers in front of taverns; archways leading to stables; boards displaying faded official notices warning of pickpockets, an illiterate population relying on the better educated clergy to read for them. Frissons of excitement ran down Marius' spine as he strolled, with no particular intention, knowing not what to expect round each new corner.

Between the ramparts and an inner road, a fast-flowing brook, slimy pondweed tugged by a swirling current, carried away the people's effluent and discharged into the river. Avignon was fortunate to avoid the usual central channel down a street clogged with excrement and household waste waiting for timely rain to wash it away out of sight. *'Fabien will grow up in clean surroundings and I hope a simple cough or cold may be the worst ailments to afflict him.* He walked on, whistling a happy tune. *What was it mother used to tell me...about Charles Marteau...no! marteau is a hammer...it was Martel, Charles Martel, that's right. He scaled the walls of the town with rope ladders, smashed through the gates with battering rams to drive out the Arabs. He burned down all within. That would be lost in the mists of time, but what a story! Hard to believe it happened, so beautiful is the Lord's Avignon this fair day.'*

An hour later he left the town through the Saint-Roch gate to find the entrance to the moorings. Two-storey warehouses lined the quays with solid oak doors of width to admit horses and carts; derricks all entwined in ropes and pulleys leaned out over the river in salute to the next loaded barge to appear. As it was with the town, the port slept still. At the far end of the marina he spied a small unobtrusive cabin distinct from the stores. That must be, he decided, the Magistrate's abode. As he neared it, wisps of white smoke rose from its doorway and, sure enough, he found the man in question, sitting on a stool before a sloping top desk, a clay stem dangling from the side of his mouth.

"Good morning, sire," Marius greeted the Justice with apprehension.

"To you as well, young man," He spoke in a rather indistinct tone, the pipe contributing to the drawl. "You seek work, am I right?" Before their meeting, Marius had an image of the man in his mind: a tall, imposing, tyrannical figure. Yet, in reality this person was short, softly-spoken and, he thought with some relief, avuncular. *'I must be wary, though, not everybody can be judged on first view. Time will tell.'*

"Indeed, you are. So…" and he was interrupted, "So, we require labourers to unload the boats' cargoes when they arrive and load them before they leave. Easy, don't you agree…and you don't need a clever head for this business, even if that might be the case…" Marius was taken aback by such a friendly, if direct, demeanour. *'It seems he will help me…again, I'm in luck!'*

"But you will be honest and a good time-keeper else you'll be out on your ear…is that clear? And if you're ever dismissed from here, you won't get work anywhere in this town, believe me."

"I do believe you, sire." Marius assured him he was of exemplary character but he needed to explain his dilemma. "My name is Nerval,

Marius Nerval. However, my situation is not straightforward." The man dipped his quill into an inkpot, preparing to copy the visitor's credentials onto a sheet he arranged on his desk, only to realise he had not asked Marius what his most unusual state could be.

"How is that, then? I am well versed in situations that are not...er...not straightforward, as you put it. A magistrate has to deal with no manner of...er...not straightforward encounters." He drew breath and puffed out his chest with pride. Marius repeated his difficulty, as he had done with the foreman.

"This morn, I have had the offer of a position at the Palace stonemason's yard, which I have accepted with gratitude. The hours will occupy me daily until three in the afternoon."

"Master Marius," the Magistrate began in a reassuring voice, "that will be commensurate...if you understand...with the time we begin our labours here. But, it means the early evening before you can return to your home. Is that suitable to you? You'll have to speak up, my hearing is not too good."

"It is, indeed, sire!" Marius confirmed, a little louder for the man's benefit.

The beak wrote down his details, still sucking on the pipe and leaning towards him as he strained to catch every word. The administration done, he looked up as if to inspect the boy.

"Good! That's settled...but just don't get ideas for pilfering...or thieving...or scrounging because *I will* find out and, if you don't take a fancy to the stocks, the robbing of the merchandises will not enter your head. We have goods here you can only imagine. Wine, cheese, wool, timber, cloth, spices, oil, livestock, iron stuff, vine poles..." He took a deep breath. "...well...we moves anything the Lord decides. It's your job to bring me the manifest from the bargee. I signs it in and you takes it off into the warehouses...d'you understand?"

"Y...yes." In truth, he did not fully comprehend, though he followed the gist.

"Fine! Fine, no doubt! I see you be a bright boy, because some of them round here don't have no brain! That's for certain! I can't be

doin' with that sort. D'you know, some of those bargees have a big
red cross painted on the boat...so we knows they are Christians and
so we can unload them. Don't matter anymore though...don't take no
notice...anything, *everything*, creature or being near by a thousand
leagues to here is Christian! The Father up in yon Palace sees to that!'
And they say this place is the *richest, most opulent, most populated
in Christendom*. Now, they're all big words to me but I'm told it's a
blessing or something similar."

"I'm sure it is. May I presume a favour of you?"

"Depends."

"Might you know of any house to rent? My wife and son will come
here once I have arranged our lodgings."

The Magistrate relit his pipe from a candle burning on the desk,
scratching his bald pate as if to jog the memory.

"Board, you say? Now, you know...or if you don't know you soon
will..." And Marius struggled to follow the thread. "...that a Magistrate such as me has a good many duties to perform. There's the docks,
the inns, the baker, the smith...in fact, I exercise justice on everything
that happens in our town! I'm even known to the Father, a fine man,
and it's not everybody can say that!" Marius nodded a gesture of ad-
miration.

"Board ain't easy because we are the Avignon that we are, if you
see? I mean all order of persons wants to live here since it's such a
good place. But, and as it happens, a landlord, Monsieur Duval, he
keeps a good house...no fightin' and only a little cursin'...but real
good ales...he has a house he rents and it's next to his inn. I'm thinkin'
it's free now. Go see him, Nerval, an' tell him the Magistrate sent ye."

"I am truly grateful to you, monsieur." The hostelry in question was
nearby, Rue de la Bourse.

"Who's sent you?"

"The Magistrate, I know not his name, though."

"Ah! I'm always minded to listen to *him*...he knows the law, a clever
man, and we depend on him to sentence assailants, pickpockets, horse
thieves, even murderers! He's a fair man, let me tell you."

"I'm sure he is," Marius said, trusting his word.

"You are fortunate today, sir. The house - and he pointed next door - is available. The previous tenants moved out last week." With that, he gave Marius a key and invited him to examine the property. It could not have been more different to their Carpentras cottage. There were two rooms downstairs, two above. The fireplace had a chimney not a pit in the centre. Shutters to the windows they had not known and, a true luxury he could only have dreamt of, a wooden front door. No straw covered the floor since animals would be neither needed nor allowed. Back in the inn, he accepted the house. They agreed a twelve-month tenancy in the first instance and the rent would be quite within his means. *'So, I am now a citizen of Avignon, the start of my new life!'* He paid the landlord one gold écu to secure the arrangement.

About to set off, in the street, a young woman, about his age appeared. Her hair was braided and shiny, her skin smooth, her smile alluring. The shawl around her shoulders was of worsted cloth, not cheap wool common people would wear. The long dress bore no stains.

"I understand we are to be neighbours," she said, a shyness in her voice.

"We are?" he asked, "I know not how you found that out so soon..."

"I clean for the landlord. He told me, but it's not a secret, is it?"

"No, of course it is not. Let me introduce myself, I am Marius."

"I'm pleased to meet you. My name is Alice." There was a pause, when neither spoke, then, for no apparent cause, she blushed and her delicate lips curled into a barely perceptible smile. Her eyes, a deep sapphire blue, caught his attention in an intense moment he could not resist. He broke the silence.

"It will be most agreeable living next to you, Alice." *'Why, in God's name have I just said that? It's not what I meant to say at all, not in that manner!'* He composed himself and continued,

"You will soon meet my family."

"'Your family?" she asked, her voice hardening.

"Yes, my wife, Dominique and my son, Fabien are to join me."

"I see," but the smile had dissolved.

Trudging back upstream along the Rhône was not a burden and a chill in the air did not bother him. Good distance made, he arrived at the old man's hut before nightfall. Inside there was a pitcher of wine, bread and cheese and fruit in a bowl, as had happened before. Mystified as to how the man knew of his presence he nonetheless ate and drank, indebted for the kindness shown him. Her sleep would be disturbed only by the next morning's dawn. It was most rewarding to have met his new landlord and neighbour, Alice. Lying on the bed of rough straw, he drifted back into cosy slumber. *'The day has gone well. The foreman, Magistrate, landlord...all honest men....and Dominique will know them in good time...and, Alice...she has a fair countenance, that's for sure.'* There was a singular mystery to this girl: she seemed out of place living in a modest rented house in an unfashionable quarter of the town. *'She seems accustomed to better,* he pondered.'

CHAPTER SIX

CARPENTRAS
1 January 1348 AD

The next morning, it was apparent Old Georges had entered the hut: on the table, he found a bowl with fresh bread, ham and fruit. There was also a pitcher of red wine. Marius was not troubled, deep in sleep, wakened only by a marauding fox scratching at the door that took flight on hearing him rise. He ate and drank, grateful once more for the old man's generosity. Refreshed after washing in the icy water of the Rhône, he pulled the cord at his waist tight, pushed in his dagger and, taking a final look around for the still absent Georges, set off to retrace the way back home to Dominique and Fabien. A childlike excitement welled within him at the thought of embracing her and revealing the news. The leagues through the forest seemed not the distance of the outward journey, the gorse less unyielding, the brambles less sharp. Elation and anticipation overwhelmed him on leaving the woodland as the wisps of smoke ahead announced the cottages of Carpentras.

Dominique dashed from the house to hold him close, kissing him full on the lips. Marius reciprocated.

"Hey, wife! What will the neighbours think?"

"To hell with them! They will not be such for much longer and I'm pleased to see you, that's all… we *are* wed, after all, are we not?"

"Trollop! Inside, and I'll tell you what's happened."

Before anything else, he went to the crib and lifted out baby Fabien. The child babbled and smiled as if recognising him. Dominique interrupted the touching scene, insisting the infant be put down and that he shared what had been accomplished. He took a tankard and slowly filled it with ale, teasing her. 'Marius! Sit down! Tell!' Enough of this, time to be serious.

"I have been to Avignon..."

"Of *course* you have, I know that much!"

"...and now, a house."

"No mistake!"

"Yes! It's next to a tavern, not that it will matter, and there are two rooms downstairs and...but, no, I'll not describe it all to you, so it will be a surprise."

Pausing for breath, her joyous face at once rewarded his efforts over the past three days.

"And it will be within our means because there is work!"

"Marius! This can be no better!"

"But, it *can*! I have not one but *two* jobs in fair Avignon."

"I am proud of you, my dear husband," and reaching across the table she squeezed his hand hard, a token expression of deep love. Fabien sleeping, they took advantage to discuss their arrangements.

"When shall we leave?"

"As soon as possible, there's naught to delay us and the date Cabasse sent us to quit has passed. They will be at our door any day." He paused. "But, we require a horse and cart to carry our belongings and ourselves..."

"None of our neighbours possess such...I'm at a loss."

"Wait! The solution! Maurice, the blacksmith who would drink with my late father, or so I believe, has a waggon, for sure. I will go and, as leverage, mention their friendship, suggesting he might grant me a favour, in father's name."

"A brainchild if ever I heard one!"

"I agree. So, it will be done, at once."

Marius had grown up with the legend that the smith's ancestors, on these same premises, had honed the spears and axes wielded by Julius Caesar's armies. True or not, his lineage boasted the craft over generations. For such, he was a valued member of Carpentras society, his skills commanded by the town's professionals, undertakers, healers, armourers, and self-styled dentists who needed metal implements and specialist objects. The smithy was open to the street, its shadowy interior a secret to curious passers-by. As Marius stepped inside it took some moments to adjust to the light then, facing him was the hearth filled with coals fanned white-hot by huge conical bellows pumped by a lad sitting at a treadle. The anvil, bright and smooth through endless blows, sat solid on the earth floor, blackened by soot given off from the blazing heat. Wooden pegs fixed to the wall held any number of horseshoes of all sizes, to shoe proud carriage-horse or humble pony, whichever. In a corner, a stack of hoops for the Cabasse cooper awaited collection.

A sexagenarian, Maurice presented the body of one half that age: broad-shouldered, sinewy bulging biceps, hands scarred by misaimed strikes to the anvil or swage block. Bald-headed, breathing heavy, rivulets of sweat from exertion and the smithy's furnace ran down his face. A leather apron protected an otherwise naked chest.

"Good day, sire," Marius greeted him, the heat warming his skin as he stepped forward, the imposing frame of the smith looming over him.

"Yes, it is. What do you want? Best not be work to be done quick. I 'ave orders for the month and more. See, that's the repute they 'olds for Maurice the Smith!"

"I'm sure it is..." His attention wandered, "...a mysterious place, without a lie, but why so dark?"

"So dark? It's a rare thing anybody comes 'ere and asks a question like that. I could spare a while to tell you...if you be minded?"

"If it's no trouble, I'd be honoured."

Maurice beckoned.

'*How it would be if I had a trade to my name, a talent? I've only worked on the vineyard and anybody can do that. I would be of service to my fellow man, to help, to comfort, I know not what, but surely there is the Lord's plan for my life? But when will it be made known? And to what purpose?*'

"Boy!" he shouted to the dullard at the treadle, "pump away!"

The bellows inflated, grey coals in the hearth changed first to red then white. The smith gripped a horseshoe with tongs in one hand, a heavy hammer in the other.

"First, I puts the shoes under the coals...pump away, boy...till it be ready...and I knows that it be ready when it changes colour and glows...and I sees that *proper* in the dark! So there's your answer!"

'I understand now, thank you.'

"Now I takes the shoe and 'olds it on the anvil and 'its it 'ard and 'ard again...tempers it...then back into 'eat and 'its it once again...all until it be the requisited shape..."

The man stuck out his chest with pride and added,

"...when I be pleased with it I quenches it in the water, see, 'ere..." In a deep stone trough, liquid the colour of rust shimmered and steamed as the malleable metal was submerged, then withdrawn to check its condition.

"If I deals with a bar, not a shoe, I puts it in an 'ole of the swage block 'ere to 'old it still. I bends it just as I likes and I knows the secret of shaping a bar, twisting a rod, smoothing a sheet, and all perfect to the limits set by the customer... but it must look right in dark. Yes, without dark I'd not be a smith!" The man halted, wiped his brow with a dirty rag and consumed the contents of a tankard in a single swallow. "I sees you admiring my tools. Them came down from my father, from 'is father and beyond. I reckons you not get finer 'tween 'ere and Marseilles."

On a long wooden bench, supporting a mighty vice, were arranged, in rows, every sort and size of metalworking utensil: hammer, tongues, rasp, chisel, pincers, saw and clamp.

"But, I do not yet know your name or the purpose of your visit."

"You might not know *me*, but you will surely recall my father, Edmond Nerval."

"Damn right I do! Nerval... we 'ad better times then, when we was young. Then you... you are 'is son?"

"The same. I am Marius."

The smith shook hands with the enthusiasm of a man finding a long lost friend.

"Edmond passed away fifteen, sixteen years since, so what would you want of me?"

"I'll come straight to it. I need a horse and cart to carry my family and chattels to a new home in Avignon. I will pay a fair price."

The smith's brow furrowed.

"More ale, boy!" Then, emptying the tankard, he spoke,

"Out of respect for your late father, I will 'elp you, and it will not be an inconvenience. Let me explain. You see that pile over there...?" He indicated a corner. "...it's pig iron I'm supposed to work on but I cannot because it's of bad quality... come from the smelting-'ouse in that state, confound 'em! Well, they can give me a decent lot and pay my boy! I'm sending 'im anyway with the 'orse and cart to Avignon for that purpose this week. You calling on me today is timely, to be sure. I'd say providence is on your side. You can take your possessions and family there, then the boy will bring back the waggon with my new iron. 'ow does that sound, Nerval? Oh, and you will owe me nothing."

"I'm lost for words. I cannot thank you enough."

"Think of it as a farewell gift to your father. 'e left of a sudden if my memory serves me. You were but a babe, your father's pride and joy... we'd drink together in all the taverns, but don't get me wrong, 'e never didn't provide for you and your mother,'e was a proper father... just that we liked to drink, see?" Marius nodded. "Then one day 'e said 'e 'ad pains... in 'is stomach... and though we paid it no 'eed, it got worse. We couldn't pay a 'ealer to look at 'im and... ever so quick 'e went, see? I never did bid 'im God Speed."

"Lend a hand, woman, it's high time you did something useful!" Marius jested, the twinkle in his eye an indication of the happiness they felt that last day in Carpentras. *'I have a faithful wife and we are blessed with our son but the time is here and we must move on. Our destiny lies in Avignon.'* He made tight the rope to hold down the tarpaulin covering their belongings to the front of the blacksmith's four-wheeled cart. A straw-filled mattress at the rear would do as seating. The boy from the forge made final adjustments to the two stout horses' tack and climbed up to take the reins.

"Be ready, 'sieur?"

"Aye! Walk on!"

The waggon lurched from side to side, its wheels following the ruts in the track hardened by the January frost. Marius and Dominique exchanged few pleasantries, his mind dwelling on what lay ahead, she cradling Fabien close to protect him from the jolting ride. The road would leave its straight course to bend around copses of ancient holm oaks or planes. From the cart, to the east and west, ancient vines planted in the mists of time stood in delineated majesty. *'Estate owners are fat on the proceeds of the grape, their only viable competitors the olive grove farmers whose planting was less regimented than the vine. Nonetheless, it was a profitable crop.' Marius mused.*

"It's hard to believe the wine we drink and the oil we cook with starts here, do you not think?" But Dominique had fallen asleep, Fabien in her arms, lulled by the motion of their travel. He did not wake her to ask either what use two upright granite stones joined by a horizontal capstone served – people called them dolmen, there forever. The boy turned round and, noticeable by a taciturn nature, informed his passengers,

"That be for the dead...a tomb...not linger near it...no! And he slapped the horses with the slack rein. Marius gave a wry smile. *'They are all foolish folk, taken in by myth and legend! Death does not frighten me one jot. Anyway, this is a most pleasant journey that chases away all morbid thoughts. I can breathe in the fragrances of herbs – lavender, rosemary, thyme. I observe the countryside – undulating, low, soft-leaved shrubs and brine ponds, beasts and wild birds of every kind... and do I see the graceful pink flamingo motionless in the marshes? I near enough taste the strawberries and melons growing around. Should I disturb her? No, there will be time anon.'* They drove on through hamlets and past solitary cottages that appeared in decent repair - flower beds weeded, vegetable plots tended. *'There is an air of pride and contentment, as if hard work merits the satisfaction they display. When I came this way before, I slept in a river man's hut, but we cannot today drive through the forest. I'll ask the lad his plans for tonight. Light is fading.'*

"Two leagues on, master, sees us at Althen-des-Paluds. Nothing much there 'cept a drinking fountain and the horses must be watered, so we break our ride and spend the night there."

"You're in charge, we go with your judgment."

Unsaddled and tethered, the animals drank with gusto and grazed on a sack of hay the boy emptied out for them. This duty done he crept under the cart, tunic pulled over and slept.

"Where there's no sense there's no feeling," quipped Marius embracing his wife, and they both fell asleep on the mattress, Fabien between them.

Next morning, the three shared bread, cheese, cooked meat, and drank red wine Dominique had brought, while the babe suckled at her breast. As they neared their destination the track widened and became less rutted, to the relief of the travellers whose bones had been shaken enough. An incline ahead, the horses snorted under the heavy load and the boy encouraged them, to their displeasure, with a stick. On the brow of the hill, they stopped to afford the beasts some respite when Dominique sat upright, scarcely believing her eyes. *'In my life, I ventured no distance from my town. I was born in Carpentras. I met Marius when we were but children and we grew up together. He was my first love and will be my last. I shall be loyal, always. To go anywhere, you needed a horse, but for our sins, we had no such means. Perchance we three will enjoy fair fortune and health in Avignon.'*

"Marius! Marius!" She shouted.

In the foreground, a vast swathe of gentle brush extended to left and right, cleared of forest that could conceal an approaching enemy, centuries ago. In the distance rose the golden defensive walls of Avignon, still magnificent in their half-built state. For the days and months to come, these were the ramparts on which he would labour.

"I am not surprised you are so charmed...it is, beyond question, a sight to behold - our new home!"

AVIGNON
2 January 1348 AD

They entered the Jewel of Provence through the north Porte de la Ligne gate. Passage along the narrow cobbled streets required the lad's best horsemanship, the houses on either side all but touching the wheels. They had not been constructed with horse and cart in mind. An old man, leaning over his balcony, raised an eyebrow; a woman in her doorway gave them a cursory glance, but the strangers attracted no real attention. The postilion reined in the horses outside the tavern. Marius jumped down to knock on the door.

"Welcome, Marius! Greetings, madam! And our thanks for the fine weather you bring today. I am pleased to meet you again, for certain." The man's salutation was polite; the two Nerval were weary.

"And you, also. Our journey has been two days and..."

"Of course," the landlord interrupted, "So, here is the key to your house and when moved in and rested a little you will dine with me this evening. I insist!"

"You are most generous and we are pleased to accept."

The men soon finished the unloading, Dominique telling them where she wanted this or that item, not that they owned more than a cart could convey – table, benches, cradle, mattress, cooking paraphernalia and bundles of clothes. This done, Marius placed a coin in the boy's hand.

"Take this as a token of our appreciation. On your return, be sure to tell your master the favour, in my father's name, has been well repaid."

"Thank you kindly, I will do as you ask." And he trundled off to collect the load of prime pig iron for the smith.

"What do you think?"

"It's a fine house! Shutters, a real door, fireplace, oven…it's more than I'd hoped for and I'm so happy you didn't describe it to me the other day. We are truly blessed."

The woman busied herself sorting pots, pans, plates and bowls on shelves, hanging clothes on hooks. Marius discovered the house had a quaint secluded courtyard to the back, shaded by the boughs of a plane tree and with a stone shed that the landlord had considerately filled with logs. The fireplace soon had a roaring fire that lifted the chill from the house. With Fabien in a peaceful sleep, oblivious to his new surroundings, the couple went to the tavern. Wearing her finest worsted blue tunic, long auburn hair brushed to a lustre, she was a lady bright.

"Your beauty takes a man's breath away,!" Marius complimented, stroking her cheek.

"Why thank you, kind sir."

"Best nobody tonight has sights on you, he'd have to account to me first!"

"Husband, you must not doubt my constancy."

The couple entered the inn.

"Call me Marcel, please, we are neighbours now, after all," the landlord invited.

"So be it."

Heads turned. Marcel first introduced his wife, Angélique, to them. Marius bowed, Dominique curtseyed.

"I always say it's that name for the angel in her." The attempt at a joke came across more apology than flattery and created no great mirth. She had heard before.

The plump round-faced woman by his side blushed but said nothing. Formalities concluded, he addressed an assembled clientele that waited with bated breath for the public announcement. Pausing, as an actor playing with his audience, then with a flourish, he proclaimed,

John Bentley

"Let me put an end to your gossip. There are, as you can see, new arrivals in our beloved town. May I present Marius and Dominique Nerval, with a minor Nerval, as should be the case with all children, sound asleep in his cradle." The customers, to a man, gave up a hearty cheer of welcome. Marcel ushered the embarrassed guests to a table laid for supper in a private alcove. He filled cups from a jug and proposed a toast, to which they raised their drinks.

"It's cider, and capital, if I say so myself. I make it on these premises but it's only served on particular occasions such as tonight. I trust it's to your taste?" Marius swallowed a draught, smacked his lips and replied,

"It's nectar, the like of which I've not known!"

"It rarely fails to impress. As a rule, it's weak ale they sup around here... ale and wine... but not wine anymore." A gulp of the cider and he continued,

"Once, we would buy wine from the Cabasse vineyard in Carpentras. Do you know of it?"

"For sure," came Marius' reply, glancing at his wife.

"As I was saying, we would order one month after the next... we are honest folk... paid the bill on time, without any problem. But, of a sudden... without warning, Cabasse wants thrice the money! Said something about a poor harvest or not enough rain... it all meant nothing to me and the result was we couldn't afford his wine... seemed to me he was being greedy, but that's that! Now it's ale or cider for special visitors, yourselves. We sell eau de vie, but it doesn't suit people."

"There is reason to dislike the man," Marius whispered.

The plump round-faced wife entered bearing a platter with an enormous roast bird surrounded by boiled potatoes, turnips, carrots and braised pears. This she placed in the middle of the table, taking a step back to admire the offering. Marcel approached, fork and carving knife in hand.

"We serve goose for festive events such as tonight. It's an Avignon tradition, and this one was honking in our yard but a week since!" With that, he proceeded to carve.

53

Later, they returned home, satisfied after much splendid food and drink. Marius closed the door behind them, commenting,

"I dared not dream of the day when I could do that." But no sooner was the key turned in the lock than someone knocked.

"Who on earth can that be at this hour?" He opened, but with caution, fearing danger. On the threshold stood a girl holding a basket of fruit, a girl he recognised.

"Alice! What brings you here?" It occurred to him this was the second time she had known of his presence.

"Marius, I pray you will forgive my intrusion, I do not wish to offend…"

"No, not at all…come in, do." Alice stepped inside.

"This is my wife, Dominique."

"Pleased to make your acquaintance, Dominique."

"You too." An awkward silence ensued.

"I will keep you no longer but, please, accept this, a home-warming gift from me to you." Passing the basket to Dominique, she looked at her directly.

"It's said to bring fortune, but I'll wish you goodnight." The girl departed, saying no more.

"What do you make of that?" Dominique asked.

"What do you mean?" he snapped, "it's a *most* kind thought, is it not?"

"I suppose it is," but with an unease and reservation in her voice.

'*My father brought me up to see the best in people and counselled me to do to others what I would have them do to me. Why, flying in the face of his wisdom, do I suspect this woman's sincerity? It's absurd. I must ensure our life here is afforded the best beginning possible.*'

CHAPTER SEVEN

AVIGNON
3 January 1348 AD

"Tarry a while, Marius, it's not yet dawn," Dominique beseeched, sliding across the mattress, drawing her body close and embracing him.

"Much as I desire, I must not be late at the foreman's office. Remember the trouble I had at the loathsome Cabasse vineyard and, while I've been assured work, I will be more at ease when I take up the offer for real. Life has a habit of kicking you when you are down. No, go back to sleep while you can. You fed Fabien twice in the night, you must be tired."

"A little, perhaps, and you're right, I should make the most of our child being quiet!"

He doused his face with cold water from the pail then wrapped the worker's staple lunch of bread and cheese in a cloth. Pulling on his tunic and a cloak round his shoulders, he left their home, taking care to not disturb his family. At that early hour, the streets were deserted, save for a cat laying down its scent to inform potential visitors of its territory. A faint, yellowish hue rising above the rooftops cast macabre shadows over the cobbles set in precise squares. He passed stone houses and try as may to resist a natural temptation to peek in through shutters that were gradually opening, curiosity prevailed.

Here, a man eating at a table; there, a woman stirring their daily meal in a pan over the fire. A portrayal of domestic happiness. Rounding a corner, he all but collided with a hooded figure that said nothing, but lowered his head – or, for all he knew - *her* head. Marius bade 'bonjour' as a politesse but there came no reply. *'I wonder who that is? I only hope the others in Avignon are more friendly! I could be mistaken in thinking him a monk in long dark robe, gliding ghost-like, but the brothers do not roam abroad when they should be wandering, instead, the cloisters of their abbeys.'*

Day had not fully broken, but finding his way northward through the town towards the Palace, along the dim streets, was not difficult. *'Keep the light to my right side and walk straight ahead,'* he reasoned. The foreman's office had its window open and a flickering candle indicated the amicable man busy writing in his ledger. As on his previous encounter, noise from the mason's yard meant the day's labour had begun. The cathedral bell sounded the angelus with a triple stroke repeated thrice, the six o'clock call to prayer, so he knew he was in time. *'I can but guess how many of the faithful attend at such an hour and the spectre I've just seen should be indoors ministering to their spiritual needs!'*

"Good morning, sire. Do you remember me, Marius?"

"Ah, quite," said the man, looking up, "so, you are arrived?"

"Thus it would seem!" Marius jested, at once regretting his disrespectful answer may have caused offence.

"Let me see now…" and he ran a finger down the neatly drawn columns of his register. "As a newcomer you will have to start at the bottom of the pile, as it were… in fact, everybody begins with the barrows, so that's where you will begin too! It's hard work, mind, very hard and there's many a young hopeful who's found it too much… but we'll give you a chance to prove yourself, I suppose."

'Sire, I will reward your faith in me, no doubt of that!'

"I hope so! I likes to get it clear. Right, go into the yard and report to Christian – for my life I don't know why he has that name… to be honest, I reckon he is the devil incarnate, not a believer. But as we toil in the Lord's name - and for sure we are in His palatial splendour here - it doesn't follow we have to believe in him... so, enough of my rambling, off you go and good luck on your first day. By the way, Christian is the smallest man in the yard, you can't miss him."

"My thanks, monsieur."

He surveyed the picture of industry in the compound: men unloading bricks from a wagon, its oxen tethered, drinking from a bucket; two workers sitting on three-legged stools either side of a long, narrow block, pushing and pulling a frame saw; sculptors wielding wooden mallets, chipping at half-finished figurines of consummate beauty. Stocky labourers hacked with hatchets to smooth down stones delivered from the quarry. Bewildered by such activity, Marius, uncertain of which direction to take, was relieved to receive a tap on his shoulder.

"Who do you seek? I can see you are a new boy."

"I'm to report to Christian," he replied to the stranger.

"Over there, the one with the compass and set square."

'Over there, he said? He's mistaken...a small man...this one is a giant! He measures over two pieds...but he holds a set square, I think.'

"Excuse me, are you Christian?"

"That's me. 'Who asks?'"

"I am Marius. I will be working here today."

"Ah, yes, the foreman mentioned your name to me."

'And I'm not dismissed yet!'

"I wager he told you to find the smallest man in the yard...well, he always says that, it's his idea of a joke because, as you are witness, I'm the *biggest!*"

"You are that."

"No time to waste, my men over at the wall need a regular, but...er...Marius...I'd better first explain what we do here."

'He speaks clearly and seems a gentle character despite his enormous size. I will listen well and learn from him. My life in Avignon depends on it.'

"I am a mason and my task at the present is to get blocks for the town ramparts cut and dressed correct for laying. Over here, I'll show you." Christian went across to the men working in pairs with saws.

"Come, Marius! Now, I mark out the right square lines for sawing. Look, these tools are my mason's trade." He held out the instruments with pride for his pupil to admire. "The master mason, he's the gentleman as lives in yonder drawing office. He gives me the plans but you'll not see him often. He instructs the monks...scribes, they call them, I think... yes, er... for the drawings of the New Chapel. They are truly wondrous creations, believe me...statues, beasts, monster faces, everything down to the humble rock for the wall. I do believe the architect...I think that's the word...is Jean de Louvres and over all my years as a journeyman - and I've worked on big churches and the like – he's the best! I met him once...he's a good'un, and clever with his ideas...he told me we raise the chapel here 'To praise God. There are not boundaries between things material and spiritual.' There! I remember fine words from a fine man, Monsieur de Louvres!" He paused for breath. "Now come with me, again. Hey, Luc!" he shouted.

A youth, who Marius thought of an age similar to his, pushed a walling stone to its position on a low cart. A donkey, harnessed between the shafts, fed from a hay net hanging on a nearby post. Hearing his name called he stood upright, wiped the sweat from his brow and approached them.

"Marius, this is Luc, your new workmate."

The two shook hands. Luc's grip was strong, his welcoming smile revealing even, white teeth. Christian's introductory duties fulfilled, he left them.

"Pleased to meet you, Marius. You will like working here. You don't have to think too much – Christian and the master mason do that for you. Turn up regular, on time, in all weather, and you won't go far wrong. The pay is reasonable as well. We have to load the cart, then take it to the north wall. We unload, come back and start again. Simple! See, here's another ready to make up six - the donkey can't pull more than that at a time. Watch me."

Luc took the animal's bridle and guided it alongside the stone. He taught his mate how to arrange the block and tackle, attach ropes and hoist it into the remaining space. An hour later, one trip and back to the yard to repeat it. When they had done this four times, they stopped for their lunch.

"I've been here for two years," Luc continued, "and the wall had barely reached the docks when I started. Though we may now be level with Clément's house, there must be still two more years left before it's done. As long as His Holiness is happy, that's what counts."

"I suppose you're right." Marius agreed, "And do you have family?"

"Yes. My wife, Marianne and son, Fabien."

"Fabien? What a chance, my own boy is called that! Perhaps it's a sign of our friendship in the future... a bond between us."

"I trust so."

"How old is your son?" Marius asked.

"Not yet three. He's a bonny lad, gets his looks from his father! But we are troubled."

"How so?"

"These past days he is feverish, his face hot then cold and he sleeps so much. Usually, he is crawling like a wild thing around the house, but not of late. They say children suffer from illnesses of no consequence, and soon see them off. But, Fabien has not been sickly from birth except a slight colic or gripe when teething. Marianne gives him herb drinks – says her grandmother swears by them – but he can't keep food down... he vomits and it causes us great distress. A healer charges more than we can afford, so..." his voice trailed away, the pain of a devoted father etched on his face.

"I hope he soon revives," Marius wished him.

"Thank you. I'm sure he will."

At two o'clock a bell rang for the end of day at the yard. Marius took his leave from Luc and set off for the docks, pleased with his efforts, though concerned for Luc's family. '*I know not the man yet but he seems sincere, someone I can trust.*' Before announcing his arrival at the Magistrate's cabin he beat the stone dust from his tunic. '*I must be presentable. I don't want him to think I'm a common vagabond.*'

"Magistrate," Marius addressed the man.

He looked up from his desk. "Ah! Young Marius, again. No need for more questions, I have it all written down... so, no further ado, follow me," he ordered, but in an affable manner. They walked along the quay to a warehouse bearing a sign for 'Pagnol Fils', its tall doors open to an unknown void within.

"Jean! You in there?" the Magistrate shouted, "he is likely taken with counting his money. I'm setting you on with the richest of all the traders around these parts, so know that, lad. He may not appear so, but he is."

At that moment, a figure emerged from the darkness. Of medium stature, bearded with sharp, darting eyes, he walked with a limp. Marius guessed him some 50 years of age. Dressed like anyone else in the town, his grey tunic, tied with a cord at the waist, fell to his calves and the sleeves were long to protect from the winter cold. Ankle-high boots with thick leather soles were the only indication of a wealthy man.

"Salut, Marius," the wool merchant greeted, "and you are, verily, most welcome." The Magistrate then excused himself, mumbling something about having to be elsewhere.

"So, I am Jean Pagnol but you may use Jean. Come inside, out of the chill."

It took a while for his eyes to adjust to the dimness of the warehouse, and Marius' first impression was of chaotic piles of fabric, the length of one side. To the other, that haphazard state was replaced by neat, orderly, square bales, each bound tight by twines. These were arranged in lines from front to rear, a space between forming aisles. '*I could be walking down towards the altar and there must be something of the church in him, to be so rich. What's that aroma... a musty, damp scent that's hard to describe? It's not unpleasant, just strange.*' He turned his nose up, like a rabbit twitching. Jean noticed his reaction,

"The Pagnol perfume, that's what they call it. You'll get used to it. But come, sit and I'll explain my business to you." He indicated a table and bench behind which stood a dresser that was more suitable in a domestic residence. The upper section displayed a variety of tankards on pegs, drinking glasses below. The lower consisted of drawers. Next to this was a rack filled with dark green bottles.

"You will join me for wine?" he asked.

"Why...yes, to be sure."

Jean selected a bottle and placed it on the table. He took a small knife and proceeded to extract the cork stopper with a dexterity born of experience. It popped out in one piece, no fragments falling into the contents. Around the neck was a label showing 'Cabasse Fils Carpentras'.

'Damn that name! Can I ever escape its clutches? It follows me like a lion stalking its prey!'

The glasses were filled to the brim with a deep purple, smooth liquid that stirred Marius' memory – *'They always say red is the best.'*

"Are you familiar? I keep a store of Cabasse vintage...payment round here is sometimes a dozen bottles of claret in lieu of money. Strange folk!" The men raised their vessels, tapping them in a toast.

"You will start your work for me in earnest tomorrow, so today let me tell you about 'Pagnol Fils'. We are wool merchants, I say 'we' because I have two partners though neither is my son, it's a trading name. There's my brother, Thomas, and the fellow Bruno Lapierre. We each have a third interest. They will both be known to you in due course. Thomas is a sail maker by craft, so when he's not working here, he's down at yon docks making sails, if you understand?"

"I do, Jean."

"Through my brother we have a ready supply of canvas and twine to pack orders...makes sense to me. And there's Bruno – he paid a third share some years ago when we needed capital to see us through a lean patch. You might spot him up in the mason's yard...he's a joiner who does woodworking jobs there and I hear he's making the formers for the vaulted ceiling in the New Chapel...well you can't get much closer to the Lord than that!" With a guffaw he took the bottle, replenished their glasses and continued,

"We live in Avignon, the three of us, in my house, Rue Limas, up near the Bénézet bridge. Then there's me. Perhaps you've noticed I'm crippled in my leg, I drags it along... it still grieves me twenty years on. I was a soldier of fortune... a freelancer they call it... with the English king, Edward the Third... I think that's his title... and his companion-in-arms Montagu when we won Nottingham castle... in the English lands. I landed a musket ball in my leg... nasty... the surgeon said it was in too deep so best leave it for flesh to heal over. It's a long tale how I came from fighting over the water to be a merchant here. I'll maybe tell you some day."

"I'd enjoy that," Marius acknowledged, enthralled by his patron's story.

"The King pensioned me off on account of my injury, and he was uncommonly grateful for my service... saw me with a handsome pension so I founded 'Pagnol Fils' and that brings us to now."

'If all this is truthful, it's an astounding descent from royal warrior to dealer in cloth. His step does falter, in fairness, so should I accept him on face value?'

"You have a fascinating history, Jean, but what will my work entail?"

"Forgive me, young man, I'm coming to that! Wool is the future as much as the present. What I mean is the noble fabric is cheap enough for everybody – it's warm and heavy, soft and light, good or bad, do you see?"

"I'm with you, so far, Jean." Marius saw this man loved the material for its qualities as for the profits it brought and he was touched by the enthusiasm for life that Jean displayed.

"Now, most wool is white so it's easy to dye with woad and it's why the tunics you see around here are a bluish-grey colour. Blankets, capes, dresses, leggings, even hats, are all made from it, and...' he paused to pour more wine, '...this is where your duties begin. We buy in the stuff... it's shipped here through Marseilles from countries across the sea like Africa, where the sailors are dark-skinned, some black as pitch. In kingdoms further away in the East, they be yellow as parchment and wear round, flat hats and have eyes like the slits in a confessional box! Every order is a job lot, a real mixed bag, so you will sort it into different er... what we call grades... then bundle it up again to send upstream to Orange, Grenoble, Valence, even Lyon, or keep it for dyers and seamstresses in the town. We have customers in all parts.' Seeing the consternation on Marius' face, he reassured him, 'Worry not! I will show you more on the morrow.'

Returning to his house, with the mouth-watering aroma of the evening's stew met Marius. He hung his cape behind the door, went over to the blazing fire and rubbed his cold hands together over the flames.

"That feels better," he declared, then taking Dominique in his arms for a lusty embrace.

"It certainly does!" she giggled, holding him tight to her, "but how was your first day in the world of the unwashed labourers? I'd ask how much work you achieved because I smell drink!"

"Only by the insistence of a certain Jean Pagnol who is, let me tell you, only the most prosperous wool merchant in... in... I was going to say in Avignon, but for all I know, in the whole world!" The afternoon's libations had left him in a mellow mood but, with just cause. *'I've done well today and I look forward to a happy life.'*

Their meal over, Dominique fed Fabien the stew, but mixed smooth in a bowl. He soon fell asleep in his crib.

"Our time now," and Marius beckoned her to join him on their bed. He drew her close, covering them with the thick, woollen blanket and began to recount his day, but it was not long before he drifted into a deep slumber induced by the flickering embers of the fire and a contentment that consumed him.

The following morning, Marius walked to the mason's yard as he would a hundred times to come. He checked in at the foreman's office where they exchanged salutations before entering the compound.

"Morning, Christian."

"Morning to you, Marius. I see being on time is not going to be a problem with you. I'm pleased about that. You can't rely on some folk, though – take Luc, for example. He knows we've got a heavy workload today but he sends in a message that he can't make it. Can't make it!" Christian repeated. "I'll have to put another lad with you and what with you only learning…"

'I've known Luc for only one day, but if I'm a judge of character, he is not the sort to fail his responsibilities without reason. What did he say… his son was unwell and he was concerned? I will ask for his house from the foreman then I may call in on my way to the docks. But there is something amiss, I sense it.'

Not long past two o'clock, Marius found himself at Luc's doorstep. He knocked gently and it seemed an age until the door opened. Luc stood trembling, his body quite out of control, tears streaming down his cheeks. With a wave of his hand he bade Marius enter. On the table in the middle of the room lay a bundle, a body-shaped form wrapped in crisp white linen. Marianne sat at the table, perfectly still, her complexion ashen with weeping, enveloped in grief. Marius took two steps forward but no more, respecting the distance between himself and the corpse.

"The fever raged through the night. Our little one tried to cry out but could not, so swollen was his throat. Of a sudden, his poor body was broken, he could endure no more. I must carry Fabien to the church. The priest will know what to do. We are, at this sad time, fortunate indeed to have the Church." Marianne was silent as that pitiful room grew into a dramatic tableau of anguish, with no-one knowing or daring to speak. It was the child's mother who found the courage, after an eternity of time frozen in the moment.

"*I* will bear him. I will do it now as I did when he was in my womb. He will rest this night under God's sacred vigilance."

Marius doubted he could have eulogised with such calm had it been his own sweet boy laying there on that table shrouded in virgin damask cloth. He felt a desperate need to express his condolences but words failed him. At that second he could think only about his own son, of the same age, of the same name. Ere long, the reality of the event overtook its fantasy and he made an offer of informing the Magistrate of the passing, as the town's edicts required.

CHAPTER EIGHT

AVIGNON
5 January 1348 AD

It was with a heavy heart that Marius approached the Magistrate's office. An icy blast bit into his face on a sad, grey, January afternoon. He should have been excited by his first day working at the docks for the wool merchant, Pagnol, but not so. *'If it were my own child, wrenched away from me in its infancy - there can be nothing under the Heavens more hideous!'* Winter daylight was fading but there was no mistaking the Justice's cabin in the distance, a candle flickering, the only light to suggest any living soul on the quay. *'Are the warehouse doors shut out of respect? No, don't be so foolish, they cannot yet know what has befallen Luc's family.'*

"Ah, Marius, good to see you. You have a manifest for me then...the bargees arrive early, and we never know from one hour to the next since it depends on the current of the river and the wind if they are under sail. Of course, the heavier their load, the longer –"

"Sire, a moment, if you will. I have no manifest nor have I yet seen Monsieur Pagnol. I come to report dreadful news, the passing of an infant." The Magistrate placed a hand on his arm in a gesture of sympathy. "It is not of my own family, but of a friend."

"I see. Let me find the register...here it is." He took down the weighty, leather-bound tome from the shelf, laid it on his desk and opened it to the next available page. Dipping a quill into the inkwell, he asked,

"What is the name?"

"Charron, Fabien Charron." The Magistrate copied it meticulously in a neat chancery script.

"The address?"

"Rue Thiers."

"And the age?"

"Two years, nearly three."

"Can't put *nearly*, has to be exact, if you see, so…two…but still a baby. This is, indeed, most unfortunate, so young and it be the first passing of the new year. I know the Charron, a decent God-fearing house, they worship at the cathedral. There, it's written. I will inform the Pope's clerk, have to do that for any demise within the town walls." Marius nodded and left the cabin without further ado. He went straight to the wool merchant's store where they exchanged greetings and the man explained how to sort a newly-shipped bale of fabrics. Marius made every effort to concentrate on his work but he was sorely distracted by the tragedy.

In the cathedral, Marianne cradled her departed son, Luc sat in silence next to her on a bench, waiting for an officiant. After a time that only compounded the couple's distress, a priest wearing a black robe that reached the floor appeared. He did not speak directly but recited a prayer for the dead in Latin that held no significance for them. '*What does all this mean? I don't understand why he's crossing his hands then pointing to the sky. Is it to where my Fabien is intended, high above in God's kingdom?*'

"He is Fabien, is he not?"

"Why…yes…but how come you know? We have had no dealing with you…"

"The Magistrate sent a runner an hour ago, so you were expected." Such efficiency was a hallmark of the town's governance.

"May the Good Lord bless this dear child, *Laudate Dominum*, Praise be to God, and may He provide succour for the parents." The priest's words rang hollow for those whose brightest star had fallen from the sky. Luc and Marianne were simple strangers to him and, while he bore them no malice, he expressed no love. He reached for the child, who she released with weeping reluctance.

"Please, follow me." He led them, in solemn procession, down the nave and turned into a side chapel. A wooden altar on one side boasted two brass candlesticks; a carved crucifix hung on the wall above; six benches in a row but no additional adornment to the cold, austere room. Placing the limp, shrouded body on the altar, he bowed his head, droning another prayer that was, again, beyond their understanding. They were distraught, heartbroken, inconsolable, fighting to make sense of the senseless. The priest turned to face them.

"Your son is in a better place, in Heaven, *Servum autem Domini,* a Servant of the Lord. The saints will cherish his soul so shed no tears. May the Lord's Grace be upon you, as with your child, now called to eternal rest. Fabien will sleep in peace in this sacred chamber until the day after tomorrow. We will conduct the funeral rites here, after nones. A grave will be prepared in the people's cemetery beyond the cathedral grounds. I understand you have donated to the Church when your means permitted, so there will be no cost for the ceremony or plot. My condolences to you both. *Vade in pace,* Go in Peace."

The next day, Monsignor Milos, Clément's assistant, tapped on the door to the Pontiff's private rooms.

"Come." As Milos entered, Clément was turning a key in a sturdy wooden cabinet, to then drop it with haste into the pouch of his robe.

"Yes? What is it?"

"Holy Father, I have the list of sermons that fall to you the coming week." He laid a parchment sheet on the desk for his master to peruse.

"I agree with them, apart from tomorrow, Friday," Clément decided in a dismissive tone.

"Sire?"

"Friday, the seventh, this week... are you hard of hearing?" His face reddened and beads of sweat moistened his forehead. "I will be confined to my chamber in solitary devotion."

"As you wish." The cleric had become accustomed to Clément retreating from contact with his congregation, as with the Palace servants, on occasions for an entire day or longer. He saw this as Papal communion with the Lord, to which he, a mere priest, could not aspire.

"Will that be all?" Clément enquired. Milos hesitated, then answered,

"No, Holy Father. A passing has been reported, this day."

"What of it? Is it not normal?" He paced to and fro as if considering the matter. Milos resumed,

"*Laudate Dominum.* God be praised. It is the first month of the year, and the deceased is an infant, aged only two. I have discussed it with a colleague monsignor and he thinks it would be appropriate, nay welcomed, if after nones when you lead Communion, the day after next, you participated in the side chapel funeral. Considering the tender age of the child, you might include reference to... well... to God's infinite Wisdom, even when taking a babe to His Kingdom. *For God so loved the world, his only Son, that whoever believes in him should not perish but have eternal life.* Saint John, Chapter Eleven, though please excuse my impudence, you need no reminding of the Gospel. We feel the congregation and, by gossip, the entire town, will approve your gesture and appreciate their Eminence all the more. Who could but not admire our tireless and esteemed Pontiff giving of his precious time to respect, in person, a child's unforeseen end?"

"Have you quite finished?" Clément asked, ever impatient, eyes darkening and his gaze fixed on the priest. His knuckles turned white as he clenched his fists in an effort to control his emotion, but to no avail. The parchment was snatched from the desk and waved through the air, as a worker might scythe wheat in a field. Such onslaughts, outpourings of his master's passion for the Word, did not surprise Milos. Today it was more extreme than anything witnessed thus far. He stepped away from the desk, fearing his own safety as Clément approached him, only to retreat and gather his composure sufficient to resume speaking to his aide,

"Each and every one of my sermons I consider with the utmost care and attention to the message I would have the people hear. You have no idea of the trouble it causes my mind, the suffering my body undergoes, how my very being trembles and dreads the task! Do you think demands we can avoid, in the form of a eulogy – and at that, for a commoner's bereavement – should not, I put it to you, Milos, be *avoided*? No! I will ignore your counsel! Give the honour to another. Are we bereft of clergy? *You* might, and it would amaze us all, have to do some work! No more! I have made my decision, so leave me." Milos took back the parchment, bowed and obeyed the order, smarting and resentful of his mistreatment.

'O help me, Lord! I beseech, help me! How I detest the pulpit! I venerate the Word but my people frighten me, I dread they do not want to hear me and would return to their homes without my blessing. With the advent of each sermon on Milos's infernal list, I am filled with a terror surpassed only by fear of Thy Presence. I lack strength, I cower. It is the potion on which I lean. I know not the way to be rid of it.'

Hands shaking, he fumbled in his robe for the key to the cabinet. It required more than one attempt to introduce it in the lock, such was his agitation. Finally, the door opened. He withdrew a dark glass bottle, sat at his desk and removed its stopper. Into a miniature silver chalice, he poured the sweet liquid, the consistency of syrup, to swallow it in a single draft. He repeated the dose, and his anger began to subside. Wiping his brow with the sleeve of his robe, he inhaled deeply and a peace of sorts regained. It was an ephemeral moment: holding the bottle up against the light, darkness on him returned. *'It is all but empty! I must send for Alice. Why does the world connive, my attendants and mere subjects plot, all to deprive me of this restorative? They will not prevent me, Lord, doing Thy Bidding. No! No! Try as they might, I will serve Thee till my end. O Mithridates, King of Pontus! If not for you, I would never have been tempted by thy evil drink!'*

SAINT MARTIAL ABBEY
1305 AD

"Where am I? Who are...?"

"Rest now, be still." The elderly infirmarian wetted a cloth in a pail and wiped cool Pierre Roger's fevered brow. The boy lay on one of six straw-filled mattresses in the abbey infirmary. He turned his head to left and right but did not recognise his surroundings. With a great effort, he tried to sit upright but his weakness was too severe and he fell back, tears running down his cheeks.

"There, it will be many lauds and complines until you have healed enough to stand and, as for walking, we trust in the Lord to bless your recovery. We can do no more than ease your pain. Here, drink." The monk supported the patient in the crook of his arm and placed a cup to his lips. "Take a few sips...that's the idea...a little more...it will relieve your misery, believe me." He lowered the boy. "Sleep now, I will return after nones."

'What is this strange world? I see dragons lined as soldiers to confound and slay me... and, lo, a terrible beast, sharp fangs and foul breath, rearing up and poised to leap upon me... then a charging warrior, sword held high, will take off my head...' He drifted into a delirium induced by his wounds and the potion administered by the infirmarian.

After attendance at nones, Brother Bertrand entered the room where Pierre Roger sometimes slept, but at intervals fitted, ranting, incoherent, possessed by the Devil for all he knew. Nothing could be done until the fever abated. The monk divided his time between wiping dry the boy's perspiring body and crushing and mixing substances with a pestle and mortar on the oak-planked table that ran the length of one wall. Drinking vessels and bowls arrayed in neat rows, pieces of white linen in a pile, indicating a well-ordered hospice. Shelves on the other wall displayed pots, bottles, phials and crocks, their contents shown on parchment labels tied with cord: saffron, sage, castor-oil, cilantro, bay, juniper, garlic, za'atur, poppy seeds and more. A low, bleating moan caused him to turn as the boy revived.

"Do not speak, nor tax your strength. I will apply salve to your wounds, be brave for the pain will lessen as days pass." He smeared a dark, unctuous ointment on the cuts to Pierre Roger's skull, chest and leg, lesions that remained gaping, the assault but a short time gone by. He was fortunate to have the resilience of youth.

"Now, a little more…do not gulp…it is a potent blend," Bertrand said in a kind tone. He snuffed out the candle, leaving the afflicted novice in peace and darkness. He returned twice during the night to check all was well, and the boy slept still, salve and potion taking effect.

After lauds in Saint Sauveur's church the next day, the brother moved along the cloister to his infirmary, head bowed as was customary. A solemn silence pervaded the ancient abbey: its Bénédictine order demanded due reverence at all times. He was glad to find Pierre Roger alert and wide-eyed, but a grimace betrayed his discomfort.

"Good morning, young man. How are you feeling today?"

"My head spins and my very being complains."

"That is no surprise, you have suffered terrible injuries."

"Injuries? How so?"

"Do you remember the attack in the forest where you were left for dead?"

"I do not. In truth, only my name comes to mind."

"As your body mends, so your memory will return. The Good Lord sees our sins and His forgiveness is a bounty to those who believe in the Word. You are barely fifteen years of age, I guess, and your natural vigour will aid your struggle, so fear not."

"Sire, pray tell me, what is this place?"

"First, let us praise the Lord." He held the boy's hand and recited a verse, finishing with *In Deo speramus, amen,* In God we trust. He crossed himself by force of habit then reached a green bottle from the shelf labelled 'theriac' and filled a small cup for Pierre Roger to drink. The liquid burned his throat but he had faith in Bertrand's competence and kindness. Staring with anticipation, he waited for the monk's explanation.

"So," Bertrand began, "this is the abbey of Saint Martial. We sent brothers to search for you when you failed to come back after visiting your family and friends in Limoges. We found you, thanks to God, but gravely afflicted by someone who had beaten you to the verge of death...yes, it was, indeed, a person and not a beast. You were borne here in all haste where you have descended in and out of consciousness for nigh on one week. I see you are most perplexed, is that not so?"

"It is so, brother," Pierre Roger replied, rolling his eyes in astonishment and pain. Bertrand continued,

"We are of the Bénédictine fellowship. Our robes are dark, in fact, they call us the Black Monks. We devote our lives to serving the Lord, in retreat, to escape a violent world and lead a peaceful existence, in silence except for communal gatherings, meals or giving instruction. All this under His perfect guidance and our Abbot's discipline. We possess no property nor do we wander outside the walls of the monastery, except with the Prior's permission. You will find some of us retire early after complines to rise in time for matins."

"This means nothing to me, but would that I may follow such a devout life."

"You will, my son, have no doubt of that," and the monk's lip curled, knowing well the difficult path ahead. He resumed,

"We each have a role within our community: washing, cooking, reaping and sowing, making wine and, believe me, that is the best duty of them all! There are scribes among us who copy manuscripts or, like myself, give medical care and hospitality to pilgrims. We are skilled at treating breaks, burns, dislocations and – as in your case – lacerations."

"This is, doubtless, a sacred home, but *why* am I here?"

"I'm coming to that. You are an *oblate...*"

"What does that mean?"

"Patience! It means you are entrusted to us by your parents, who have great aspirations for you, to receive an education in the Way of the Lord, and the arts of mathematics and science. You are first named *postulant,* then *novice* until you have proved yourself worthy, after one year. Next, you will undergo four years of Piety, Chastity and Obedience before you are admitted, after vows, a *monk.* This explains why you are here, does it not?" Pierre Roger swooned, such was the mountain ahead.

'*Can I achieve what lies before me? It is, certainly, too much! However, it is convenient they live in silence, as I do not enjoy facing others.*'

"Worry not. You will recall everything in due course. But, let us see if you can consume some food. The potion alone is too heady for one so young. You have made weird utterances in your fever... repeating the name Edmond. I know not who this person is." The monk broke a small piece off a flat loaf, dipped it into red wine he had poured into a bowl and helped the boy to eat a little.

"You are progressing well. A few drops of our theriac again and you will rest."

The routine of salve, bread, liquor and sleep continued for two weeks until he was strong enough to leave his bed. After a time he resumed his studies and prayer with the other postulants. His physical wounds healed but there were recurring headaches and bouts of dizziness, causing him to visit the infirmary each time to partake of the theriac. Bertrand, fulfilling his obligation as the abbey's physician, administered the medicine that he trusted without reservation.

"Of what is its composition?" Pierre Roger asked, "for I would learn."

"You would *not!* You need *not!*" the monk retorted in a sharp manner, "the recipe is passed to me by a late brother, the infirmarian before me, and so it goes on. Nowhere is it written down."

"So, it is a secret?"

"If you call prayer a secret, then it is such. The ingredients for theriac are natural in origin, but its efficacy comes from the blending. Saint Hildegard of Bingen, two hundred years past, and a most popular saint among those seeking spiritual enlightenment, bequeathed us a fine treatise on herbal medicine. I have read it many times and without it, I don't know how I could call myself a *healer*. She advocates everything on this earth comes from God, so we should profit from the fruits and flowers of the land. There is also..." He paused.

"Do carry on."

"...there is also an uncommon recipe. Thus I describe it because not every physician or apothecary knows of it. The sap and seeds of the poppy combined with henbane, crushed amber and – not always easy to obtain - the viper's flesh, in particular measures with the theriac gives *laudanum*. Mixed with wine, or better still the spirit eau de vie, the result is a remedy to govern the worst pain or illness of the mind."

"Do you dispense it?"

"Not often. It is a costly medicine, so I keep it secure. Be it known, our souls submit to His governance and wisdom, this is beyond dispute, but our bodies are ruled by the Four Humors: blood, phlegm, yellow and black bile. A good healer understands the balance of the Humors and treats the patient with this knowledge. But, enough! Does it ease the hurt in your head?"

"I fear not. Pray, let me drink laudanum." The monk, seeing no harm, took a phial concealed behind larger bottles on the shelf. He filled the bowl of a wooden spoon and passed it to Pierre Roger. In moments, his mind was animated, inspired, emboldened through the power of the opium elixir. His nervous state was, equally, calmed; his confidence, restored.

COLLEGE DE SORBONNE, PARIS
1307 AD

"We are most thankful the Abbot, our esteemed brother from Saint Martial, has sent you to us with the intention of completing your novitiate, to then accept vows. From his letter of introduction, we note your future in Orders will be best fulfilled here, where our founder, Robert de Sorbon, decreed the Gospel be taught within our walls but also broadcast across all Paris." The Provisor of the College touched Pierre Roger's head, genuflected and stepped back with a welcoming smile.

'*Are they aware I detest the thought of speaking in public? How do they think I can spread the Word, whence will that courage come?*' As his training progressed, leading to communion, he would be expected to evangelize. An acute sense of panic enveloped him. '*But, it is as if the Lord is watching over me and knows my weakness. Was I not calmed with Bertrand's theriac? And yet greater was the power of laudanum. I'll wager the infirmarian of this college will offer the same cure. I will say to him that pain still pervades my head and ask whether he could...offer me a crock to keep next to my bed and, so, not bother him in his work: nobody need know the arrangement.'*

ABBEY OF FECAMP
1324 AD

"I trust the chamber pleases our new Abbot?" the assistant monk asked Pierre Roger.

"It does. On the morrow, I will provide you with a list of our where-withal that I may suitably receive visiting clergy, of whom there will be many. The items are to be charged to Abbey revenues."

"I shall see to it, personally, sire."

The Abbot sat at his desk, picked up a quill and wrote his list on a parchment sheet:

- Bible Historiale, version of 1297, Guyart des Moulins

- Silver drinking chalices – 6- white linen serviettes

- Skin of good claret wine

- 6 crocks each of laudanum and theriac

- 3 bottles of eau de vie

'Here, they abstain from quarrels, slanderous talk and gossip. That will mean less conversation for I shall leave that to others. But there is noise of bringing the English King Edward to this land to pay homage to our good King Philippe, and the Holy Father expects me to do the bidding! I trust not my nerve alone to carry out such a mission, so laudanum will be my crutch. The infirmarian here will not question it, considering my injuries and their lasting hurt. I am to ease my complaint with the substance, a stimulant of miraculous faculty!'

Pierre Roger's behaviour in his subsequent positions at Arras, Sens and Rouen, exhibited similar traits. Abbots, then bishops needed to instil the highest confidence in their peers as in their flocks. They had a duty to preach the Gospel from the pulpit, with gusto and conviction: this bishop, Pierre Roger, new in his post, could not evade his responsibility.

AVIGNON
6 January 1348 AD

"Milos! Milos! Attend me, at once!" Pope Clément bellowed. The priest entered.

"Excellency?"

"Entrust this note to a postulant. He will deliver it to the landlord of the hostelry on Rue de la Bourse, a Monsieur Duval. He must then tell him a young woman will present herself. As on previous occasions, no names are to be revealed. Do I make myself clear? You do not need to understand, either, why I ask this. Trust in your Holy Father."

"It will be done, as you instruct, sire."

'*Alice will go to the apothecary, the most skilled in town at crushing and blending herbs, amber and the rest. He has influence enough to obtain viper's flesh and, I hear it adds to the prescription, cow's intestine! A curse of the Devil or marvel sent by God? I care not which! She will enter by the palace's secret passageway to bring me my precious laudanum and no-one is the wiser! I, Clément, am to give a eulogy in memory of the deceased infant of a poor family. But am I to blame for the condition of my mind? Have I sinned that the Lord punishes me, sending demons that haunt, voices that ring in my head louder than the bells of my Palace? No! It is not my fault that night descends to obscure the path to righteousness. It is Edmond - for certain residing in the Hall of Hades where the Furies with their blood-shot eyes, bats wings and snakes for hair do their worst, in such a heathen place. Hades sends plagues of locusts that bite and sting me and the curse lives on through his son, innocent by birth, guilty by association! Men ought to know, but do not, that from the brain arises all pleasure, joy, laughter and jest, as well as our sorrow, grief and tears. Through it, we see, hear, think and distinguish the ugly from the beautiful, the bad from good, the pleasant from the unpleasant, the Godly from the Pagan. It makes us mad and delirious, inspires us with dread and fear. O Lord! Thy sublime power and glory alone does not reach my inner sense, I require more!'*

His meditation was abruptly interrupted by three sharp knocks at his chamber door that opened into the secret passage-way known only to Clément and a trusted friend. He regained his calm and slid back the bolt.

"Come in, Alice."

She removed the hood that hid her face, shook her dark tresses free and approached the Pontiff.

"I have the vessel you requested, Holy Father. As for its contents, I cannot say. It is not my place to ask." She passed him the crock, wrapped in sack-cloth.

"You have done well, Alice... and no-one saw you?"

"Not a soul, rest assured."

"May the Lord bless you, my child."

"Amen to that," she replied, staring into his eyes, a provocative smile on her lips.

"Will that be all?"

"For today, Alice, it will. I have a sermon to prepare and must give it my full attention. Your presence would not be conducive to Godly writing."

"Indeed. I will take my leave." She gave a respectful bow and left down the dark passage. He pushed home the bolt in the door, sat at his desk and unwrapped the crock, sighing with relief that his supply of laudanum was replenished. He poured a measure into a silver chalice and drank. A new parchment sheet laid out before him, he began to compose his sermon and eulogy for the following day.

CHAPTER NINE

At three in the afternoon, Marius and Dominique, Fabien in her arms, left their house to walk to the cathedral and attend Luc's family bereavement service. A sharp pain erupted in a troublesome tooth and Marius rubbed his cheek against the bitter cold, tugging down his hood. Dominique held her child tight to her bosom, ensuring her shawl covered every part of him. Neither spoke. Silence expressed their emotions more than words.

The setting sun bathed the rooftops in a warm orange glow; the chimneys stood upright as if saluting the citizens below, peaceful and content. And, this on a day the people had no right to feel thus. One street or two away from their doorsteps, the lifeless bodies of an innocent boy or girl awaited interment in the cloying earth. The warm embrace of their inconsolable parents soon exchanged for an uncaring, anonymous churchyard. Their grave would be marked only by wooden stakes, no headstones for ordinary folk. Few people roamed about at this hour, it being neither light of day nor dark of night, the one betwixt and between the other. The street sloping uphill meant the Pope's Palace would be visible round a bend.

"Not far now," Marius said to his wife, to encourage her. She nodded but still said nothing. The building loomed ahead, massive, imposing, regal, its stern military aspect suggesting fierce swordsmen and warriors within more than venerable clerics. The slits in the walls, designed for archers to fire their arrows down into an approaching enemy. Crenellations atop the building permitted boiling oil and pitch to be poured out and scald, rendering senseless any soldiers below, brave enough to have come so near. Its windows showed no light, no sign of life, no glimmer of humanity. The couple skirted the palace to arrive at the cathedral of Notre Dame des Doms behind and under the protection of the Pope's residence. A fine Romanesque edifice overlooking the Rhône valley. The west entrance, after the chill of the town, came as a relief. They felt the intensity of the ordeal ahead grow with every minute.

Inside the church, Marius removed his hood and Dominique took the shawl from around Fabien. The sheer beauty of the place astounded them. To left and right, arched aisles flanked the nave in perfect symmetry; an ornate boss, decorated with carvings, secured each vault. Rich, embroidered hangings adorned the walls. At the east end, the grey granite altar, draped in a golden-threaded linen cloth, bore a heavy brass crucifix, two candles burning on either side. They marvelled at the apse, painted with biblical scenes embellished in precious gold leaf. They blinked in the flickering light of torches.

"Have you ever seen the equal?" Marius asked his wife in a hushed tone.

"I have not. It's truly beautiful," she responded, "but who is the master of it all? The Lord? Thor? If we asked Luc and Marianne, likely they would reply *Satan*! And, no doubt, it would affect us in a similar fashion!"

"Quiet! Not so loud!" Marius urged. "Such talk is blasphemy in a holy house and you would be severely punished should an authority hear. That said, I must agree with you. Death and beauty should not belong together." Their eyes focused in the dim interior on a group before the altar. They made the sound of a monotone chanting. Marius and Dominique watched and heard it move down the nave. A priest, his head crowned with a black tonsure – a custom decreed by the Pope – led the procession. He wore a long, white robe for the purity of the deceased, belted with a leather thong. Aloft, he held a brass cross fixed on a pole, much as a soldier would flaunt the symbolic colours of an army entering the fray. Behind the priest, an old man pushed a creaking wooden bier bearing a human form wrapped in a coarse, brown winding sheet. Three elderly people and a younger man made up the solemn cortege.

A tap on the shoulder caused Marius to turn round. The Magistrate, black tunic and cap worn only on formal occasions, greeted them,

"You are come to witness the funeral of Luc and Marianne's child?"

"Yes, justice."

"The service in the nave, must first be conducted, so there is a short delay until the priest returns from the cemetery. Luc's party is in the side chapel, and I fear the wait will prolong their grief."

"I understand but, may I ask, who is the old man?"

"Cédric. He sold vegetables from a barrow since long before my tenure, until he retired to enjoy time with his wife. A noble ambition, do you not think? He is a good man, but we know the Grim Reaper will collect us all, in the end. It is, nonetheless, a battle we fight to hold on to life and escape his calling. As I see it, she passed away through old age, nothing surprising in that..."

"There is not, unlike little Fabien."

"Quite another matter, I'd say, but...be quiet now."

The white-robed priest, followed by the old man labouring with the heavy trolley and its burden, left the cathedral. The cleric's continual droning created a religious mysticism with which to bid *adieu* to the cadaver. Marius shivered from the sound that resonated, even as they moved away.

"Let us join Luc now," the Magistrate said, his manner calm and reassuring as he ushered them into the chapel.

On the front bench sat Luc and Marianne, she sobbing in between breaths, her anguish doleful and heart-rending. She pleaded time could revert to when they might have prevented the loss. But there was nothing she could have done. Her husband tried as may to placate her distress, with little success. *Rigor mortis* made the infant's corpse stiff beneath its white shroud of purity, on the altar placed two days earlier. In the half-light from the chapel candles, the clear shapes of people eluded Marius who the Magistrate had shown to a rear seat.

'I recall him telling me, when we first met, he had the ear of the Holy Father. He's in command of affairs, that's clear.'

Of the mourners, Marius recognised but a few: Christian the mason, his bald head glimmering; the innkeeper, Marcel; Carel Rostand, the beggar he had not seen since his first visit to Avignon. The others he did not know whether family or friends, but it mattered little. Weepers and wailers, mothers, fathers, sons and daughters filled the small chapel. Each mourner had his own view on death but despaired equally, in unison and sympathy for an infant's soul soon to fly its mortal coil.

Baby Fabien woke, and started to wriggle and murmur in his mother's arms. She shushed him, singing a lullaby so gentle only he could hear. Marius looked at his wife and son, and in front of him to where Luc and Marianne waited in sadness.

'How can it be? Who has decided their child perishes while mine lives still? What being says to one man you shall be happy, but to the other your lot is misery? Does any man possess such power and, if so, why does he choose to inflict suffering, pain, fear, and horror? The answer is beyond a simple boy like me, but I am minded, one day, to ask a priest - they are the wise ones.' His gaze roamed around the room and he wondered why the innkeeper and the beggar attended the service. *'Pity the poor parents who have lost a child! I cannot imagine their hurt. If it were in my gift to prevent suffering...'* At that moment, a door behind the altar opened and, the same priest who had lead the funeral cortege for the old woman entered. He moved to stand in front of Luc and Marianne. They began to rise but he gestured they should remain seated. Leaning slightly forward, his dominance was both physical and spiritual: a well-rehearsed ritual. All whispering and shuffling ceased. The con-

gregation's jaws dropped, eyes wide open. They expected, with impatience, the sombre tragedy to unfold, resentful of the injustice that had brought them to the cathedral: the death of a child.

The cleric, wearing the same white robe, clasped and twisted his hands together, head thrown back, but silently, invoking heavenly intervention. His body trembled, his eyes opened and closed as if overcome by a convulsion. An unintelligible message escaped his mouth until, quite suddenly, he became still. He represented a player standing centre stage in a drama that in a just world would not have been performed. Speaking in a tone barely audible but stirring, he pronounced,

"*Brevis ipsa vita est sed malis fit longior* – Our life is short but is made longer by misfortunes – *Integer vitae scelerisque purus* – Blameless of life and free from crime – *Vita mutatur, non tollitur* – Life is changed, not taken away." Only the priest understood the Latin utterances but the people nodded in affirmation, such was his control of the moment. He paused, gathered his composure, and continued,

"We are here to glorify the soul of the deceased, Fabien Charron, that sin in Purgatory is extinguished. We provide condolences and comfort for his parents, Luc and Marianne."

The mother rocked to and fro, crying and quaking, scarcely able to contain her grief. Marius sat upright, glaring at the priest when he heard 'sin' pronounced,

'*Sin! How dare the man use that word? Does he know the 'deceased', as he puts it, is a mere child, not of this earth long enough to sin? If he says it again I fear I might rip out his tongue!*'

"O God, whose attribute it is to show mercy and to forgive, we humbly present our prayer to Thee for the spirit of Thy servant, Fabien, whom Thou hast called to Thy house. We beseech Thee to deliver it not into the hands of the common enemy, nor to forget it ever, but to order Thy holy angels to receive and bear it to Paradise. It had believed and hoped in Thee, so may it be spared from the gates of hell and inherit perpetual life, through Christ our Lord. Amen."

"Amen," came the reply. They understood the gist of the eulogy if not the detail.

After leading communion at nones, Clément had left the palace and gone to his private rooms. He removed his mozetta and zuchetta and took out a key from the pouch in his white robe, worn for everyday services. Unlocking the cabinet on the wall, he reached in for the crock and placed it with due reverence on his desk. Pouring a good measure of potion into a small silver chalice, he sipped, then breathed a sigh of relief.

'*That tastes good... not many worshippers for nones today... perhaps thirty in my church that can seat five hundred... but, why should I worry? The townsfolk will reap the wrath of the Lord come the Day of Judgment.*' He took another draught of the special elixir. '*Now, I must think about my message for the Charron child. With each sermon I give, the harder the task becomes, and the more I fear my flock... is fear the correct word? I know not, but, my heart races, I perspire and shake like the leaves on the trees whipped by the Mistral! Then I calm down to a state fit to face the congregation... but only after this infernal liquor has passed my lips. O, how I resent that man, Edmond, who, even from his grave puts me through this agony! I am sure he cares not a jot! May Satan cast him into the lake of everlasting fire and brimstone that froths and boils in the netherworld that is hell!*' He drank again, and thought, '*That is much better. My head is clearer and my body soothed. I will pronounce words that are suitable for the sad occasion. I do not perform this duty often – that is why I employ priests – but, Milos was right... what did he say... ah, yes, the entire town will appreciate their esteemed and tireless Pontiff... let me find the passage from Saint John's gospel.*' He pulled down a parchment scroll from a shelf and untied its ribbon. He sought chapter eleven. While laudanum affected the body and mind of its frequenters, in Clément's case his memory remained unimpaired. He remembered with vivid precision his last encounter with Marius' father. A knock came at the door,

"Sire, they await you."

"I will attend in five minutes." He put on the stole, embroidered in red and gold thread, and replaced the white skullcap with purple. Attired in the appropriate funeral dress, he left his study and walked through the body of the cathedral to the chapel. As he entered, the priest bowed and his subjects gasped, hardly believing their eyes to see Clément. They stood, at once, to attention.

"This was not expected...the Pope!" Marius whispered to his wife.

"Be seated," Clément instructed and, as he genuflected, the people copied him. "For God so loved the world He gave his one and only Son, that whoever believes in Him shall not perish but have eternal life.' If Marius and the rest followed the sermon, Luc and Marianne ceased to pay heed: they wished for the affair to be concluded so they could mourn in private. They knew not how long the Pontiff spoke, and they emerged from their emotional stupor only when he raised his voice and offered his outstretched arms to the sky, a sign for his audience to stand.

"*Pater noster, qui est in Caelis* Our father, who art in Heaven. Then, *Gloria Patri, et Filio, et Spiritui Sancto*...In the name of the Father, and of the Son, and of the Holy Ghost...*Semper beatus* Eternally blessed. *Requiescat in pace* Rest in peace." Delineating a cross in the air, he bowed, turned and left by the door whence he had come, murmuring under his breath, '*Milos was right, they were, indeed, impressed, I can tell that...I will thank him for his wise counsel. When my body is calm, I have a gift...a talent for speaking.*'

The priest stepped forward and, with nothing further to add, motioned Luc to approach. He gave instructions in a hushed tone and Luc carefully took up his child. An altar boy in white surplice headed the suite, a candle held high. The priest came next with the same brass cross on a pole he had used an hour before. Luc, bore Fabien and, finally, came Marianne and the others.

Filing with measured step, they made the short way to the walled cemetery. A verger's torch lit the burial plot, prepared that same morning. Darkness and shadows cast by the flame chased around like spectres, fiendish ogres abroad to ensnare the living and thrust their victims deep into the cold frosty ground. The mourners grouped around the grave but at a respectful distance, allowing Luc to climb in the pit and lay down little Fabien. He and Marianne scattered a handful of soil over the corpse as the priest repeated Clément's '*Requiescat in pace* Rest in Peace' and the proceedings ended. Before the verger took away his torch, Marcel, the innkeeper, to general surprise, spoke up above the polite, joyless silence,

"My friends, night has drawn in and it is royal cold. May I invite you all to my tavern where my wife has made a roaring fire. My finest cider will be served – at modest cost – and you can all... er... console one to the other, as it were, in the warmth and convivial atmosphere of my humble establishment. You know which inn is mine, I'm sure."

'*So, now I see why Marcel is here! Marius realised.' Touting for trade! I cannot believe any man would profit from another's misfortune! And I'll wager he addressed the previous funeral party in a similar manner. Our first night here in Avignon, when he asked us to dine with him and his fat wife, I suspected he was an insincere man.*' Marcel's commercial acumen was vindicated as most of the mourners accepted his invitation and retired to the inn. The place was abuzz with stupor at the unexpected appearance of the Pope in the cathedral. His fine cider sold well. The ambiance was warm and sympathetic, unlike the cold of the huge church, priest, and Pope. Marius went from one person to another, to find his arrival in Avignon and renting the house was common knowledge. It did not worry him, he cared not who knew his identity, why should he? Cédric, the former vegetable seller, now a widower, but a friendly old man, was quite willing to engage in conversation about his late wife.

"My heartfelt condolences to you," Marius said, shaking the man's hand.

"Thank you for your kindness. Do you know, I gave my barrow and, thus, the business to my son. My wife and I hoped the rest of our lives, together... she wanted to visit Marseilles where she has cousins, but that was not to be. The Good Lord saw a different journey for us... I had a yearning to discover my family lineage. We came from Arles and my father took me there when I was fourteen or fifteen years old where we lodged with my grandfather. Every day, we carried our rods, lines, bait, all the fishing tackle, down to the river – such good times.

We would catch pike, trout, and sender that grandmother cooked. Did you know Julius Caesar watched chariot races and gladiators fighting in the amphitheatre there? My loved one said, in jest, I'd look a picture with a trident in one hand and a net in the other! She had a good sense of humour."

"I did not know that, Cédric."

"My wife says – no, I meant *said, I...*" Tears welled in his eyes, overflowing with despair and running down his weather-beaten face. "I'm sorry, such feebleness is not becoming." Then, pulling back his shoulders, straight and alert, he concluded "death is a natural end to a complete life, bless her.

"Whilst she was three score and ten years, she had no ailment or malady - hale and hearty as they say. I told her many times she would see me to my grave. And so, her passing is all the more shocking: one day fine, the next, gone to the Lord. She showed a fever that raged without respite through the day, later her throat became swollen so she could neither speak nor cry. That's how she left us." '*A fever, then throat badly swollen... these are the same signs young Fabien displayed. Strange, but I suppose it's the way life goes and, as the Magistrate said to me in the cathedral, the Grim Reaper collects us all sooner or later,*' Marius pondered, then moved away from Cedric, as many folk waited to console him. He spoke, in polite tones, with the Magistrate, still sporting his badge of office – the black tunic and hat. After that, he exchanged words with the priest. '*Now, where is Luc? Ah, yes, by the fire.*'

"Luc, I can do nothing to console you, but please accept mine and Dominique's sympathies."

"You are very kind. See, over there, our wives are sharing their thoughts and that will help Marianne express her melancholy but, and take no offence, I am best alone at this moment."

"I understand, Luc." He embraced his friend and left him in peace to take a solitary seat at a table in a corner of the room. The Magistrate did not delay in approaching him, as he had with every other person.

"A rum affair, do you not think, Marius? Two dead in two days! If it carries on like this I'll have my work cut out, that's for sure! I'll need a new ledger!"

"You will, for a fact, Magistrate, but with your experience in these matters... you will account well for yourself."

"Good of you to say so," he answered, embarrassed by the compliment, "but life goes on, as they say. That much I've learned."

A voice behind caught his attention - Rostand, the beggar, a wooden bowl in his hand, saying,

"... you speak good things about the old woman... did you know her well?... your opinion of her says much for yourself and your caring, thoughtful, generous view on the wonder of the Lord... Cédric is moved by your attending today... may I pass on his thanks to you?... " He bowed, fawning, his face contorted with sympathy and the bowl proffered imperceptibly towards the other person. Motionless, he waited for the message to be understood. A coin clinked into the receptacle and Rostand nodded in gratitude: in fact, the most he had to do with either Cédric or his wife being one day when he stole a melon from the man's barrow, his back being turned. But, today, everyone in the tavern suffered from sadness. They did not discriminate between an expression of genuine concern and a man taking advantage of the situation to inveigle money.

'Thanks? What on earth is Rostand saying? I will have more than words with the charlatan when next I find him begging in the street!' Marius filled his tankard from the jug on the table, drank and withdrew into his meditation, to be disturbed by a soft, female voice,

"Marius Nerval, may I sit with you?" He looked up, it was his neighbour, Alice.

"Why... er... yes, please do." He replied. He was taken aback as he had not seen her earlier in the day.

"Nerval is your family name, is it not?"

"It is so." He stared into her eyes but saw darkness, not pleasant green or blue.

"You will not mind me asking how you have settled here in Avignon?"

"I do not mind at all, Alice. We find the town to our liking, the people most charming. I assume you are speaking to me as any kind neighbour does. The accommodation suits us – by *us*, I mean my wife and son, of course."

"That is good. And how goes your work?" At this point, he was feeling somewhat uneasy with her questions.

"Although it has only been two days, I am enjoying it and I find it rewarding."

"You are employed at the stonemason's yard?"

"Why yes, but I know not how you have been informed."

"Avignon is a small town - news and gossip soon find their way around. Do you have any other employ?" His unease now changed to suspicion. '*Why does she ask me so many questions? That I am her new neighbour should be all she needs to know, until we become friends or enemies, as is the natural way. She is, though, a beautiful woman... high cheekbones, a slender nose, and tantalising smile. I wonder... she appears to be not wed.*'

"Yes, Alice, I also work for the wool merchant at the docks. If that is all, I prefer my own company this day."

She stood, bid him farewell, and left as requested. One hour later, she knocked on the secret door to Clément's study.

CHAPTER TEN

AVIGNON
CLEMENT'S STUDY
7 January 1348 AD

"...come in, Alice." The two sat at Clément's desk, their heads close, she speaking in a low voice, he listening with great attention. "...yes, that is well said, my dear, and I thank you. Now, will you take wine with me? I have an hour away from my duties."

"I am not worthy, but your cellar is too good to refuse." She savoured his claret, he enjoyed her body. When she left, her clothes were in disarray, her face aglow. Breathing hard, she pulled the cowl of her cloak over her head before exiting the door into the wooded Rocher des Doms. She walked down through the town to her house next door but one from Marius and Dominique's.

Clément's sermons had fatigued him. He had kept his own company for two days in his private rooms. Without sleep, he immersed himself in astrological theses constituting a large part of his library. He sought answers to matters religious that the Bible seemed unable to provide. As his paranoia deepened, he perceived threats to his authority all around from anyone and knew not friend from foe. Beneath the veiled persona of papal power coursed fears and negative emotions. A nervous state of self-delusion, induced by regular use of laudanum, made him behave erratically and impulsively. His aides and others close to him watched this deterioration with growing dismay but nobody questioned the Pope. He was the Holy Father and there was but one more powerful than he, the Lord God. On the second day of seclusion, after consulting the charts and scrolls that filled his collection, he determined the moons of Jupiter and Mars were aligned on a favourable pathway and his spirits rose. Slaking his thirst with fine claret, he then sipped a little laudanum and ate bread and cheese. Opening the bible anew, his disposition became more joyous - the extreme nature of a troubled brain - from depression to rapture.

"See my chapel is prepared, for today I shall pray," he ordered an attendant. And, although out of general view, ritual was ever important to him. Being denuded of his robes was akin to denial of the Faith. His garment brought, he retired alone to his personal niche. With reverence, he recited Romans 8:38-39,

"For I am convinced neither death nor life, neither angels nor demons, neither the present nor the future, nor any powers, neither height nor depth, nor anything else in all creation, will be able to separate us from the love of God."

'This must be the strength that drives me on these hard days and I thank Thee for Thy patience.' His belief in the message he preached the previous nones was sincere. It was *not* the Lord's fault, who loved them always, but the sinner's: the name *Nerval* permeated his essence. Alice confirmed his suspicion and the seed of revenge, planted in the past, now started to flower. *'I must devise a plan, a method to execute my hatred and so, at last, alleviate my bitterness. But my spirit grows weary with the heavy load and I barely dare ask Thee for help. It is an affair I must resolve by my own devious, if justified, means.'*

Clément's respect for the power of evangelism began in his days as a novice under the tutelage of the Abbot of Limoges. Face to face delivery of the scriptures to the individual man, he believed to be as effective as talking to one hundred. The latter was fearsome anathema with the passing years. His intellect and spirit oversaw ordinary folk, who had little or no education – the Church's haughty appreciation of its laity - one of its less appealing characteristics. He did not trust in the judgment of his cardinals or bishops to spread the Word as he saw it. He held regular tutorials in his library with three chosen, handsome, young men, at a time. He did scarcely more than quote the Bible, blandly offered guidance, then blessed and sent them on their way. He gleaned satisfaction from the exercise. Rome did not approve, but Rome did not rule the Church, Avignon did and he persisted.

The Pontiff depended on the recommendation of the Magistrate in selecting the men who were to report to the palace and the relationship grew out of mutual trust. On this occasion, he had, with suitable caution, requested one man in particular to be included: Marius Nerval. By chance, he saw the name on a register of men employed for work on the New Chapel. *Nerval* struck a chord. The new meeting room, as with his private quarters, was almost completed, in accordance with his design. It had two monumental entrance doors to the outside world; an immense vaulted wooden roof; square stone slabs to the floor. This, as with the entire architecture of the palace, represented the role and power of the Catholic Church. One might have thought it the mansion of a warrior king, not the spiritual home of Christendom. An iron-bound door, defended by two papal guards whenever he was present, opened into a hallway. Rich embroideries, hangings, and paintings from his collection shone against the typical Provençal sable-coloured rendering. A simple stone altar wrapped with a silk-woven cloth bore a brass cross and heavy Paris bible. To the right was a short bench behind a desk laden with religious texts. A cardinal had once questioned his extravagant taste for fine art and exquisite tapestries, suggesting that as the Lord's life was exemplified by poverty, so should be the Pope's. This enraged Clément,

"What sort of imbecile are you? It is clear to a man with half a mind that art is beauty and we worship the beauty of the Lord. So it is! Art, music, the best wine, attractive women... all are beauty our Lord, in his bounty, provides!" A logical, apologetic man, his anachronistic nature had tried him all his life, from first entering the Faith. He fought demons and wrestled with a darkness known to himself alone or, crucially, by Edmond Nerval back in his childhood. His new tower of the Garde-Robe and the sweeping Grand Staircase for which he was responsible testified the pontifical liking of display and ceremony.

THE MEETING ROOM
8 January 1348 AD

The three chosen subjects lined up, their apprehension palpable.

"I don't like this at all. Why us?" Breton asked under his breath.

"No idea," Lacroix answered, "I saw Clément for the first time at nones in the cathedral the other evening, but you can't say no to him."

"You're right there," Marius said, "his eyes are too close together for my liking... my mother told me that father always said to not trust a fellow with eyes like that, and he wasn't too often wrong."

"Does your father live here?" Breton asked, for no particular reason.

"No, he died in my youth, so I don't remember him," Marius answered. There were others who did.

"Should I call them in? They've been waiting these three hours..." the guard asked his sergeant.

"Yes, His Holiness should have finished his business by now. A chalice of best claret and he'll be set up... doesn't care to bide time though."

"Late, today... perhaps there's a change of plan?"

"Don't be stupid!" the sergeant scolded, "it's in his power to delay if he wants... idiot!"

"I suppose you're right but it's so dreary... standing... bored... guarding... and why does he need armed men?"

"Hold your tongue! You don't know when you're well off! Would you rather be outside chasing pickpockets, or maybe helping the Magistrate's men chain some wretch in the stocks?"

"Course not."

"And, what's more, it's an honour to be in his guard. He's told me, himself, that all sorts of ruffian could be out to get him, so, even if he's not liked by everybody, he *is* the Pope! You'd realise as much if you spent time on deep thinking like me..." the sergeant boasted with the air of one who plays the occasional philosopher. Their conversation was halted by two raps at the door – the signal for the guards to show the men in to the sanctum.

"Come!" boomed a voice and the three men shuffled in, the door closing behind them. Clément had total ecclesiastical authority few would emulate.

"Sit, my sons." They obeyed, one of them wiping the sweat from his brow, one rolling his head from side to side, the third rubbing his palms together.

"Do not be feared, you have done nothing wrong, except in the eyes of Our Lord and, in that, we are all guilty. I tell you, *this* is your time! If you will allow the light into your hearts, you will be forgiven your sins to enter the next world cleansed. Our Father, we beseech Thee…but, no!" The pontiff curtailed an increasingly frenetic exhortation, "No! You have yet to identify yourselves," and pointing at one of the fearful men, he enquired "What name is yours? I will hear your name!"

"My lord…" began the first.

"Do *not* use that word! I am *not* your Lord…there is but one Lord, our Lord in Heaven. Say *Your Holiness* when you address me."

"S…sorry. I am Breton."

"Mmm…Breton…and are your family from Avignon?"

"Y…yes, over many generations." Clement turned to the next man, "And you, boy?"

"They call me Lacroix."

"I once knew a respectable house under that name, but they hailed from Montpellier…is that your line?"

"Nay, I too am of Avignon stock." He looked at Marius, of a sudden, saw himself as Pierre Roger, so many years ago, and he felt each blow to his head and kick to his body. He had put up no defence but accepted the beating, spineless and cowardly, lying on the ground bleeding, bones broken. '*Why, O why did I not fight back at Edmond? The wounds he inflicted cause me agony to the present day. My headaches… shaking and sweating…stuttering in private like a deranged madman, afraid to face my congregations until I have swallowed my potion - all the fault* of Edmond! Ay, there's the blame! And he darkens my name by dying before I could exact just revenge for his acts! Lord above! I may be the greatest of sinners among sinners, that I do not deny, but, I pray, see my life, devoted selflessly to Thee and forgive me.'

Marius felt the cold stare of the Pope on him. '*Why does he look at me so, his gaze piercing my countenance, angry and foul, as if he loathes me?*' It was his turn and he started before Clément had time to ask,

"I am Nerval, Marius Nerval."

"Your surname suffices! Nerval…I see…"

"I am from Limoges, by the river north."

"I *know* where that place is. Do not insult my intelligence!" Marius continued,

"My kin moved to Limoges seeking work on the vineyards."

"And prior to that?" Marius did not understand Clément's train of thought.

"Am I surrounded by dullards? Half-wits, cretins, and heathens to boot! Ye Heavens save me!" This was a moment he had dreamt of and such was his ecstasy he close on revealed all. Inhaling deeply, he composed himself. God's mercy came through his beloved Jesus Christ for the enlightenment and salvation of man on earth. But, his own unfulfilled vengeance for Edmond might at last be realised: Nerval, before him! Triumph rose in his breast, his soul inflamed by uncharitable spite, the object of his ire kneeling at the papal command! His religion upheld mercy, compassion and forgiveness as its keystones, so how could he reconcile the contradictory emotions that seized him? The promise of a fleeting, temporary victory would not suffice.

He wrestled with this dilemma: '*If it be in my gift, what punishment can I mete on a man who shares no fault for the deeds of his deceased father, who is innocent of a feud long since passed?*' He heard nothing of Marius' answer, for his suspicions had been confirmed. Edmond's son! '*After all these years! The boy was Edmond's pride and joy, so what do I see in him now? I don't know… it's too much to take in! Dear Lord, forgive me for what I might do, absolve me, I plead.*'

"My sons, Breton, Lacroix and Nerval, you will hear the Word of our Lord Jesus, the Word will be your peace and the peace will be your salvation. Hear the Word, kneel in supplication, fear, and reverence! Believe and tell others you have, this day, seen the light!"

The higher Clément's voice rose, the more terrified his three subjects became. He reflected later that his intake of wine and laudanum had, that day, been excessive – he should have anticipated its effect. Unrolling a scroll, he recited verses in a monotone voice. To their astonishment, he flailed his arms and parchment in a grandiose arc, adding to the surreal drama confronting three bemused men. But, as swiftly as the business had begun, it ceased, an oppressive silence filling the meeting room. Approaching the bench and placing a hand on each head in blessing, he offered his gold ring of office to be kissed in gratitude and acceptance, according to custom. In pressing the band to his lips, he afforded more time to Marius than the others. *'I'm not imagining it but he's lingering over me... what's his game?'* he thought.

"Stand! Return to your families, companions, e'en your enemies to recount your union with the Lord. Encourage, as Jesus did, entreat disbelievers to open their hearts and save their very existence!"

Sitting at the desk, his fist banged to summon the guards.

"The matter is complete. Escort them out!"

As they left the room, Clément's gaze fixed on Marius. *'I will consult the stars and the planets once more. The Curia tells me what they think I want to hear, and the Good Book contains no solution for my woes.'*

Bowing his head, alone and deep in thought, he stroked the ring that had touched Marius' lips. The offspring of a man he hated with venom, in spite of so long a time, was within reach. The boy lived in *his* town and was in *his* service. This must be divine intervention, a miracle no less!

Clément passed a hand over his perspiring brow. His silken sleeve, moments before , had brushed the grimy fustian of Marius' garment. *'In the infinitesimal, the momentous begins.'* Drinking more laudanum, his nervous state calmed.

CHAPTER ELEVEN

AVIGNON
CLEMENT'S CHAMBER AND STUDY
9 January 1348 AD

Motes of dust danced in the yellow light cast by the four torches blazing in their hangers, one on each wall of the chamber. The hypnotic effect of the flickering particles on Pope Clément must be, or so he thought, due to a night of troubled sleep. He yawned and rubbed his eyes, in turmoil after the momentous encounter with Marius Nerval. His mind, tormented by hatred and paranoia, brought him to the verge of physical collapse. Not knowing which direction to take enervated his spirit.

On waking, he could hardly believe he had laid hands on Marius, son of his detested, erstwhile companion. '*Surely it's a dream, or a visitation as when the Lord sends his angels into the world to instruct and give guidance to mere mortals? No, Clément! Come to your senses! It was, indeed, Marius before you. Yet, he did not fawn like a returning prodigal son, nor did he entreat as did Lazarus pleading of Jesus – none of that. He impressed me by his honest manner... but, you, Edmond, if only you were here today! How I would confront you and have you pay for your crime... and, should the law not punish you, the fury of the Almighty would exact fearsome vengeance!*'

Still in his nightgown, he paced in his chamber until there came a sharp knock at the door.

"Good morrow, Father. I have brought you food." The cleric bowed and placed a board with bread, cheese, and fruit on a side table.

"Do you require anything more?"

"No, you may go." No-one ought to be privy to what his mind craved. Food featured low in his list of priorities. He slipped off the gown and splashed cold water on his face. A clean, white linen robe soothed his skin that burned hotter than a blacksmith's furnace. He examined the board without any desire to eat. Instead, he gathered parchment scrolls scattered on his desk and replaced them on the shelf of his library in an adjoining annex. His Paris Bible and two candles, one to the left the other to the right, remained. "That's better," he nodded, turning to the wall cabinet which he unlocked, withdrawing his cherished crock of laudanum. This, along with a silver chalice, he positioned, with precision, on a centre point of the desk. The wax lights on either side of the bible stood like guards protecting their king. *'Good order, everything in its place. But, would that the events in my life were as uncomplicated.'*

He placed a spill into the dying embers of his hearth and lit the candle. After the wick burned with a steady flame, he took a brass snuffer and, one by one, extinguished the torches on the walls. The room at once transformed into another world, a cave without issue, a dungeon, a prison for those whose debts would never be honoured. He watched, with an intense curiosity, the smoke from the fading torches spiral upwards to dissipate on touching the ceiling. Gaze fixed on the Heavens, he swayed from side to side like a stook in a wheat field blown by the wind. He knew the time to act was nigh. His emotions of resentment, bitterness, and humiliation, sensations that gnaw at a man's soul will end only in a tragic resolution.

Sitting at his desk, he peered through the candlelight to the shadows beyond: inanimate blurs adopting human forms, people with whom he was compelled to converse. He filled the chalice with the silky potion and replaced the stopper in the crock. As he sipped the liquid with respect, it was like a priest conducting the Eucharist, drinking the blood of Christ. He inhaled deeply and prepared to speak. These visions he recognised not as hallucinations – though they were so – but as a pathway into a world beyond. Therein, he might see, hear, smell, taste and feel things that did not exist on the earth he inhabited. '*The disciples saw an apparition of the Lord Jesus, his face shining as the sun, his garments brilliant white...they heard voices from Heaven...such a miracle...would that our Saviour appeared to me...*'

The abstractions in the study taunted him, and he knew not which to address first. The moment was frozen in time and, although he was alone in the room, in his mind doubts and uncertainties confounded. He drank more laudanum.

"Be you friend or foe?" he asked, seized by panic, "ah...I see Satan! You are a fallen angel, the serpent in the Garden of Eden, the dragon in Revelations! Shall I call you Lucifer, Beelzebub or plain wicked one, the abhorrent tempter? For an instant, I see Edmond in you...but no...o foul being with horns, tail and goat's body...animal hair...all covered with boils and scars. Satan! Purveyor of black magic, a plague of locusts on thee! But, wait, do I see a woman? Salome, daughter of Herod! You danced for him and demanded the head of good John the Baptist on a platter. Unfathomable evil! Or, maybe, there hides Delilah in the corner, who sold Samson's secret to the Philistines, and all for a tribute of silver pieces. His locks shorn, strength wasted, how did she defend her deception? Or are you Athaliah, descendant from the line of David and Queen of Israel? Unrestrained ambition led you to slay your grandchildren to claim the throne: aberration and paltry contempt!"

Leaning back in his chair, he drew breath and swallowed a further draught of the elixir. "Satan, Salome, Delilah, Athaliah, answer me! Why do you place temptation before me? Your wickedness renders me weak since my thirst for revenge is not quenched." He squinted hard, trying to account for the grey illusions cavorting against the wall.

"Ah!" he cried out, venom in his voice. "Peter! Why did you thrice deny the Christ? You swore you did not know the man, despite his prophecy that you would disown Him. Where? Why? But...wait...you are gone from my sight and...and Herod takes your place! *Great* they called you, though you murdered your family and put innocent babes to the sword. Do not look at me so! Now, others appear... Cain who killed Abel; Judas Iscariot whose treachery betrayed the Lord; Jezebel, you worshipped the Devil and... last in line, a Bokor! No! No, I do not believe my eyes! Bokor, the Voudou sorcerer, who brings fresh blood to cadavers with a deadening liqueur. I have read of your malevolence, how you administer drugs to the corpse such that it will rise from the grave to do your bidding! *Zombies* are their name... the potion presides over the brain and... " But, of a sudden, the mirages vanished, sublimated, leaving Clément exhausted, perspiring and trembling with passion.

"The soothing syrup controls my spirit and I cannot survive without its sustenance. These demons, this day invading my being, will assist my resolve, of that I am certain. An old abbot told me *it's not your enemies who betray you, but your friends.* I will send for Alice."

Two hours later, the torches on the walls were lit again, religious scrolls arranged on the desk, the crock and chalice locked away from prying eyes. The Magistrate arrived for his regular meeting to keep Clément abreast of town affairs.

"It is early, perhaps, but would you join me in wine, Magistrate?"

"Your Eminence knows wine is my Achilles' heel."

"Why, such erudition from a common justice! I was not aware Greek mythology was of interest to you. No matter, take wine with me." The men emptied their goblets and Clement continued,

"So, what do you have to report?"

"The town sleeps in winter." He passed over a parchment sheet for Clément's perusal. "As you see, crimes are one each of drunkenness and gossip last week, nothing more serious. One birth and two deaths notified to me since you conducted the Charron child's funeral, but two nones past – both young men... fever and dark patches to the arms... not common, I'd say..."

"It is, truly, curious, but the Good Lord decides when our time has come," Clément answered in a dismissive tone, "His awesome power carries off saints as with sinners."

"You have the right, Father. I will depart. I have matters to attend at my office."

{that afternoon}

The Pope watched Alice pull on her spotless, white dress, as he poured *eau de vie* into two small cups. He liked to vary his beverage. She was, undeniably, a fine young woman. He admired her curvaceous figure, lustrous hair reaching her waist, cherry-red lips and a tantalising smile that drew him to her. *'You flaunt your attraction like a dangerous Siren, luring unfortunate sailors to founder on the rocky coast with weird voices and music.'* She sat on the edge of the bed, her gaze lowered with seductive, false modesty, and asked,

"How did you first espy a harlot like me?"

"Do not say *harlot*! You are a woman sent to me in God's greater plan, and we must succumb to His will –"

"If any man understands God's will, it is you," she interjected, smiling.

"Quite, Alice. I recall noticing you from the pulpit giving my first sermon as Pope Clément VI. Your beauty stirred carnal desires in the lusty youth from Limoges, that I cannot deny." He paused, an expression of guilt clouding his countenance. "However, the Lord moves in a mysterious ways. As a novice, new in my position, the Curia advised me on bulls, canon law, foreign affairs and the rest, but they have no local knowledge, if you follow. I chose you, child, as my...er...apocryphal assistant in the Faith."

"You speak words of wisdom."

"I do, but..." and with an impatient edge to his voice, he looked into her dark, searching eyes. "Enough of this idle talk. I have an important task for you."

"A task? What do you mean by that?"

"Listen carefully, I will explain. You have observed Marius Nerval – at my behest – the fellow residing in the house next to yours..."

"That is so, and I have informed you about him."

"You have, Alice. Now, I require more…"

She tied the cord round her dress and straightened, attentive, wondering what was to come.

"Did you find Marius a…how shall I say…a handsome man?"

"That is a strange question. Why yes, though when men are the question, I set high standards."

"Of course, you do," Clément said, missing the irony of her words. "I would like you to know him better…er…with greater intimacy. The chase will not prove too onerous for an *agent provocatrice* possessing charms like yours. If he is desirable, you will achieve a union of the Faith and –"

"Sire! Are you suggesting I should lie with him? He is married with a young son…"

"That is precisely what I am suggesting, Alice. I have good reason to ask this of you, trust me, although such reason need not concern you. The union will be illicit, of course, and it must remain an absolute secret. What say you?" He replenished their cups and stared at her with both anticipation and dread for the transgression he was about to conceive.

"If it is your wish, I cannot refuse."

"Excellent!" he exclaimed, clapping his hands with infantile glee, "I will not be party to your method but, may I propose the inn as a fruitful place to introduce yourself to him anew, to start your…advances…to ply him, so as to put it. In that case, you will incur expenses – ale, cider, eau de vie, food, whatever – so, take this." He handed her a purse. "Here is adequate coin. I do not expect you to fall into debt on my behalf."

She accepted the money without comment. "Will you drink more?" he asked, pouring brandy into her cup before she could reply.

"Have you had occasion to meet his wife, Dominique?"

"Yes." She had no idea where this was leading, "I welcomed her to Avignon on their arrival and made her a gift of fruit. By chance, our paths crossed the other day at the market. She stood by the fishmonger's stall and, seeing the woman was unsure what to buy, I offered assistance. She had no appreciation of fish so I advised her on the best sort, the freshest. She was most grateful for my help. After all, it would not do to serve Marius river eel a week old that should be thrown back whence it came."

"Certainly not... that is interesting. It would seem you have already gained her trust, and, if not, you soon will – this is of crucial importance. But, excuse my riddles, Alice. I expect to see you again, without too long a delay, and bearing good news. So, you may now depart." He held out his hand for her to kiss his ring of office.

"I will do my best for you."

In the street leading home, she stepped aside, out of respect for a funeral cortege making its way to the cathedral. The cart, pulled by two mules, bore a crude wooden coffin draped with olive branches – a symbol of peace and virginity. *'It is unusual to see a coffin instead of a shroud for burial, and, also* two *mules. Must be a person of some wealth...'* The cortege passed and Alice spoke with a woman standing in her doorway.

"Do you know the deceased?" Alice asked.

"She is Anne, daughter of the baker on Rue Thiers. May the Lord save us! She was barely twenty-four years of age, a mere girl and an only child. Her father is heartbroken and, worse, it came without warning... taken in the night with nothing more sinister than a fever, but soon, black lumps in the groin."

Alice nodded and carried on her way. Her thoughts were now focused on the pending seduction of Marius. *'Why have I consented to become enmeshed in a plot as dark as night? And with a man as gentle and honest as Marius?'*

In his lonely chamber, Clément drank another cup of eau de vie. A feeling of smugness overwhelmed him: his plan was beginning. *'I wager theirs will not be a happy home when Dominique discovers her husband is unfaithful. He that chastiseth the one, amendeth the many. Take heed Edmond, my old friend.'*

CHAPTER TWELVE

AVIGNON, THE DOCKS
10 January 1348 AD

The day broke as Jean Pagnol, the wool merchant, and his brother the sail maker, Thomas, left their house on Rue Limas. They walked towards the Porte du Rocher where they intended to examine the state of the river Rhone that morning, expecting a barge at the docks, laden with a consignment of cloths. Its time of arrival was determined by the flow of the water as by the prevailing wind.

"Good morning, Jean and Thomas," hailed a man leaning from his window – a habit of observing his neighbours out of curiosity, "you're up and about early today."

"Yes, and you should be aware the Devil finds work for idle hands... you might try working instead of wasting time away!" Jean quipped, easily recognised by dragging a crippled leg, lame from his service as a mercenary for the English King Edward.

"Come, Jean, he's not worth your breath." Thomas urged his brother, "and we have much to do."

The street opened into the pretty, tree-lined Place Châatelet, pink mimosas, the sleeping tree that folds up its leaves at night. They waited for the spring to blossom and shade from the sun women sitting on benches, exchanging local small talk. White and purple lilac bushes gave off a scent that would attract hummingbirds, butterflies, and bees in the warmer months. The simple beauty of the square epitomised the glorious contentment of the dwellers of Avignon. The balmy fragrance would rise above the people, living oblivious to adversity ahead. As the brothers passed through the Rocher Gate, Jean dropped a coin into a bowl next to a wizened old man on a stool. His duty, conferred by the Magistrate, was to report visitors and residents leaving or entering the town. The justice, however, heard little since his representative spent much of the day sleeping. The townsfolk admired his peculiar ability to doze in an upright position. Avignon vaunted as much to be praised as despised.

On the Saint Bénézet bridge, traders were setting out their stalls while the rest of the world slept. Sellers of fish, fruit, ironware, vegetables, wine, clothing, herbs, and potions: all for sale or barter. "The bridge will be swarming when the sun has risen. I wonder where they all come from," Jean mused. "You have the right there," Thomas replied, "but, it's them *underneath* I don't hold with. Don't know why the Magistrate never acts... you can buy, and easy, goods from wine that's not as strong as it should be, to bars that glisten but aren't gold, least not solid all the way through..." Jean continued, "Ay, wine that's been watered down and ingots empty in the middle! How folk are duped amazes me, taken in by a *bargain!* The rogues set up under the arches where they can hide from the beak... I believe they be trolls from the caves in Arles and charlatans from Limoges... for sure, they aren't locals like the traders above. Now, *their* honesty is such to make 'em dance if you get my meaning?" "I know you well enough by now to understand your strange riddles: it's Heaven above but Hell below – a fact you can't ignore."

"Ay, you're correct."

"How's your family, Roul?" asked a cheesemaker from Villeneuve-lès-Avignon, on the west bank of the river. "Well, thank you," replied Amis, a baker who lived within the walls of the old town.

Jean and Thomas reached the centre of the bridge and leaned over the parapet to study the water below at its deepest point.

"What do you say, Thomas?" He had confidence in his brother's knowledge and experience. A man who sewed sails understood their purpose and the strains they would endure against wind, rain and the flow of the river. Thomas peered into the swirling runs and eddies. The current was as dark and dangerous as life for any fool who disrespected the power and majesty of the great Rhône. He threw, with all his strength, a piece of branch to watch its direction and movement. He concluded, "it goes strong down to the south, stronger than I've known for many years…the snows in the north are likely melting early. But, I'll wager it's not as angry closer to the bank…see, Jean, over there…" He pointed to the water's edge.

"I'll take your word for it, Thomas. What of the wind?" The brother licked his forefinger and held it above his head, "It blows hard southwesterly and that's not good for a boat under sail, even with skilful tacking. No, he will be using horses along the towpath."

"Confound it!" Jean cursed, "that will cost us dear."

"Maybe, but tomorrow, another of our boats from Lyon will come downstream under sail, without that problem."

"You have the right of it, and I would guess he should be at the quay after sext – if he set off these three days since and has not had rogues ambush or wild boar consume him! Let's be off."

Turning their backs on the bridge, they regained Rue Limas, a biting wind blowing in their faces. The leather soles of Jean's boots tapped a rhythmical cadence as they walked down the cobbled street. They crossed but two people en route, but, at the quay, gangs of workers tied up barges and winched cargo out of holds. Foremen barked orders, arms waving about, and cusses filled the cold morning air. Flames given off iron braziers augmented the still faint dawn light, only men huddled around the same warmed hands and exchanged news. The brothers went first to their warehouse and drew open the immense wooden doors. Thomas banged two flints together, the spark igniting prepared tinder in the open hearth. Soon, a fire took the chill off the cold within the building. Meantime, Jean lit a candle in the office. Taking a parchment from a pile on his desk, he ran his finger down the list of wools they expected that day. "Be a good day's toil for Marius... see what he's made of..."Jean shouted, but Thomas was in the bowels of the cavernous shed and did not hear. The cry of 'wine', however, as if by a miracle, reached him forthwith. He joined his brother to share a bottle of claret: a drink to numb the senses against the bitter weather outside. Refreshed, they set about sorting a bale of assorted wools – of woollen, worsted, and in-between quality. The silence was broken only when Jean aimed a blow with a cudgel at a scurrying rat, disturbed from its sleep inside the warm bale.

"Drat!" he exclaimed, "I'll see you off later, my little friend!"

"You're slowing in your dotage, brother! Time was you would have separated that fellow's head from its body!"

The wool arranged into proper bundles, the men sat down once more at the table. Jean refilled their glasses. The peals of the bells in a nearby church sounded – three rings, three times followed by twenty-five in succession. sext, announced for devout folk inclined to offer prayers in the middle of the day.

"Far away across the fields
The tolling of the iron bell
Calls the faithful to their knees
To hear the softly spoken magic spells." Thomas recited a verse he had learned as a child -

"I agree, brother, except 'softly spoken' is not the manner those roughneck stevedores will talk until they are paid off... and, they are surely anything but 'faithful'. Enough of your ballads!"

The Pagnol's bargee, a bull-necked sailor, was born aboard a boat and would likely end his days on the same. Biceps rippling, his brow screwed into perspiring furrows. With both hands gripping the handle, he winched one bale after another onto the quayside. Deep in the hold, four labourers of indeterminate origin, forced hooks as sharp as dragon's teeth into the loads and waited for the bargee to lower the winch ropes once more. The procedure continued until fifteen bales were stacked up on the quayside by the winch. Jean and Thomas observed the unloading with indifference. They knew better than to interfere with the fellow plying his craft. When the hold was empty, he acknowledged his two employers.

"My respects, Pagnols," and he extended a grimy hand.

"To you also, Mahi," Jean reciprocated, shaking the hand and giving a wide smile to a man he knew since childhood, broken by his service over the seas as a mercenary. He continued,

"The ostler has led the horses to the stables...there's hay and the farrier is arranged."

"As it should be, Jean." He faced Thomas and hit his arm with a clenched fist, in friendship, not enmity. "Marius and Bruno will cart the bales to the warehouse after nones. For now, join us for a drink. You've earned it today."

"I'll not refuse such an invitation."

Mahi and Thomas sat at the table while Jean removed the cork from a dusty bottle of wine: the best was such, being undisturbed for years. He filled three goblets he reserved for guests and retreated to his office, from where the rattle of coins was heard. On exiting, he tossed a money pouch to Mahi. "That will cover fifteen bales, not forgetting the adjustment for the hay and farrier. No need to count it, I'm feeling generous today!"

"My thanks, Jean, and I'll see my men get a fair wage," Mahi said, tying the pouch to his waistband. He raised his goblet in a toast.

"What news from Marseilles?" Thomas asked. There followed a silence.

"Strange times around the place...evil times..."

"Tell, then! What are you saying?" Mahi drained his goblet and pushed it across the table.

"I was fortunate to muster a crew these two weeks passed. There are not sufficient men...or, what I mean is there *are*, but not those willing to come to the port...they're afraid, suspicious, angry...it's hard to explain... They have seen their family members, neighbours, friends...taken! Dead! There be a scourge afflicting Marseilles. Don't know what or why, but, men, women, children...the smith, the cooper, the priest...makes no difference! Lord have mercy upon us! It's a sad sight and the first kind in my remembrance, such that, I've put my meagre estate in order. For all I know, it will please Him to call me to His glory!" He drank two draughts of wine and gathered himself,

"It came last summer, the hottest I've ever felt and it grew mightily… four dead, then ten, then thirty, then… hundreds throughout the city – too many to have any bell toll their passing. It rages to this day. First, it shows – and I watched it with my own brother – with a fever of hot and cold fits and an awful shivering. Such melancholy! Swarms of rats, as plenty as nests of ants, descended on us and scurried in and out of the houses, churches, shops, all at will." Jean and Thomas listened, mouths open in disbelief of the horror described by the bargee.

"I found the four men you've seen on the boat… they were as pleased to escape the city as to earn money. A bite from a rat… swelling, painful growths, most often in the groin, on the thigh, in the armpit or on the neck. My brother had those lumps, hard, would not break open and… the Devil's agony! Four days on and he had expired. In the end, his release from the pestilence was a mercy. It spread like a raging forest fire, nothing standing in its way! Imagine, your ship's hold full of black and brown rats, and so it goes on! I'm afeard to return to Marseilles so I will moor up here till it's safe again."

"You are welcome to stay as long as you desire," Jean offered, "our association with you goes back many years. To help you in a time of need is what the Lord would want, nothing less."

"You are most kind, Jean, but I don't trust much in the Lord after the sights I've witnessed."

{earlier that day – the stonemason's yard}

"Good morning, Luc," Marius greeted his friend.

"And to you."

"How is it with you at home? Is Marianne coping?" He at once realised the crass nature of his question.

"I'm not sure the word is *coping*. We go from day to day but it's a shadow, a dark cloud over our heads. However, it was the Lord's will, so we must accept it."

"I cannot imagine your pain, Luc, and if there be anything Dominique and I can do to help, we are here for you."

"Thank you. A day's hard work takes the mind off my sadness. Let's be about it."

They started to manhandle blocks of wall stone, dressed the previous shift, when a tall, lean, angular man approached. He stopped in between the blocks and the cart they were loading, forcing them to stop and acknowledge him. Marius did not know the stranger, though Luc had seen him around the yard. The mallet in his hand and a setsquare dangling on a cord from his waistband told them he was the joiner.

"I am Bruno. We have not met. My trade is wood. Anything wooden in the palace is likely down to me. Grotesques, goblins, leaves, letters… all mine! I hang doors and mend benches, but my true love is carving… what I does best –"

"Ah… Bruno…" Marius interrupted, "I work for Jean Pagnol at the docks, so, you are his partner, is that correct?"

"It is." He stuck out his jaw and continued, a pride in his voice, "I share an interest in the business. I will accompany you to the river this afternoon. Jean tells me a delivery will arrive, so, you will appreciate any assistance."

"I am sure your experience far exceeds mine."

"Yes, it does. Until later." Bruno turned to return to his joinery shop across the yard but stopped and spoke again, "I am alone today."

"Alone, Bruno?"

"Yes. Heard this morning my apprentice, young Onfroi, passed away last night. Rum affair. Twenty and two years old. Rum, no doubt. The best I've had in many moons. Hard position to fill." Bruno's short, sharp manner of speaking served to add gravity to his message. "Meet at the gate before nones. Walk to the quays together."

Marius and Bruno exchanged not a word as they moved through the town. A light burned in the Magistrate's office where he was deep in conversation with the wool merchant, Jean, and his brother Thomas. They entered to be met with ashen faces.

"What's the matter?" Bruno asked, expecting the price of cloth to have risen or a rogue apprehended. They were not prepared for the Magistrate's grim announcement.

"Four more deaths reported to me this day before prime. Father Colbert of the Saint Symphorien church saw me in person. The four passed are from his parish, two men, one woman and one babe. That makes six this week! I have met the sexton of the cathedral who bemoans the sudden increase in the number of graves he must dig. He refuses, on his paltry stipend, as he puts it, to work without a mate hired. I conceded. They are both digging as we speak."

They all agreed it was a lamentable state of affairs, but, felt the *status quo* would soon resume. They left the office apart from Marius who held back.

"Magistrate, is there anything I can do to be of service to you?"

"Why, Marius, I had not foreseen such circumstances and... er... you could do me a great favour, so as to put it."

"Name it, sire."

"As I was leaving my house this morning, a runner accosted me. Gasping for breath and face as red as claret, he told me there be a corpse on the steps from Place Pie. No-one knows his name... a vagrant, for certain. Now, a kindly washerwoman nearby has covered him with sackcloth to preserve his dignity. He can't be left like that yet there's not a person brave enough to move the body. It has perplexed me forever that the dead are feared more than the living... no sense in it. However, as I was saying, it would be a great benefit to me if you could carry the unfortunate to the cathedral for burial. What say you, young man? I will arrange that Jean releases you early from your duties before nightfall. There are barrows outside the office." Marius agreed without a second thought.

He had no difficulty locating the cadaver. A gaggle of women chattering and wringing their hands together had congregated at the foot of the steps leading up from the square in question. As he approached, the women parted to let him through.

"Nothing better to do, ladies? One of you can help me get him on the cart." At first, nobody volunteered, so he chose the stockiest woman and pushed her onto the steps.

"He'll not bite you, mistress! He's all stiff, so you take the head and I the feet...that's the idea...now onto the barrow...good, my thanks to you."

The streets were now in darkness. No funeral procession for that poor soul. Marius wheeled him, slowly, to the cathedral. Within were forty or fifty mourners, sat in four groups representing the four people deceased, as described by the Magistrate. The priest finished the prayers and eulogy for one, who was removed to the cemetery. Immediately, the next service began: a lineage of death.

After one sad hour, there remained but Marius and his mortal load. The priest left the altar and came towards him.

"Father, the Magistrate has given me instructions to bear this defunct person to your good offices."

"His name?" The priest's tone was dismissive.

"Unknown. Magistrate calls him a vagabond, that's all I can say." The cleric opened his bible at any page whatsoever, made the sign of the cross, and mumbled a few Latin words. '*He shows no respect for the poor wretch! He could just as well be buying fruit from a market stall...no human warmth, no name to refer to...*'

"Take him away, now," the minister ordered, turning his back on Marius and the body.

Outside, the wind howled and icy rain soaked through clothing. Only the Devil would parade in such pitiless weather. Behind the cathedral, a grave awaited the vagrant's body. The two sextons heaved it off the cart, as they would unload a sack of potatoes, and all but dropped it into the hole. It was left to Marius to cast a handful of earth, in respect, before the men covered it over.

"Is that the last one?"

"It better be, I've no strength to dig more!"

The following day, and every day thereafter, Marius called in at the Magistrate's office.

"No deaths today," he was informed, and the Magistrate sounded a cautious optimism. So it continued: the infection had come to an end as rapidly as it had arrived. Throughout the months of February and March, deaths were of a normal figure for a town the size of Avignon. Marius, Dominique and baby Fabien read the bill posted on the cathedral door, announcing mortalities for every fortnight. They perused the causes of death:

Aged 1

Childbed 1

Gangrene 1

Wormes 1

Buried –

Males 2

Women 1

Total – 3

"*And they assembled them at the place that in Hebrew is called Harmagedon*"

The war had been proclaimed though not a battle had yet been fought. Neither man nor beast in Avignon had a care in the world.

CHAPTER THIRTEEN

AVIGNON, THE TOWN
15 January 1348 AD

Alice was a woman recognised by but not known to the people of Avignon. She appeared amongst them as if from nowhere. Her past was the subject of much conjecture, based on scant evidence, by the townswomen who thrived on gossip. Walking out from her house, adjacent to Marcel's inn, she wore a black robe that enveloped her body, reaching the ground. Long, dark hair partly concealed her face so, as she was unknown, she was unseen.

"A sailor from the barges told me she is a Sicani woman from a tribe of pagans on the island of Sicily. Said he once sailed there and saw them dance round campfires and make sacrifices to their gods!" revealed one busybody.

"I've heard her family blood-line goes back to Hugh of Arles, the Duke of Provence. Close to royalty as makes no difference," pronounced another.

"My cousin reckons she's a witch with power over our minds, bodies, and property. Even uses malicious magic to force us against our will...can make animals sick, bring bad luck...for certain, she knows evil ways that can cause sudden death!" was the opinion of a third woman.

Alice lived alone. She would not be seen carousing with menfolk in the drinking houses of the poor quarter of the town, as did many women, for their pleasure. Contrary to myth, she was devout, that they could not deny – proven by her worshipping in the cathedral most days, twice on a Sunday. The congregation departed, she remained to engage in conversation with the officiants. People wondered what right a plain woman like her had to keep company with the clergy. But, she did not mix with others: an enigma in black, Alice did not reveal the slightest intimation of who she was or whence she came.

The landlord received his rent on the first Monday of the month and she did not fall into arrears. This day, taking the money to him after she had prayed at sext, the inn was deserted, apart from an incoherent, wizened crone in the corner, muttering strange words to the jug of ale in front of her.

"How are you today, Alice?" Marcel enquired, leaving the counter, aiming a vicious kick at the house cat.

"I'm well, thank you." Placing coins in his outstretched palm, she turned to leave.

"Why! So soon? Sit with me a while, my wife is away for the day and I have finished my chores. Not often do we have the chance to... er... talk."

"It's true," she agreed. Sitting at a table by the hearth, she undid the cord and loosened her cloak. With a shake of her head, her long, silken tresses fell free. Her gaze did not move off Marcel as he took a bottle from the shelf, approached the table, and placed it with two glasses in front of her. He filled them in silence before joining her close on the bench. She reacted at once, shuffling away from him to show physical contact was unwelcome. Appreciating his lecherous intent to be a misjudgement, he moved to the seat opposite.

"Meant no disrespect, my dear, I ain't that sort of fellow. Forgive me." A fawning smile exposed broken, yellow teeth, beads of sweat forming on his brow. As he stared at her, his breathing deepened and became more rapid. The woman leaned back to increase the distance between herself and the innkeeper's sour breath. She could not help but compare this repulsive man with the wholesome, attractive Marius. Raising his glass, he proposed a toast,

"Here's to you, Alice, and..." But, she did not heed him, her thoughts were elsewhere.

'Clément said the inn would be a suitable place to first befriend Marius. But, what does he know? He will not be part of it, it depends on me. If I flirt with him in a place where people gather, such as this, he will surely suspect my motives. No, not like that... to start, I must gain his trust, as with Dominique. When I am accepted as a friend of their family, my web will be much easier to weave. Husband and wife neither should know, too soon, the feelings of the other. When his infidelity is at last revealed, the consequences will be as Clément desires. The Holy Father makes few demands of his subjects and, in this, I am a woman blessed.'
Marcel tapped his glass on the table for a second toast.

"Your health, Alice."

"Yes... yes, and yours too," she replied, her reverie disturbed.

"You should frequent my humble establishment more often. A pretty face will always brighten up the winter's gloom." Marcel cared not whence came his customers: mourners at a wake, ruffians from the docks - to him, trade was trade. "My patrons are all fine sorts and, as far as I am aware, not one of 'em a felon!" he continued. "You have lived here now for two, maybe three years, yet we scarcely know you..."

"You do not, Marcel, and that suits me well! Understand?" Her sharp tone surprised him,

"Of course I do. I did not intend to... er... pry..."

'I will need to become more sociable in their eyes,' she thought, *'and it will not be done in an instant. Come in here occasionally and befriend Marius, but the others too. Yes, that's the way. They will see me as a sisterly person and, though I may tease their menfolk, I will not give the women further reason to think of me as loose. To them, as to Marius, the unusual Alice is a harmless girl who has likely known hard times. Yes! They can feel sorry for me!'*

"... your business is your own," he concluded.

{19 January}

Alice sat in her sparsely furnished, one-storey house. She ran a bone comb repeatedly through her hair. The flickering flames of the fire reflected in its auburn sheen. Since visiting the inn, she focused her attention on the plot to seduce Marius. Its execution would need to be subtle, gradual, cunning, for maximum effect, as Clément desired. The Pontiff wielded sovereign authority, be it over his flock or private acquaintances. But, this particular quest was beyond his sphere of influence.

Two benches sat either side of a rough-hewn table, a pitcher on the floor next to a small cabinet and washbowl with a flannel dangling from a hook to its side. In one corner was a lay, straw-filled mattress covered with a blanket of neither coarse sackcloth nor fine worsted – adequate to ward off the cold when the embers of the fire had died. Against one wall stood an iron-bound wooden chest, with a pile of neatly folded clothes on top: a sturdy trunk, but unsuited to the simple quality of the house. From three pegs hung a cloak, a robe, and a nightdress. From the fourth, attire of a quite different nature. A white dress embroidered in silver with a fillet of gold. Small sleeves, reaching from elbow to wrist, in red and white check; on its bodice, a blue shield with golden fleur-de-lis. The garment appeared, again, incompatible with its unassuming surroundings.

She gave a shudder and dragged the bench closer to the fire. From a nearby church chimed the bell for matins. At this hour, only the ordained gathered in the cathedral.

'*A time for saints or sinners, none halfway,*' Alice reflected, '*and the Lord above knows which am I.*' Warmed, she poured a measure of eau de vie from a stone jar and set her mind to the pressing *affaire de coeur.* '*I must, first, observe his daily behaviour. When does he leave the house, the route to his workplace, what time does he return home? Does he walk out with Dominique. How does he spend his evenings? Yes, understanding his usual customs will give me the advantage to lead him astray. An opportunity to meet him, as if by accident, will be the first move of my mission.'*

Marius heard the distinctive thud of mallet on chisel coming from the joinery shop walking across the yard. Within, Bruno was engrossed in carving an oak tracery panel. He chipped away two or three times before stepping back to study and determine where his next cuts would be made. In silence, Marius watched the skill of a master woodcarver, his artistry practised since antiquity, here toiling in a humble, provincial atelier. Sensing Marius' presence, he turned to face him and, placing his tools on the bench, greeted,

"Hello, Marius."

"Hello to you, Bruno. I can but marvel at your talent. This work is truly beautiful."

"Why, thank you. It's one of twelve for a rood screen twixt nave and private side chapel. Commissioned by Clément himself."

"Then, it's surely an important assignment?"

"Ay... called me to his office. More usual that I confer with prelates, cardinals and the like... them of a lesser position, if you understand. Anyway, there were illuminated parchments on the desk – plants, flowers and the like, all drawn fancy... and, he wanted 'em put into carvings... never seen so many to copy..."

"What kind?"

"Lilies, crocuses, almond blossom, brambles, vines, rushes... hope he be pleased."

"Bruno! If every panel is as well-crafted as this one, you have nothing to fear."

The joiner breathed a sigh of relief and paused before saying, in a sad tone,

"I miss Onfroi."

"Your apprentice?"

"Ay, him. I'd have turned him into a carver. He had a real gift."

"I'm sure he did. Taken so young and without warning – and the same age as me. A great loss."

As Marius left the yard at nones, he met the Magistrate. They exchanged a few words and went about their business.

'*It's welcome news. The spate of deaths has ceased. It was nought but a temporary difficulty, I suppose, in the life of any town. We will carry on, regardless, and we can breathe again.*'

The next morning, at first light, Alice peered through her shutters, no candle betraying her vigil. She heard Marius' door open and close. Seconds later, he passed her house on his way to the yard. She waited till he was nearly out of sight before stepping outside to follow his progress through the town. Keeping in the shadows of the houses, she ensured he would not notice her: secrecy was paramount. He soon branched off the main street and crossed a square she did not know. '*I must make certain this is his normal route... this, though, will suit my intentions.*' Always holding back, lest he spotted her, she watched him report to the foreman's hut and, by terce, enter the stonemason's yard. '*Men are creatures of habit and Marius is no exception. I will observe him tomorrow, but I wager he will make the same journey.*' At nones, she hid behind trees near the entrance to the yard to see him leave. As she thought, he walked the same streets going down to the docks for his afternoon employment. '*Although I live next door to the Nerval family, I have not seen Marius since the day he arrived. The time has come to put the situation to rights.*'

The following day, she left her house, again, as Marius' door closed. They all but collided – as planned – and she started, her cry of surprise rending the silent morning air.

"Marius! I did not expect to meet you so early. You made me jump!"

"Sorry, Alice. My labours call, but, how are you?"

"I thank you for enquiring, I am keeping well."

"And, what brings *you* out at this hour?"

"I visit an old lady, infirm, who does not get out of the house. We sit and chatter. She enjoys the company as there is no-one in the world to take an interest in her and relieve her loneliness."

"It is, undeniably, very kind of you to give of your time. Would that there were more like you."

"It's no sacrifice to help those less fortunate than ourselves, do you not agree?"

"I do, Alice. Now, will you walk with me – that is, if you are going my way?"

"Even if I am not, I accept. I am pleased to see you again," she smiled, her dark eyes looking into his. '*It's proceeding as I have planned.*'

They set off together and she asked him about his family and she listened to his answers with interest. Her facial expressions exuded charm, her body language unmistakable as she let her arm touch his, but, with a casual movement. Choosing a random moment, her tone gently reluctant,

"This is where we part, Marius. I have enjoyed talking with you."

"And you, too, Alice. I hope you have a pleasant day." The woman nodded, turned, and went to minister to the fabled old lady, thinking,

'*I am now in his thoughts. He will wonder he's met me by chance...I am familiar with the minds of men. At nones, I will be sitting, resting a little, then he will join me.*' To assist her trickery, she went home and rinsed her hair with fragrant rose water and pinned a sachet of scented, dried lavender to the collar of her clean, white dress. Before setting off, she threw a fine damask silk shawl around her shoulders. '*Who can resist such an enticing woman? Man is a hunter, they say, and, ever has he been so! I must repay the Holy Father for the faith endowed in me.*'

"See you tomorrow," Luc said in valediction to his friend at the end of their shift moving stone blocks for building the town walls.

"Yes, goodbye, Luc."

Shortly, Marius was surprised to see Alice on a bench in a square she frequented and where she knew he would pass. '*My luck is in... twice, today*' he thought in a pleased but involuntary reaction.

"Hello again, Alice." Approaching her, grace and prettiness engulfed him. Of a sudden, and beyond his control, it was with fear as much as anticipation that he sat down beside her, without an invitation.

"Master! Do you not respect an innocent maiden?"

"No, I –" He was at first taken aback by her question, and about to apologise, until the flirtatious smile told him it was just banter. She began to speak with the familiarity of well-established friends,

"How has your day been?"

"We – that is my partner and me – have scarcely stopped for breath. We have to make sure the stone-layer is kept with enough stones to lay…" Alice laughed.

"What is it that amuses you?"

"It's the way you put things…no matter, do carry on."

"So, busy, and my hands are red raw."

"Let me see." He held out his chafed hands, palms upwards.

"Ooh! They are indeed sore. You must ask your lady wife to apply ointment. All wives worthy of the name keep balm in store." She took his hands in hers, eyes meeting his and lingering with an endearing tenderness.

"Yes…er…I suppose she has some." But, Marius, not worldly-wise, failed to realise she was creating temptation by inferring Dominique might be inadequate as a spouse.

"Forgive me, Marius. You will have affairs to attend to. I do not wish to detain you."

"You are not, Alice… " At once, he knew his reply was inappropriate. *'Why on earth did I say that? I am too close to this woman. I am married with a child, so this is not proper.'*

"…the wool merchant has no need of me this afternoon, but I must away to Dominique and Fabien."

"Of course. I have enjoyed talking with you, but, goodbye." Her voice expressed a reluctance at their parting.

"Goodbye, Alice."

As she watched him leave the square, she pondered, *'He is an honest, upright man. But the Holy Father knows best. I must satisfy his will.'*

Late that night, she had put on her nightgown and was about to re-tire. There came a knock at the door. A man in a brown, monk's habit pushed past her and entered the house. She recognised him. Around the town, the people saw a simple monk, of which there were many, suspecting no subterfuge, his true identity concealed. The prelate carried messages to and from Clément.

"Mademoiselle Alice." She nodded, folding her arms across her bosom, with false modesty. The man handed her a small parchment, a red wax seal keeping it closed and secret.

"I must return with your response." Sitting at the table, in the light of a candle, she broke the seal, unfolded the document, and read: *'Alice, if you are making progress, tell him yes. If not, then, no. That is all he needs to know. C.'*

Looking up, she told him 'yes'.

"Thank you. I wish you a peaceful night." Upon which, he left the house.

Alone, she blew out the candle and lay on the bed, but a dilemma prevented her from falling asleep. *'I cannot help but feel sorrow for the man, his wife, and son. By my persuasion and cunning, I must besmirch his family name, and for I know not what reason, I will create a dark intrigue to satisfy an old man's whim. Within myself, it does not sit well but, I have to yield to his greater wisdom. He is God's omnipotent servant on Earth and I, a lowly peasant girl – as I am seen – will not deny his authority.'*

At home, Marius ate his supper with Dominique – a fish stew. "Alice told me the best fish to buy," his wife commented, "she is a kind, thoughtful neighbour, do you not think?"

"No mistake," he replied, a guilty sense of impending disaster confusing his domestic happiness.

CHAPTER FOURTEEN

AVIGNON – THE TOWN
January, February, March 1348 AD

The cold, biting winds and sleet of the winter months did little to hinder the trade and daily lives of the inhabitants of Avignon. All nature of goods for consumption or sale arrived down the river from as far north as Lyon, upstream from Marseilles, and across the Saint Bénézet bridge from France to the west. The high living of the town bought salted fish from Brittany when the icy river inhibited the fresh variety. The three bakers within the walls loaded their stalls to breaking with newly baked loaves and pastries. Vegetable growers brought in potatoes, carrots, onions, broccoli, courgettes, and squash to the Saturday market on the bridge. Guy, the vintner, provided the people with beverages, from red and white wines to cider and distilled liqueurs. They believed the intake of alcohol warded off coughs and sneezes and he boasted the best cellar in all Provence. The fine, proud cart-horses worked until dropping in the summer. Winter was a season of rest for them but, a time of full orders for the farrier and the blacksmith, shoeing at the stables, hammering in the forge.

Men, women, children, young and old, enjoyed the privileges and benefits of a successful town: no-one starved, there few robberies or murders. They had food and drink in plenty, and spiritual succour was readily accessible in the numerous churches. They portrayed a satisfied population. But, for those unwilling to earn an honest coin, begging – though officially prohibited – and minor pilfering or picking pockets was an alternative employment. It ensured the Magistrate and his deputies had enough to occupy their time enforcing the rules and regulations that governed the place.

"How is trade?" Guy, the carter, asked his friend, the baker.

"They eat more bread when it's cold weather, that's for certain! This week I've had the oven going three times a day."

"Less of your idling!" a man jested to the blacksmith in his forge.

"Idling?" he retorted, "I swear the 'orses 'ave five legs, the rate I'm turning out shoes for 'em!"

"I hope you're not wanting brandy today, Guillaume?" the vintner asked his customer, "sold clean out, no more till the cart delivers, and that'll be next week. They all be drinking it for *medicinal purposes*, as they puts it. Believe that if you will!"

The Magistrate was happy; Pope Clément was thankful; only the sexton bemoaned there were few corpses to bury, and his wages were down.

After supper, Marius would go to the inn. He was, by now, regarded as a local person rather than a visitor.

"Evening, Marius," the landlord, Marcel, said in a welcoming tone. The greeting was returned as he sat at his usual table by the fire. His order of a tankard of ale was shortly placed before him. '*I think I've earned this, today*' he told himself, pondering over his exertions at the stonemason's yard and the docks. '*I wonder if Alice frequents this inn…I have not seen her since our encounter in the square…*' His thought was casual but, nonetheless, serious. Taking a full draught of his ale, he leaned forward and gazed at the ceiling, in a contented frame of mind. It was but minutes later that his daydream was interrupted by a soft voice behind him. Turning round, a tall, thin man stood, towering above him.

"Do you mind if I join you? It is Marius, is it not?"

"Yes, it is, but to what do I owe this honour, we have not met, have we?"

"I suppose we have not, in the literal meaning of the word...that is to say, we have not been introduced. I will put that matter to right. My name is Rostand, Carel Rostand." He held out his hand which, Marius, not without reservation, shook. The stranger continued,

"I have observed you, your wife, and child, in the church on several occasions. You work for the stonemason and the wool merchant."

"How do you know?" Marius felt threatened by this intrusion into his privacy.

"Let me tell you, Marius. It's my business to know who people are and what they do. You could say it's an aptitude, a predisposition, a skill. Yes, any of those words fit Carel Rostand." He sat down opposite and beckoned the landlord to bring a pitcher of ale.

"There is no need," Marius tried to decline but, too late, the drink was served. Rostand raised his tankard in a toast, to which he, half-heartedly, reciprocated. There followed an awkward silence during which he studied the man's countenance. A floppy, velvet hat fell to one side of his forehead; eyes dark as jet; a narrow nose and chin; pinched lips; white, even teeth. His boots came to his calves. He removed his cape to reveal a tunic of decent cloth.

"You do not recognise me, do you?"

"Ah!" and Marius recalled seeing him, "now I do, you are a beggar and I've noticed you around the town."

"It is true and, I thank you, for you have dropped the occasional coin into my bowl. The clothes I wear when I am begging are threadbare, worthy only of a poor man. When I keep company though, as this evening, I like to present myself in a more favourable light." Marius took an immediate dislike to this contradictory man, who it seemed had the means to dress well. He could pay for ale by night, but, by day, sat cross-legged at the town's gateways without a penny, at the mercy of generous, gullible passers-by. Noting he had agitated Marius, he carried on,

"You see, I am no fool. Yet, the world brands me as such. This gives me the upper hand when it comes to persuading folk to part with their money...you could say it's my superior intelligence. It's a game, is it not? My mind over theirs. Let me explain why I am successful as a beggar..." He paused to drink from the tankard.

"Do tell me, pray, though your story is not one that impresses me."

"I am sure it does not, but, that's because you are a moral person...how shall I put it...a man with well-defined standards of right and wrong. Life is not thus. My own degrees of decency vary according to the situation. Answer me this, Monsieur Marius: is it wrong to usurp the wealthy of their money? No, it is not! I only play my game with those who can afford to part with it. I watch them – in the church, the town, the street, wherever – and I overhear their conversations. To My Lady this or My Seigneur that, I will say "Was it not a moving sermon? The word of the Lord is mighty powerful." They behold a devout man, but one who has known hard times...and they feel sorry for me. The Lady's fancy purse is undone! What do you think, am I a bad person?"

"Your reasoning suits your purpose, Rostand, but it is, nevertheless, begging and that is against the law."

"Your answer is as I would expect. But, you are not experienced, like me. You will learn that, sometimes, what's wrong is right and we make perverse, capricious choices."

'*He is correct, by Satan! Does he know I have wicked feelings for the temptress, Alice? As yet, though, I have done nothing untoward.*'

"My cardinal advantage," Rostand continued, "is that I do not *need* their money. It's a matter of indifference to me whether they give or do not give. The only thing that's damaged is my pride!"

'*Pride? Is he talking about me? What has he seen?*' So he asked,

"What are you saying, that you have no *need* of their donations?"

"Ah! They do not realise this *fool* is not a fool, nor that his family line has breeding beyond their petty, bourgeois titles."

"Do you say..."

"You have it, Marius! Well done! In Fort Saint Martin, on the west bank of the river, resided the Count of Provence. In collusion with the Bishop of Notre-Dame des Doms in Avignon, he was granted the power, jurisdiction, and seigniory over our town. The Count's wealth came down the lineage..." Marius had to control his surprise,

'The Count of Provence?'

"Ay! My family, although, nowadays, it's the Pope who holds the authority, the glory, and the money - but hush, I trust you not to broadcast my story."

'He trusts me? If so, he knows me also. I must be cautious.'

The evening passed and the two men discussed and argued the case for mendicancy. It was the first chance, in his young life, he had conversed on an adult, sophisticated level. Though they disagreed on fundamental premises, he was enjoying the intellectual challenge. Engrossed in this discourse, he failed to notice a woman sitting in a far corner of the inn. It was Alice. She flirted and jested with two men who hung on her every word. She got up to leave but stopped at Marius' table.

"Hello, Marius. I did not see you here or I would have spoken to you earlier. Excuse my rudeness, I do not mean to intrude. I have to go. Goodnight to you and to your companion." She left before Marius could reply.

"That woman, Alice," Rostand said, hand over his mouth to keep his words confidential, "Do you know her?"

"Not well. She lives next door to me, though... *why does he ask me that?'*

"Be wary, my friend. Remember, folk are not always as they seem. As with many other residents of our town, I have observed Mistress Alice. Take care, that is all I will say." Marius did not appreciate the warning. He had done nothing wrong and he knew nothing of her designs. Thus, proceedings drew to a close.

The bakers, vegetable growers, vintner, smith, and farrier, all were content with their lives.

Days went by and Alice did not appear as Marius walked, daily, to and from his work. He had found himself looking for her, smelling for her scent, picking her out from other women with anticipation, only to be disappointed. It was with a frisson of excitement and latent desire that he eventually espied her on the bench in the square. They talked and she held his hand, tenderly. Biding her time, she now decided to escalate their friendship from its platonic state. Her master had encouraged her of late, anxious for news he could consider favourable.

Clément's involvement in the vengeful plot was distracted when, at the beginning of March, as spring sunlight warmed the yellow stone of old Avignon, the Magistrate requested an audience. He reported four unexplained deaths within a single day.

"The sexton is pleased, Holy Father, but it is most unusual, do you not agree? Our people do not pass away at such an unforeseen, unpleasant rate."

"Clearly not." He added,

"Four, you say... they will be miscreant men or wanton women, no doubt?"

"Sire, you do the deceased an injustice, if I may speak with candour. They were two men and two women, but, all from virtuous, God-fearing homes."

The Pope lowered his head in acknowledgment of his tasteless observation.

CHAPTER FIFTEEN

AVIGNON
March, 1348 AD

The next morning, there came a knock at the door to Clément's study. A flustered guard bowed and spoke,

"Sire, the Magistrate is without, says he must talk with you and it's urgent."

Clément hastily pushed a bottle on his desk out of sight behind a pile of parchments.

"Admit him." This interruption displeased the Pontiff.

"What do you want, Magistrate? It is barely twenty-four hours since you were here. Do you not know I have a sermon to prepare for the sext service?"

"My apologies, Sire, but I have received grave news. After the deaths of last week, today there are more. A woman and her two children, then two sailors at the docks..."

Clément narrowed his gaze to the man.

"This is, as you say, serious news. Would it seem there's something afoot?"

"We have not known so many deaths, now almost daily, for...er...not in my memory. But, we will face adversity, as we always do, with God's grace."

"Amen to that."

"I propose we conduct burials, if more there be, in the cathedral. The graveyard is adjacent and the clergy there will officiate. It will allow Sire to devote his time and effort to Palace ceremonies."

"I agree, Magistrate. Is that all? I am occupied today."

"You may have every confidence in your humble servant to arrange all that is necessary. However, I require your consent to hire additional grave-diggers. There be two sextons but they will not be sufficient if the situation remains as it is. They can't be digging graves *and* pushing carts. I need one more carter to assist young Marius, who has kindly accepted my request for his services –"

"Marius, you said?" Clément pricked up his ears at the name.

"Yes, Sire, Marius Nerval. A fine, upstanding lad if ever I saw one."

"I am sure he is, but come to the point, man, what do you ask?" There followed a short pause. The Magistrate knew full well the Holy Father detested parting with money, so he breathed in before continuing,

"While the Church pays the priests' stipends and one sexton, occasional workers will increase your expenditure. With your permission, I will deal with the matter."

"You have it." Clément consented, reluctantly. "I trust you to take whatever measures are needed."

The Magistrate had asked Marius to meet him at the cathedral. Excused his duties by the stonemason, he approached the thatch-covered lychgate as a group of mourners, with great solemnity and sadness, were leaving. The justice remained sitting on the wooden bench inside the gate, head lowered, tears running down his cheeks. Marius sat beside him and waited till the man was ready to speak.

"I am sorely grieved, Marius. I have performed all nature of public functions over the years, but today has moved me in the extreme. On this very seat," he touched it, "laid out... the mother with the children either side. Others... friends... caressed the bodies as they passed. Such distress, such melancholy. The priest ordered them to pick up their beloved and take them in... all shrouded in white." The cleric spoke but nobody heard him above the woeful clamour, only his valedictory *Requiesce in pace* that we recognised, but nothing further."

Marius too was on the verge of crying, this account so terrible – one he would hear with heart-rending monotony over the weeks and months to come. The Magistrate continued,

"The wretched husband, bereft of his family, muffled in a coarse, brown cloak, moaned with misery! Strength had departed his body and he remained upright only with the support of his friends, a truly sorry sight. He followed the buriers taking the deceased out to the graveyard where they were lowered, with dignity, I should say, into the grave. The mother first, the children laid atop her. The father roared and screamed, heartbroken, oppressed with the dreadful weight of desperation." Regaining his composure, he exclaimed, "Hey! What use is a troubled magistrate, I ask you? We have each to perform our offices as best we can, nothing more, nothing less, boy! But, I have a proposition."

"What is that, Magistrate?"

"In the town, death is coming every day, for what reason I know not. To make it worse, the number rises, so I must act for the benefit of the people."

"I do not see how this affects me."

"Marius, I have had the time and occasion to appraise you… er… as a man."

"Magistrate?"

"You are who I was forty years ago: honest, strong and caring. I must appoint someone to oversee, as it were, the measures to deal with this sickness. To my shame, we were unprepared and now we have to act. Most urgent is the need to carry the corpses to the cathedral without delay. I require you to ensure we have sufficient carts and men to push them. What say you?"

"I am too humble, but I accept. However, there is my employment –"

"I will accommodate the stonemason and the wool merchant and also pay you a wage. You will, then, work for me. Understand? Before coming here this morning, a lad informed me there be bodies to attend to at the docks. That is all I know. Take a cart from outside my cabin and commandeer casual labourers to assist you, with my blessing."

"At once," Marius said. Unnoticed in a secluded corner of the church-yard, Carel Rostand observed them.

Marius passed by the bridge and stopped short. It was market day. The calls of the traders and laughter of the children rang out in sharp contrast to the sombre cathedral scene. Beneath the spans of the bridge built into the river bank, disreputable merchants sold spurious wares: in good times or bad, people are deceived and abused through the temptation of a cheap deal. At the quayside, he was beckoned over by Bruno who was with Mahi, the bargee at his moorings. They shook hands but their faces showed no pleasure.

"Ah, Marius, we were expecting you. They are in the boat."

"I beg your pardon?" Marius asked. Mahi spoke up,

"My two hands, down there." He pointed into the open hold of the barge. "We had just sailed out of Marseilles when one of them started to talk like he'd been drinking strong liqueur. Can't have been so because there's none on my boat – I learned about drunken sailors years ago. He made no sense. Then the other lad had fits of real bad coughing and a fever... but, worse was the swellings, lumps, like, in his neck. Hard to the touch, they were too... and fiery hot... spread all under his arms. I've seen some sights in my life, battles, riots, but naught like this! We'd not made three days upstream when the two of 'em howled, like wild wolves, until they keeled over, dead!"

"Terrible, it is true," Marius responded and, adopting his new, official role, instructed the sailor,

"Get down below and lift them as high as you can. I'll take their arms and haul them out."

The bodies were heavy but they eventually removed them to be placed, side by side, on the cart.

"Find me sackcloth to cover them... that's right... now, you must assist me to push them to the cathedral."

"Willingly, for the poor souls... but there's one more thing –"

"What's that?" Mahi lowered himself into the hold and, a few moments later, clambered out with an animal in his arms, black as night and rigid. The man stroked it gently, then revealed,

"It's the ship's cat, Eloise. Been with me for six years and more, so decent age. Used to keep her to kill rats, and damned good at it she was!" The muscular, swarthy seaman hesitated, his eyes moist, and concluded,

"Found her this morning, cold and still. Suppose she had to go one day, but the same time as those two...? Put her on the cart with them, master Marius, please." Marius did as requested. A steady rain fell as they made their way through the town, he taking one handle, Mahi the other. At the lychgate, they were grateful for its shelter and waited until the priest appeared,

"Two more. Any family?"

"None. Sailors from a boat this morning, and a cat." The cleric raised his eyebrows.

"A cat?" Mahi stepped forward,

"She was mine, but close to the men as well, so it's the decent thing to do, lay her down with them."

"I concur. The Lord tells us there will be animals in Heaven." He turned to Marius, "No service since there's no family. Take them to the graves, behind the apse. My blessing concludes matters."

Mahi and Marius pushed the cart around the cathedral to where the sexton and his mate had just finished digging the two pits, one for each man. "Be a luxury soon...one each I mean. If it carries on at this rate we'll run out of space," declared the gravedigger, leaning on his spade. They lowered the bodies, heads facing west, feet to the east, as was the Christian custom, into the holes that had filled with rainwater, turning the soil into a cloying mud. The cat lay on top. The priest threw a handful of earth over both, mumbled a few *requiem* verses, bowed, crossed himself and departed the miserable scene. The five funerals conducted that day had drained the emotion from him and he felt pangs of physical and spiritual inadequacy. '*Only the Lord knows whether I am made of the right stuff to face such duties should they continue – and there's nothing that tells me they will not,*' he wondered. The sexton tapped Marius on the shoulder,

"I would introduce myself. My name is Alban." He wiped his soil-caked hand on his tunic and proffered it towards Marius, who accepted, and he continued,

"I am told you are to be in charge of delivering the unfortunates to me – or, should I say, to the *priest,* first, if he's to do a ceremony. That's only when the collection bowl receives a coin or two, if you follow... otherwise, it's straight to me, like..." Marius studied the sexton. His was a short, rotund figure with curvature of the spine that belied his capacity for grave digging, "...now, my job starts and ends at yon lychgate, within the grounds. Outside of that, it's your business. And, I understand I will have extra men since there are too many graves for me and my fellow... is that correct?"

"It is, Alban,"

"Good. I trust our association will be a happy one – as far as this line of work *can* be so!" Marius said nothing, at once disliking the man's attitude but understanding his pragmatic opinion.

The same evening, he went to the tavern, in need of drink stronger than the ale in his own house. Events weighed heavy and he questioned his strength of character to perform the onerous undertaking the Magistrate had bestowed on him. Earlier, when he returned from the cathedral, Dominique greeted him with a smile and embrace to which he did not properly respond. Thoughts raced through his mind in a chaotic jumble and, to her curiosity and disappointment, he told her only that his work had changed and he would explain later. This she accepted, knowing her husband always did what was in the best interests of her and Fabien.

"A bottle of eau de vie," he called to Marcel as he sat at his usual table. The landlord put one down, as told, and a glass.

"Are you celebrating, Marius? Fear not, I shall charge only what you drink from it."

"Damn you! You are a buffoon whose equal I have not known! Do not bother me any more tonight, else I may not be responsible for my actions!" Marcel was shocked by Marius – normally the mildest of men – speaking to him with such vehemence. He withdrew behind the safety of the counter.

Marius drank three glasses of the liqueur, in quick succession. Ale or cider was his preferred tipple, and he was not accustomed to anything stronger. The alcohol, though, had the desired effect: he felt more relaxed and prepared to consider all that was happening, at this dreadful time no-one had expected. *'The Magistrate has placed a rare burden on me and, I pray to God, I do not fail. It is a cavernous leap from unloading wool on the barges and moving stone, to transporting dead folk to their final resting place. I have never shied away from hard work, but this is different. It's not a simple job... it's viewing at close quarters, and touching the very soul of the person gone before. I know nothing of death. It's an occurrence, until now, I cannot recall confronting me. My father died when I was but a child and I remember it not. Does the deceased rise up to Heaven? What if he has led an unworthy life on earth... a trickster or even a murderer? Will he be refused entry through the pearly gates? If not, what will he – or she – do in that case? What is Hell like? Where... but, Marius, control yourself! You'll not help man or beast if the mourners see you in this state – whimpering, doubting, questioning. You must be strong!'* Then, he admitted, *'All this religion is beyond me, the Bible, the Lord... in truth, I am afeard of it. I do not like all those fancy words, bowing and crossing, sitting and standing, arms flailing like a windmill. But, enough!'*

Marcel came over to put more logs on the fire, this time with discretion, seeking to avoid his previous reprimand. He uttered not a single word. Sparks leapt up, consumed by the wide chimney and the embers became flames. His thoughts embraced his uncertainty.

The inn filled with patrons of all classes, from the lowly to the affluent. They were united, though, by shared talk of how and why people were dying, and at an unprecedented rate.

"He was a man in his prime, all to live for and now he's gone," one customer said to another.

"She was my neighbour... lived next door to her for thirty years... no, more!"

"What about Agnès? She's left her three children behind and the husband must bring them up alone."

News of the rising toll of death quickly got around the town. In ordinary times, its citizens' cares and tribulations focused on the price of bread, the grape harvest, or the latest reprobate to be shackled in the stocks. But, these were not ordinary times. Although there was not panic, to any degree, it was impossible to not detect anxiety, surprise, or morbid interest. Reports of the agony of people in their final hour – distorted bodies; hard, purple lumps; fever as hot as Satan's fire – were on everyone's tongue.

At the same time, the Magistrate stood in the cathedral lychgate, in animated conversation with the priest.

"How can this be? Tell me, what number is laid out inside?" the justice asked.

"Twelve. But I now have word of twenty more and from all parts of the town...Saint Bénézet bridge down to the Porte Saint Michel, Oratoire across to Rue des Lices. It's as if an avalanche is pounding us, in torrents and all of a sudden! At first light, they must be carried here. We will bury throughout the morning, but, as it is, interments will run into evensong."

"So be it," the Magistrate agreed, ashen-faced.

"The sexton," the priest continued, "has hired four hands to assist with the grave digging and they work with admirable vigour to keep apace of the funerals. However..." He paused in reflection, "if it goes on like this, I know not if we will cope. See the list." He ran his finger down the names and handed over the parchment. "Twenty souls passed, their bodies still warm, I'd say, not yet brought to the shelter of the Lord."

"Fear not, father, we will endure. Be assured, for Avignon is an orderly, law-abiding town – by and large – due to our dedication and devotion to duty. *You* fulfil a religious need, *I* cater to more earthly demands...but, I have met nothing of this sort. It increases by the day with a virulence exceeding any expectation. The bargees tell me tales of an awesome scourge that blights towns, cities, villages alike down river near the sea, and we must pray that..." At which point, he seized the parchment from the priest and, waving it towards the sky, raised his voice,

"Where is he?"

"Magistrate?"

"My runner! The boy knows he is to meet me here every day and at this time. He delivers my messages and instructions so people are informed. As I said, my office is well executed." His anger mounted, "and Marius *must* have the list!"

Alice emerged from the concealed passageway into the wooded Rocher des Doms. She had spent time with the Pontiff: certain bounties did not, he would acknowledge if ever pressed, always come from the Good Lord. Still, his parting words rang in her ears, "Make more progress with Marius, woman!" Walking past the lychgate, she could not help but hear Marius' name, so she eavesdropped the exchange between the Magistrate and the priest. In an instant, her cunning nature saw an opportunity. She approached the two men and, pulling back her hood, asked,

"Gentlemen, I mean no disrespect and I dare say you do not recognise me, but I could not fail to catch the name *Marius*. Will that be Marius Nerval? If so, he is my neighbour and I am returning to my house forthwith. It would be no inconvenience to deliver the letter. But, no, forgive me, for a humble girl should not be so bold –"

At first surprised, the Magistrate was relieved that Marius would soon receive the list. The whereabouts of his unreliable runner in doubt, he accepted her kind offer.

"Your boldness is excused, and most welcome, mistress. I thank you, but ensure it is given to Monsieur Nerval personally. It is a matter of great importance."

"You can trust me." With the parchment tucked under her robe, she bowed and departed. She was confident he would be in the tavern and this was confirmed when she heard his door open then close.

Her dancing voice drifted over to Marius, but in a tone that struck him as inappropriate given the main topic of conversation: death. The drinkers, with a natural innocence, grasped any moments to deny a growing reality. Laughter, nervous insecurity, moral insensibility, all coloured the thinking of a township reluctant to address a disease that was starting to overrun their complacency. With a delicate waft of rosewater scent Alice sat beside him without a word. He did not acknowledge her presence, engrossed in thought until she leaned her shoulder against him.

"How are you, Marius?"

"Ah...hello, Alice, I didn't notice you."

"Do I have that effect on men?" she asked, in a teasing voice.

"Just the opposite," he answered. "Bring a glass and join me, will you not?" She needed no further encouragement.

"I have a parchment from the Magistrate. He says it's most important you have it." She placed the document on the table. He read its contents and deliberated, struggling to absorb its severity:

'*Colbert – Rue Violette*
Woman and child – Rue Louis
Woman – Place Pie
Sarrasin, man – Rue Vialla...and so the list went on, name after name, street after street. At the end, the Magistrate had written,

'*Essential the bodies be carried to the cathedral as soon as possible –*
civic duty – hand over to priest at the church – their concern then
Take on labourers to assist – as many as you decide, with my sanction
Use carts from quayside
You may direct this sad task from my cabin'

"Bad news?"

"The likes Avignon has never experienced! Death all around. More with each day. I have to take bodies to the cathedral." She listened and sympathised – two requirements to win over men that she had learned early in life. They emptied the bottle, and as he got to his feet as if to leave, she asked,

"You will not allow a poor, defenceless woman out alone at this hour, will you?"

"What are you suggesting?" he said through a haze induced by the eau de vie.

"That you see me to my door."

"Why of course, forgive me."

Outside, she held his hand and led them down an alleyway, both with unsteady gait, to where they entered her house through a back door, unnoticed by anyone. It was easy to consummate her seduction. She pushed the half-drunk, lustful man onto her bed.

"...why...what, Alice...what are you doing?"

"If you need telling, you are the man desire." She leaned over and kissed him hard on his mouth until he responded and was unable to resist her any longer. A tug at the cord round his waist and she removed his tunic. She caressed his strong shoulders, her kiss now moving to his chest and lower. Marius revived from the alcoholic torpor under her passionate embraces. He collaborated without encouragement in this sexual infatuation for a shameless trollop, now all-consuming. Their union complete, he rolled off her body and, lying at her side, he touched her face.

"Alice, we should not – She stopped his protestation, a finger closing his lips,

"Say nothing, my dearest Marius, enjoy the moment."

Dominique asked why he was so late, to which he replied,

"I have been drinking – as *you* would, woman, if you bore the responsibility I have to face. Let me be, I'm tired and will explain all tomorrow." He slept, but his mind was overwhelmed with guilt for his weakness and fear for what lay ahead. Holding clear views about what was right and wrong, his infidelity was a sin, of that he was in no doubt. '*When Dominique discovers my wicked deed, how will I justify it? I love her and Fabien...not Alice. They are my family and deserve my respect and care, above all others! And this at a time when tragedy begins to engulf the town.*' Alice looked forward to ingratiating herself more with Clément when she would give him the good news.

CHAPTER SIXTEEN

AVIGNON
March, 1348 AD

Marius woke at first light. Dominique was already sitting at the table, Fabien in her arms. She fed her son soup from a wooden bowl. In between mouthfuls, he gurgled contentedly, a healthy, young boy.

"How did you sleep last night, Marius...well, I'd say, you were maudlin from drink?"

"So I was," came the sheepish reply.

"You must tell me about your new *responsibility*, as you called it."

'Can I believe my liaison with Alice?' He thought. 'Surely, it's but a dream...but no! And there's no doubt I'm blameworthy – for Alice and my unfaithful act.'

"You've heard about deaths in the town over the last week...well, the Magistrate asked me to carry two deceased sailors from the docks to the cathedral. It was a case of me being there at the time and he requesting a favour. I agreed. He has placed his office at my disposal when I work for him. As from today I am his deputy. Times are changing."

"*Changing,* what do you mean by that?"

"The things I see are not usual, they are...different...changed. A woman and her two children struck dead – but not by a cutthroat! If you had been at the service…her man left alone in the world! Only the heartless would not have wept."

"So, that's five souls departed."

"You count well, Dominique! But the tally is, as we speak, greater than that." There was an edge to his voice, a discourtesy he was not accustomed to using when speaking to her.

"Greater?" she asked.

"That is what I said!" He all but spat out the words.

"Let me explain. See the list the Magistrate sent to me last evening." He took the parchment, still in the pocket of his tunic, and placed it in front of his wife. Her eyes scanned the names, stopping when she had counted twelve. Her countenance betrayed disbelief.

"How can this be so? Fair Avignon is a town for the living, where our children may thrive and outlast their *parents*."

"It is so – or should I say *was*! To answer your question, yes, life itself is transformed. They are young and old, rich and poor who have met the Lord, and before their due moment. But, hey, do you hear that noise outside?" He opened the door to see two men pushing a cart laden with what was, by their shape, bodies. The wheels' iron hoops clanked on the cobbled street as it approached their house, the sound a *danse macabre* to accompany a funeral procession.

"The Magistrate has sent out a wain even before dawn. This evil becomes darker by the hour." He took his cloak from a hook on the wall, wrapped it around his shoulders, and, kissing Dominique on the forehead, said,

"I have to go to the docks. I predict there will be increasing mortality. I intend to repay the Magistrate's trust in me, if God so pleases. I expect to be away until evening."

Outside, the winter Mistral wind blew incessantly down the narrow streets. Shutters closed tight, the only sign of life was white smoke spiralling upwards from chimneys. They lit fires in the houses early this bitterly, cold morning. No human voice to be heard, the only disturbance to an eerie silence coming from the occasional stray dog or cat, sniffing, listening, watching, spreading scent to mark their territories.

Marius sensed the distinctive rumble of a second carriage before it came into view. It trundled out of a side street and creaked slowly towards him, weighed down with however many victims he could not count with precision. Close up, he raised a hand, requesting the men to halt.

"Good morning to you."

"And to you," they replied in unison. To rest a while and regain their strength, they needed no persuasion.

"Where have you come from?"

"The east side of the town," one continued, "two houses, close together, the addresses given us by the Magistrate...but...are you not Marius? Yes, I believe you are! Yon justice gave us your name and said to make your acquaintance if our paths crossed, and that they have! You need not know what they call us, we are simple hands at the warehouses and don't earn much so when this chance came along...we gets well paid for pushing a barrow, so it's good luck for us if not for them piled up..."

"Enough! Speak with respect for the dead else one word from me to the Magistrate and you will be lucky, I warrant, to sweep the streets of rubbish!"

"Beg your pardon, Marius," the man said, embarrassed, "I meant nothing wrong. As I was saying, four wasted in one house, three in the other. *Announce yourselves as my representative,* the justice told us. *We've come to take your departed, under the instruction of the Town Magistrate, to the cathedral for proper burial,* we say to the householders. If they are not wound by their family, we are to cover them with sackcloth. It's heavy work, you see, but it has to be done if we are to get our wages! We found both residences and, within, we were met with grief and howling that near burst your ears. In one, the man had laid out his wife and two children; in another, two aged grandparents, a child, and a maidservant. However, please excuse us for we must press on without delay. When these be given over, we are to return since he has many more reported."

"Of course," and Marius stepped aside to allow the cart passage.

Out of earshot, the labourers struck up a conversation. "I know we'll earn good money for moving these corpses, but...it's creepy, do you not think?" one asked. "Creepy?" asked the other. "Yes, till this morning I'd never smelt a stiff, let alone manhandled one! And the wife, I swear she was watching me, scolding me for intruding in her house...before the husband put coins on her eyes. Those youngsters looked like...er...them cherubs painted on the palace ceiling, all peaceful and holy, if you get my drift?" 'I do not!" came the response, "if you're going to be so soft, we'll be no use at all to the Magistrate and we'll not be paid a penny!" "I suppose you're right." "Yes, I am! Now come on, get pushing!"

A light flickered in the office, creating weird shadows. To muffled voices inside, Marius entered and nodded in the direction of the Magistrate who was pointing at a parchment, explaining the procedure for three unkempt, broad-shouldered youths to follow.

"Take a dolly, each, from behind the office and be away with all haste. When you have delivered your load, return here. There are ample trips to fill the whole day, so be off." Then he noticed Marius.

"Ah! It's good to see you," and he ushered out the three recruits before pulling another stool over to his desk. "Sit, please." He took a bottle and glasses from a cupboard and poured them a tot of a dark green liquid that Marius sniffed, with suspicion, before drinking. "Not seen that before?" "I have not," was the reply, although a smile confirmed his approval. "I don't know its name," the Magistrate explained, "but I buy it from a particular bargee who sails from somewhere north upstream. We are, to be sure, in need of its sustenance today. See here, the list sent me by the priest...deaths during the night." Marius put down his glass and studied the parchment pushed in his direction. He could scarcely believe what he saw: twenty-four names and addresses.

"I am, in truth, shocked! So many and all of a sudden. Neither floods nor famine would smite our fellows in such numbers. Have you, in your long and distinguished service, known the like?"

"No," came the gloomy answer. "This is why I have made you my assistant. I'm too old for lugging but not so to prevent me dealing with...er...administration, as they call it..." His voice tailed off and he sipped the coloured spirit. "...a justice is not worthy of the title unless he is versed in lists, young man. Sometimes it's offenders or barrels, other times vegetables or marriages...all kinds, but they have to come to me on a list, do you see?"

"If you say so, but –"

"Forgive me," he cut in. "It's not a time for idle prattle, there's more urgent matters."

"You speak true! But how are we to..." Again, he was interrupted, "Look outside, what do you see?" Marius saw six men in a silent line.

"I put the word around last night, offering good money to workers who want to earn more than they can on the boats. So, we are not short of labourers. Your job is to organise them, send them to the houses where deaths are notified and take the bodies to the church. I trust a man of your intelligence can perform this gruesome duty?"

"I will do my best, sire."

"I am sure you will. And tell them there's no wages until you are satisfied with their work...bound to be some slackers among them. Now, I have three carts. One is enough to carry four bodies with more on top. One is smaller and...I'll leave it to you to decide how to best use them. You have my authority to commandeer trucks from the warehouses. And, the same for sackcloth to bind them with some respect, at least. Do you have any questions?" Marius took a deep breath, "No, I understand." The Magistrate leaned back in his chair, relieved to have a man like Marius at his side. His life had been to serve, assist, organise and, often, to mete out punishments to any errant Avignonnais. Among the latter, he was extolled for his fairness and, when appropriate, clemency. In addition to mundane matters of taxes, goods imported to the docks and the lackeys who stood guard at the town gates, he sat one day a month to hear causes and offences. Whether passing judgment on miscreants who had contravened civic regulations or a fellow who had argument with a neighbour, he was even-handed. An honest man, he had not married, his magistrate's commitments were, in his opinion, quite sufficient to occupy his time, so he quipped. It was said his ear could be bent by the occasional dressed pheasant or basket of truffles – a perk of his trade. He executed his judicial function fearful of the Lord.

"I wish you good fortune, Marius, and the way deaths are rising, you will be in sore need of it! I must seek advice from the Holy Father, and sooner the better. His prayers cannot but help the situation..." But, his voice was not confident. "I suspect trundling bodies to be buried may prove an inadequate action to deal with this calamity, however, we will see what the days bring." The pen dipped in ink, he went back to marking the list, sorting names street by street.

As dawn broke, Marius gave instructions to the men. "You, take the two-wheeled to Rue Saint-Joseph... you, use the big, flat-bed to..." Thus, the work began – and hard drudge it was. Bodies in such number were soon viewed by the men handling them as chattels, cargo, commodities to be toted from house to resting place. The more they died, the less due ceremony could be afforded them. Their ultimate treatment became, of necessity, sanitized, and despite innate goodness and respect for the fellow man, pragmatism dominated idealism.

"You must have the priest sign for those on your parchment, then go to the next houses, until your list is completed. At the sext bell, visit the nearest tavern, order bread, ale, and whatever food they offer. Tell the landlord the Magistrate will settle their account – no-one will argue with that." Marius possessed a natural talent for delegation and organisation, tempered by compassion denying his tender years. The contagion, to his eyes, was a wrong inflicted from on high: only the greater wisdom of a cleric could explain its gratuitous arrival. God had a reason for everything, that he accepted, and mortals like him did not doubt His supremacy. Their fate was a blessing, perverse and unfathomable, to be embraced with all their heart: comforting his companion in times of trouble was an opportunity to thank Him for His abundant bounty.

"Before you begin, I ask you to not discuss your employment with family, friends or strangers. Although we face days of deepest darkness, we should not cause a stir. It is better one side of the town remains ignorant of the plight of the other. Panic will serve no purpose."

Pope Clément knew, before they spoke, that the Magistrate had come concerning the deaths and he began the meeting with two questions,

"So, Magistrate, how many do we have and will you take wine with me?"

"Holy Father, I cannot refuse such an offer." Clément uncorked a bottle and filled two goblets. "You know – or may not know - the number rises daily…" and the Magistrate hesitated, lips pinched tight closed as he did the calculation,

"…two score and nine but the report this morning says it will be more than four score. They all die, without exception, displaying the same symptoms: swollen lumps in the groin and under the arms or on the neck – hard, that will not break. Terrible pain with a violent coughing and fever…"

"Heaven preserve us."

"Amen to that, sire."

"And the healers?" The Magistrate grimaced,

"There are only four or five in the entire town, too few to attend so many sick people. For those with the means to pay, these physicians have administered the usual salves and medicines. However, these are *unusual* times. In my opinion, they rarely cure a common cold, so – Clement interrupted,

"I understand what you are saying. The Church suffers physicians, surgeons, quacks and the like, *but* – His voice became altogether more passionate, "these practitioners can never be a substitute for the power of prayer and devotion to the Scriptures."

"My Lord is familiar with such matters. *I* have to confront the real world and, in my estimation, we do not have the luxury of prayer. The town is in need of more immediate assistance."

"I take your point.' Clément ceded – not the reaction the Magistrate had expected, "We will, nonetheless, pray for the deceased, as for the living. Tell me now, what more do you require of us?"

"I have Marius Nerval as my deputy and have conferred judicial authority on him, as is permissible in an emergency. He is brave, steadfast, and I could not wish for a better man for the circumstances that confront us."

"Ah, the Nerval boy!" Clément's gaze hardened.

"The same. He is, at this moment, organising carts and men to bring the dead to the cathedral. There, we have three sextons and three men to dig the graves. The priest has called on two clerics from the other churches within the walls to conduct funerals..."

"Yes?" Clement asked, his patience waning the more wine he drank.

"We may need to take greater measures, and I have plans in mind. We will go through the next few days but... I see no sign of an abatement and the graveyard is fast filling."

"Magistrate, you have my complete confidence and support. Do as you judge fit and inform me when we can act further to help you. Meantime, we *will* pray. Kneel, my son." The Pontiff placed a hand on the man's head, mumbled a prayer, and offered his signet ring for the ceremonial kiss. The Magistrate bowed, turned and left, nodding to the guards as he passed. He went straight to the nearby cathedral to collect the daily list.

'*Nerval! Damn him! The Magistrate rings his praises – he would not if he knew the father as I do. In my eyes, his offspring is not worthy of the slightest flattery! But I will prepare a sermon, for the people will expect me to offer them hope and consolation. I will be ready.*'

On the quayside, Marius dispatched the last bearer of the morning. He wiped beads of emotional sweat from his brow when a man appeared through the rolling sea mist. Jean Pagnol, the wool merchant, announced himself,

"Good morning, Marius. So, this is why the Magistrate has purloined you from my service?"

"Ah, hello Jean. Yes, you know –"

"Of course I do – the whole town knows, so many families have been afflicted."

"That is the word!"

"I might well have laid you off anyway, so few boats moor here since... it seems as if the world is in a fright. Men sailing out of Marseilles have heard deplorable stories of those stricken by the... er... malady, and they refuse to dock there or here either. Bad for business, I can tell you –"

"*What* do you say, man?" Marius lurched forward to growl the words into his face, indifferent to the fact he was addressing his employer thus. "How on earth dare you consider your livelihood when fellow Avignonnais fall at our feet, smitten without mercy! Man, woman, husband, wife, child... a plague on your game, Pagnol! May a swarm of locusts and famine descend on your household, for if the weightiest of worries on your mind today is your vile trade alone –"

"Marius! Forgive me, I was not thinking, the people owe you a debt of gratitude."

Marius inhaled deeply, regaining his composure,

"I need not gratitude, rather a cure to offer them. As you say, they are *in a fright,* and with very good reason."

The wool merchant paused, accepting this admonishment, albeit with a guilty humour as if he was about to make a confession whatever,

"I've lived my life with brother Thomas in our house and have never dreamed of any danger. The Magistrate can muster armed men if invaders threatened. The esteemed Counts of Provence and Toulouse, protectors under good Charles of Anjou and Alphonse of Poitiers, have since long guaranteed the independence and safety of the town. With the deaths, though, I admit my brother and me have become sore afraid ourselves, not knowing whether it might be our turn next. We have moved a few chattels and the strongbox out of our house to live on the barge, moored at the end of the wooden pier, away from any infected folk. We have not returned to the town except for most urgent matters – of which there are none."

"What are you telling me, sire?"

"Our decision was taken out of fear, simple as that. Is it reason enough?"

"I say *not*! In truth, you and your brother are turning your backs on the scourge, leaving us here to cope as best we can - I call that *cowardice,* Pagnol, faint heart, absence of courage, timidity...whatever you like! If this is your resolve, better you sail your boat down the river, and take your chattels and strongbox with you, lest we set eyes on you again!" Pagnol turned and walked, head lowered and shoulders stooped, into the mist whence he came.

With fear grew suspicion. The people who lost members of their family knew, at painful first hand, about the dreadful disease. Their loved ones buried, they ventured out from their houses only for essential supplies such as bread, oil, and salt-fish. Those wealthy enough to hire servants sent them out on errands. Mistrust spread and divided the population: one neighbour knew not if the infection had visited the other. A trader from the market on the bridge might contaminate them, or so they thought, by his call for custom: rumour prevailed that the germ was carried by foul vapours and unpleasant odours from stinking breath. Healers recommended patients to keep mouths tight shut in the street. It was said that a gentle, faithful dog, once poisoned, became a ferocious wild hound. They avoided a stranger's handshake, and even an innocent greeting was given from a distance. Terror gripped the town born out of an uncertain future.

CHAPTER SEVENTEEN

AVIGNON
April, 1348 AD

Prior to January, 1348 AD, Avignon had been thought of as cosmopolitan, with justification. Its people came and went through the gates in the town walls with abandon. Their lives were uncomplicated to the point of serenity. They neither sought nor, to their detriment, recognised danger: death in their midst was accepted as part of the Good Lord's ordinance. Traders of sundry nationality sailed up the river Rhône from Marseilles, the Mediterranean and beyond. Across the Bénézet bridge roamed itinerant merchants and visitors alike from the western provinces of greater France. Upstream, on tracks well worn, arrived daily, sellers of wine, hawkers of crafted jewellery, purveyors of salt meat and fish. Cowherds and shepherds drove sheep and cattle of all breeds for sale at the livestock market near to the bridge. Strangers welcomed, relied on for their continued prosperity. The more unknown faces there were, the more the coffers swelled. The populace, from lowly labourer to venerated cleric, received their education in life by exposure to the outside world. Before the events of a few weeks previous, Jacques was sociable; Jeanne was lively; children, in the games they played learned the benefits of cooperation and tolerance. Whereas the actions of some provided suitable fodder for the

Church's frequents rants, Avignon society was, for the most part, law-abiding. The judicial powers dealt with contraventions of the town's bye-laws, disputes over land rights, or arguments for a pitch on the market, with an even hand.

An old man, sitting on a bench outside his house, commented to a neighbour,

"My father spun yarns to me and my brother when we were youngsters... stories about King Clovis who defeated the Visigoths and ruled all lands to the west of the river. Then... let me think... Hannibal's battles and Emperor Caesar's victories as a soldier. He told me those famous generals all had their greatest triumphs when the enemy was most content: they lowered their guard and happiness meant they were at their most vulnerable. I've no reason to doubt the truth of it." His friend nodded in agreement.

Alice led Marius by the hand down an overgrown path deep into the woods of the Rocher des Doms. From the cathedral behind them sounded the bell for prime. The pale, spring morning had not yet penetrated the canopy above. They stumbled over fallen branches and brambles scratched their legs.

"Where are you taking me?" asked Marius, excited and intrigued as he was, always, in her presence.

"You'll find out" she replied, mischief in her voice.

The pathway opened into a clearing where he made out a hut.

"Come, come" she encouraged him. Within, she picked up two flints and, striking one against the other, lit a candle. As its flame brightened and his eyes adjusted to its flickering illumination, he saw nothing apart from a bench and three large, straw-filled sacks on the floor in a corner. To his surprise, she took a pitcher and filled two wooden cups. Passing one to Marius, she observed the confounded expression on his face.

"Will my lord take wine?" She teased. "I have it ready for you."

"Indeed I will, but what is this place?"

"It's a drover's cabin no longer used. The cattlemen tethered their beasts to graze while they laid down to rest after a journey of... I don't know... many leagues. Nowadays, they go down the better tracks that follow the river. So, you see, we have this to ourselves." She was familiar with the hut since it stood on the path to the secret door of the Pope's rooms. It did not cross Marius' mind she may have availed herself of it before, concealed as it was from the public gaze. However, he was under no illusion regarding her intentions for him today.

"Drink up," she instructed, untying the cord around her waist and letting her tunic fall to the ground. Her perfect figure complemented skin the colour of pure-white marble. He drained his cup and pushed her, but with tenderness, on the sacks. His own tunic came off and the two held each other in a naked, passionate embrace although, in his consciousness, he felt an acute, bittersweet guilt. It was his lechery to betray Dominique but it diverted attention from the duty he had to care for his fellows of Avignon. Their union completed, she stroked his brow and placed her lips on his. With their ardour diminishing, the chill of the morning urged them to dress.

"I hear you have been entrusted with seeing the bodies are taken –"

"How do you know?" But nothing is hidden in these times. Yes, I have been given that task, and hideous it is!"

"I can but imagine," she said, holding his hand and looking, with concern and interest, into his eyes.

"I have to meet the Magistrate within the hour, although, having called at the cathedral today, the situation is even more inauspicious than I thought. I am honoured to serve our people in their moment of need but, at home..."

"...at home, Marius? Do you have a problem there?"

"It's complicated, Alice. Pass me the wine." He drank half a cup, then resumed,

"Dominique does not believe I should have anything to do with dead folk. She says '*Leave it to the others! I will never forgive you if you bring the curse into our home. You should consider me and Fabien first!*' I understand what she says, but I have no choice! This business concerns us all. I have seen it take richest, poorest, youngest, oldest... it makes no distinction so we must unite to survive it! The Lord has chosen me, this I feel – don't look like that, of course, I don't mean as a saint or similar. He just wants me to do what's right. Makes no difference the Scriptures have not been explained to me." He paused and drank more wine. "Dominique has told me to decide between her and Fabien or my work for the Magistrate." His lover squeezed his hand tight, eyes open wide, expressing support and encouragement.

"How can she ask that of you? It is not a reasonable –" Marius hushed her,

"If she had witnessed the scene in the cathedral but two hours ago, she would sympathise with me more!"

"Tell me, do." The affinity she showed him was part of the ruse, hatched and developed at the behest of the Holy Father. There were occasions of reflection when she was not at all sure of the motives for the seduction: this doubt increased the more her relationship with Marius blossomed. "Pray, carry on."

"I am familiar with the priests, the sexton and his assistants, everyone, and they perform their duties without complaint: they are worthy citizens, Alice, they give of their best. I fear mere goodwill does not have the power to overcome the evil surrounding us. You should spread the word that we each have a part to play according to the steps described by the Magistrate and town elders – whosoever they may be."

"I saw for myself, last evening in the cathedral, the awful state we have now reached. First, I heard the bell rung by the carter as he approached. At the lychgate, the family and friends unloaded the corpses. I am sorrowful the carter had to lay hands on them more than was needed, but so it is. They proceeded into the building lit by flaming torches like an Inferno ruled by the Devil and not a Christian sanctuary at all. Before the altar are rows of benches, one for each body. The priests have no time to offer more than a brief, mysterious blessing in the strange foreign tongue we understand as Latin. The sexton's men came to take those beloved folk out to their final resting place. The mourners followed on, holding candles that shone scant hope in a hopeless gloom. Alice, you had to behold the grief, nay anger, roaring out of those people who watched their dead son, daughter, parent lowered onto bodies already laid down. Yet they stood upright and proud, like vines on a trellis. A scattering of earth then on to the next until the grave was full to within a hand's span from the level ground. Our companions are dying in such numbers that we are now piling them up like flatbreads in a baker's shop! The sexton told me they dig every hole deep, but when they hit sandstone that is the bedrock of Avignon, they can go down no further. He orders six adults or twelve children to a plot and it will not be long before the whole graveyard is full. What else can they do?"

"Nothing more," answered Alice, "these are truly frightening times but consider your words. Why should *we* resent the pleasure you and I bring each other in the midst of such melancholy?" Marius said nothing, but thought, '*Under these circumstances, we should not be sinning as we surely are! I have to put an end to it lest Dominique finds me out.*'

The woman shook his arm to disturb his dreaming. "It is nearly light, Marius." "So it is! I have to go to the Magistrate. A priest gave me a message that there is a matter of the gravest import." He pulled on his cloak and boots, leaving her in the cabin to ponder the situation. '*I feel change in my heart, this man is in my thoughts day and night. Clément sent me on a mission for his own reasons, not caring this vulnerable damsel might fall, enamoured, with handsome, intelligent, lustful Marius. I doubt I can lie with him and usurp his innocence while an elderly pontiff sits in his palace, rubbing his hands with curious glee every time I tell him how the seduction goes.*'

As he made his way to the docks, towards him trundled one death cart after another, laden to breaking apart. Their pushers grunted and groaned with the effort required to keep them rolling. By contrast, those going in the same direction as him, free from their load, moved along without difficulty. He thought, '*they could be trains of ants, each following the next, blind, without reason, oblivious to the horror ahead.*' For a fleeting moment, he rose with majesty above the rooftops. His soul transcended those below who succumbed to his jurisdiction. The view from the heavens bode ill: at every house, square, street corner lay shrouded forms, still and serene, but unaware of their fate in the cold, cloying ground. His vision encompassed the town, a panoramic picture of the helpless crowd below. How he wished for a godly power – the strength of Hercules, the might of Goliath – that he could exorcise its vile contamination.

His descent to the road was as sudden as the rising. Snapped out of his imaginary elevation by a carter cussing him to move out of the way, he thought '*We will survive, mark my words Satan!*'

"Enter, Marius, do." The Magistrate took him by the arm and pulled him into the office, anxious to talk. "Sit, please," he invited, his mind elsewhere. The desk, usually neat and well arranged, was covered with parchment sheets strewn in a haphazard fashion.

"Lists, Marius! We cannot avoid them for they are essential – couldn't do without them. I yearn for better times - though, for the present, we must face reality. Do you know how many deaths have occurred in less than two months?"

"Many, Magistrate."

"*Many*, he says!" His eyes rolled upwards, "since the first, there have been six hundred and sixty-four and they multiply by the day!" Marius ground his teeth in disbelief. '*I have allowed my work to cloud how the numbers deluge and abominate like the river in flood.*' The Magistrate continued, "It is our duty to remain calm. To this end, I have this morning visited the Holy Father to inform him of the measures we will now enforce. The same will carry legal status and their contravention will be punished at the stocks or by incarceration."

Marius' jaw dropped as he listened to the justice speak with such imperious conviction, who resumed,

"I have mulled over my plans for no short time, praying they might not be necessary, but no longer! We must act! The names of the victims of the plague – and henceforth it must be known by this term – are to be posted outside the cathedral each day to quash rumour and let the people see the rate of mortality. You could think of this as the action of an old functionary, obsessed with lists – not so! Our people will seek out this or that missing man or woman – out of natural curiosity. By informing them thus, all doubt as to the gravity of our lot may be done with…and there are those who, even confronted by the processions of death carts, view the business as a little temporary inconvenience! I wager you have experienced the same? We will not triumph over adversity with our eyes closed. We have to *see* the Devil before we can slay him.

"The master of the household - or mistress, if appropriate – will report every passing within twelve hours and that house to be shut for fourteen days. Such closure, I understand, may be hard for those affected, but there will be no argument. Yes, I foresee resentment but it cannot be helped. The displeasure of a few is for the good of the many, and may the Lord have mercy. Surviving members of the family are forbidden to exit, as are any visitors to enter. Watchmen are to patrol the streets, some night sentinels, others for the day. These men can run errands on behalf of that abominable house and are permitted to accept gratuities when offered.

"A cross in red dye is to be painted for all to see on the door to the building. Should one be not locked, that man is liable to a public flogging. It is many a long year since I have been minded to deliver such punishment but, deliver it I will! Marius, you may raise any concerns you have in a while but…hey, young man! Is it not time for refreshment?" He went over to the cupboard, took out a bottle of his favourite green liqueur, and filled two glasses. Marius needed no encouragement to partake.

"Now, carters - or *buriers* as they will be called – are to carry a red pole, as both a symbol of their important function and, as I suspect, a cudgel to repel distraught folk seeking to lay hands on the bodies the buriers alone are permitted to handle at this point. To my thinking, the colour red signifies danger, blood that is shed in battle, if you like. May the brandishing of the herald's wand keep them at a safe and respectful distance.

"All bedding and clothing will be seized by the buriers and burned. Any attempt to trade this stuff will result in fines. The years have taught me humanity hides a dark side. I do not pretend to understand how the plight of one unfortunate is turned into profit, but such greed exists! Any man who sells his soul for reward merits contempt... what do you think, Marius?" But he continued, without waiting for a reply, so urgent were his pronouncements.

"Bodies must be bound by the family with whatever cloth is to hand. Burials are to take place only before dawn or after dark, periods when least folk congregate. One family member is to accompany the deceased to the grave: all this to promote the general safety of the people and prevent the plague from spreading."

"Magistrate, it would be a madman who disputed anything you have said."

"That is true. In addition, I order no cats or dogs to be let loose on the street – and the surface, in front of every house, must be kept well swept.

"Should any citizen suspect his neighbour to have yielded to the plague, he shall report him at once to my office. We will send *searchers* – healers wanting to assist – to examine that person and proclaim yea or nay.

"My decision for the present, and I anticipate it will be resented above all others, is to close the town gates save two. Guards with weapons are to ensure they remain closed. We are ignorant as to where the plague owes its origins so, the fewer men or women intruding, the better. Furthermore, I suspect there are the lily-livered among us who do not have the heart for a struggle alongside their fellow brothers and sisters. For those deserters, the gates will open but they will not be received back should they change their mind."

Avignon, previously outward-looking and adventurous, now portrayed introversion and fear.

"The Porte du Rocher gate to the Bénézet bridge and the market will allow traders to sell and servants or watchmen to purchase provisions. Any person continuing across the bridge to the west bank will be refused entry back into the town. They can dance and entertain us on Bénézet as long as they like but, their fate is sealed! I will not permit the risk of infection to be greater than it already is.

"The still open Porte Saint Charles gate to the docks is for people to report to my office. Do, you see, Marius, I have had these plans ready for no short time. Now is the moment to execute them. I invest you as my deputy and, as such, you may wield judicial authority to appoint or, as appropriate, conscribe our townsfolk to the duties I have explained. Do you have any questions?"

"Magistrate, I applaud your intentions. You have my unreserved loyalty."

Sitting alone in the tavern that evening, despair overwhelmed the young man with so heavy a burden. Marcel brought over a second pitcher of ale, removing the empty one from his table. They exchanged not a word. Raised voices from the other side of the room caught Marius' attention.

"I heard a decent man buried his entire family and, afterwards, went to a hostelry near to the cathedral to drink away his sorrow. Anybody can understand that, I vouch. Although it is a reputable inn, one of the customers had earlier noticed the death cart pass by. I know not his reason, it may have been influenced by the ale, but he turned on the poor man, cussing God and shouting the wretch should have jumped into the grave with his kin! All rebukes by the landlord were met with foul contempt for our Father, with curses and swearing."

"What happened to him?" another customer asked with baited breath. Assuming the question concerned the blasphemer, the reply came in a soft, frightened tone,

"The next day he was struck down by the plague. Got what he deserved, if you ask me! Let it be a lesson for any man who takes the name of the Lord in vain." The men became silent.

A piper sat in the street, his eyes covered with a strip of cloth, feigning blindness to beg for alms. The priest warned him it was forbidden but the player ignored him. Later in the day, he fell asleep. The door to the house behind him opened and a corpse was laid out for collection alongside him. When the buriers came they put them both on their cart, thinking them both dead. At the cathedral, earth was tossed into the grave and only then did the piper awake to escape certain peril.

{Clément's private rooms}

"We thank you for your effort, as for that of the soldiers you have assembled, for soldiers they be to fight the good fight," Clément addressed the Magistrate. "Now, take on volunteers, enlist the uncertain, turn away the unworthy! Do whatever you and the boy, Marius, deem necessary to defeat the illness. Also, we concur with your suggestion concerning an extraordinary church service I will conduct, in person. You may leave us." Clément stood behind the desk, his upright posture bringing dignity to the audience. The Magistrate bowed and retired.

"Guard!" The Pontiff called.

"Sire?"

"See I am not disturbed until lauds."

"As you request."

Clément paced to and fro in his study, mumbling questions under his breath without finding answers. In spite of the fateful happenings in the town, his hatred for Edmond Nerval was never far from his mind. He sought retribution still for the odious attack on him when they were boys and bided his moment to expose Marius' infidelity. More immediate was the sermon he was obliged to prepare. Since the outbreak of the plague, the Church, in his personification, had failed to pronounce either consolation or hope. But that time had come. Fumbling in the pocket of his robe he found the key to the wall cupboard. The bottle of laudanum was removed and placed on the desk with a reverence he usually paid to arranging celebratory objects on the altar for mass. The prospect of preaching a sermon filled him with dread, and the *nectar*, as he referred to it privately, calmed his nerves and focused his spirit. After a glass he opened his leather-bound Paris bible to Jeremiah 5. With a steady, measured tone he read out the verse,

'*Shall I not visit for these things? saith the Lord: shall not my soul be avenged on such a nation as this?*'

More laudanum and his mood lightened. '*Now the theme of my sermon is clear,*' he thought, '*my flock are to be chastised for their wickedness.*'

CHAPTER EIGHTEEN

AVIGNON
early May, 1348 AD

The Grand Audience of the palace was full to capacity. Those who had arrived too late to claim a seat stood in the side aisles. The people awaited the entrance of the Holy Father, Clément Vl, with an acute sense expectancy. Few would have risen in time for the early morning prime service, but, being the choice of Clément for his much-anticipated sermon, they attended with due grace.

Marius, with Dominique and Fabien, from their bench to the rear of the chamber, recognised neighbours and friends. Present were buriers, night and day watchers, sextons and priests from churches now redundant, only the cathedral and Audience remaining for worshippers. The Magistrate and the wool merchants sat two rows in front; Bruno the carver; his friend, Luc, and wife, Marianne; the landlord Marcel, accompanied by the rotund lady; Rostand the beggar. Alice looked towards Marius, the coy expression giving no suggestion of the secret only he and the Pontiff knew. In the shadows of the arches, the mysterious observer, ordered by Clément, stared straight at Marius. So, the congregation consisted of men and women from all social classes and persuasions: individuals, united in a common fear and despair.

After a very short time from the first deaths, the mortality rate, day by day, reached the hundreds. The Magistrate had ceased posting names and addresses at the cathedral lychgate - space on the board did not permit. Instead, he wrote only the date and number: '12 May, 1348 AD: 164'. The cemetery, able to cope with burials in normal times, soon had no ground left, even after the sextons had resorted to piling bodies into the same grave. The incessant procession of the dead carried for interment would have defied the comprehension of any town, village or hamlet afflicted by such a catastrophic epidemic. By order of the Magistrate, the sextons and their diggers excavated deep pits outside the churchyard. In a hurry, they bundled up the people who died in the night, if the family had not the means for winding sheets. Buriers threw them into the hole. They shovelled earth on top, repeating this, layer by layer of loved ones. The priest, and all associated persons, hated this procedure but, they had no choice: the plague did not afford them any luxury. One sexton denied a report saying the corpses, so sparsely covered with soil that ravenous dogs dragged them forth and devoured them throughout the town. '*Not so,* protested the sacristan, '*the Justice has forbidden hounds in the streets so where are they? We are all law-abiding and God-fearing. But, happy posterity, who will not experience such abysmal woe and will look upon our testimony as a fable!'* They removed the debris, making a mound running along the north edge of the trough. Among the myriad superstitions and falsehoods surrounding the blight, they feared the infection was spread on the breeze. Disagreeable vapours and fumes from the decaying remains carried minute particles, fanned by the wind, that penetrated the vital organs of the living, or so they thought. Blood surged through the veins in turmoil. It went about the agitated spirit was borne in the air by insects and invisible creatures, entering the man or woman and generating poisonous eggs. As they cried out for cures, so they searched for causes. The devil they neither saw nor heard dumfounded the highest intellect to the dullest fool. '*Make a bank that will be a windbreak along the ditch*' – that's what the priest instructed me!' a digger related to his mate, '*Stuff and nonsense if you ask me!*'

For many of the gathering, this was their first experience of religious pomp and ceremony. Understandable apprehension became in-

tensified by the rising incantations of the choir. Pungent sandalwood
and camphor diffused from the swinging censer and a bell, tolling slow
and menacing, wrote an awe-inspiring drama. The players performed,
on the Audience's stage, a piece of theatre with a prologue but no dis-
cernible end game. Still no sign of the principal actor, Clément. But
why were *they* present? Had they come to worship? Did they expect
a marvel? None of these, only the need for solace and, should it be
provided by a cleric they knew not, nor believed in, then it was of
small matter. Hope sprang regardless of its origin. The scriptures are
unfamiliar yet they begged human nature would survive adversity.

All of a sudden, the cantors fell quiet. All shuffling and murmuring
ceased as a door to the right of the altar creaked open. The church-
goers rose at a signal given by the assistant prelate. They watched for
the Pontiff to come into view. Their wait was over as the tall, gaunt
figure of Clément moved, ghost-like, to the centre of the raised step on
which stood the stone altar. Facing his flock, he lifted his right hand to
make a sign of the cross in the air. With the same movement, his head
jerked backwards in supplication, staring to the heavens. His countenance betrayed no emotion, his features stern, lips drawn tight. With
a bow, he turned and knelt. Throughout the ritual, silence dominated
the hall - no soul dared make a sound such was his authority and their
acceptance of his importance. He wore a shining white under-robe
that touched the ground. A shawl of red velour edged with gold braid
covered his shoulders. The mark of his office, a white skull-cap, and
a heavy golden crucifix hanging round his neck completed the papal
regalia.

He made his way, with perfect appreciation of the moment, to the
pulpit, an imposing structure of finely carved mahogany. Four treads
lead up to the lectern, from where he overlooked the assembled mass.
Without noise, without movement, there was nothing to mar the Pontiff's address. The wretched citizens of Avignon craved his words
would engage their resolve and give encouragement to combat the
evil surrounding them.

Clément's shaky, clenched hands and the beads of perspiration on his forehead went unnoticed. How he hated this requirement of papacy, but it could not be avoided. Everyone present felt transfixed by the well-practiced, steely gaze scanning the assemblage from left to right, farthest to nearest. Taking a deep breath, he began,

"*Kyrie, ignis divine, eleison!* Lord, divine fire, have mercy! People, pray the Almighty spares you eternal purgatory for your sins! Kneel before the Lord!" As one, they knelt, in fear of the threat they, simple folk, believed. "The pestilence is sent from above to punish your affluence and complacency and, it is not unforeseen. The Scriptures give you fair warning but, you have ignored their wisdom. Pray! In Revelations, the apocalypse is promised to mankind and that time has come. Let anyone who has an ear listen to what the Spirit is saying." He paused, a perfect quiet pervading the charged atmosphere, enabling him to increase the tension. "You must be brave, as I am." An undercurrent of whispering, then gasps, moved along the benches: ordinary beings, brows frowning, eyes open wide. "Coming before you this morning, I risk infection since this is not a safe place. But, let it be known, I do it for *you! Deus tibi sit propitious eris.* May God forgive you and protect Clément, your leader on earth. I have faith I will prevail, with your earnest supplication." On hearing these words, Marius was mesmerised, unable to believe the head of his Church had expressed such desire for self-preservation, with no apparent thought for his flock. He looked around and saw contempt, disbelief, and confusion. They came together for fleeting respite from the detestation, with no high hopes but, Clement chided them, sneering at the daily horror they faced.

From his place close to the altar, the Magistrate turned and met Marius' glance. The two men confronted death in every street. They witnessed unfathomable sorrow and, indeed, felt the same despair as the families whose cadavers they touched and lowered into the pitiless ground. The teams of volunteers demonstrated abundant strength of character. '*What is this game Clément plays?*' Marius thought, bewildered, '*and what message does he give?*'

Soft, muffled tones could be heard from all corners of the Audience as the Pope continued,

"*Et peccaverint tibi.* You have all sinned, James said and, if any of you lacks wisdom, let him ask God who gives generously to all without reproach, and it will be given! So, if you are invited as a guest to a wedding, go humbly and take the lowest seat. Wait to be honoured and later promoted to a higher one. Make no foolish assumption of your importance. Do not merit disgrace, humiliation or embarrassment. Be of modest nature, to please God. *Laudate Dominum!* Praise the Lord!" His hands signed a cross and he waited for complete hush before resuming,

"*I am the vine, you are the branches. If you remain in me, and I in you, you will bear much fruit.* Sow your seed on decent ground and hear the word of the Lord! The Good Samaritan bandaged a wounded man: you too must love your neighbour as your God. Is anyone among you in trouble? Let him pray. Is anyone among you sick? Let him call the elders of the church to pray over him, so said James. *Gloria Patri,* Glory to the Father." Clement rocked to and fro, closed eyes adding force to his words. But the throng, simmering, was perplexed. Try as they might, the public could make no sense of the Pontiff's homily. Did he scold them? Were they not brave, in coming together in mass, rubbing shoulders with a neighbour they knew not? "And so I say…" But his sermon was no longer heard. The citizens turned to each other with anguished, distraught expressions. Instead of answers, however few, they had been served questions. The Magistrate noted Clément's agitation, hands trembling, inhaling the clamour he had provoked, with not a single reference to the curse. The justice, a self-taught man, who had gained his education via the duties he performed and the humanity he encountered. He had minimal knowledge of the Bible, its lessons understood through anecdotes and attendance at church services. With what little appreciation of the Scriptures he possessed, he heard Clément's words as irrational with morsels of the Gospels plucked at random, following no logical thread. His mind was awhirl,

'*This holy man is not worthy of our respect. He is, surely, under the influence of the grape. Our revered leader of the Faith a devotee of Bacchus! He is a souse who has partaken either of strong liqueur, or a forager eating poisonous fungi like the mad wood dwellers in the north!*'

"*Cave, cave, Deus videt!* Beware, beware, God sees, then *Animabus propitietur Deus noster* May God save our souls." With these valedictions, Pope Clément stepped down from the pulpit, bowing first to the altar then to the congregation. He disappeared from view as mysteriously as he had arrived and everyone filed out of the Audience with a heavy heart. The Magistrate caught up with Marius and Dominique,

"Ah, Marius – and madam – I saw your face and, though I be no mind reader, it was not hard to guess your thoughts."

"Indeed," Marius agreed, "and has he helped or hindered our work? Our despair can only deepen through his ill-chosen rambling!"

"I'm afraid you are correct. But I followed Clément's rise to supremacy with great interest. I think of him as a friend – although the Holy One is not permitted 'friends', not like you and me understand it, if you follow. I would describe him as an intelligent, well-read man, as you might expect, and who are we to comment?"

Alone in his study, the Pope unlocked the cupboard for the bottle of laudanum. After two large glasses of the potion, he leaned back in his chair and breathed hard, grateful the morning's ordeal was over. '*Most satisfactory! I have discharged my responsibility as the Magistrate thought I should and, I will sleep well tonight.*' Both his private life and history had been so well protected that few in the town or country at large had the slightest suspicion he was driven by vengeance and liqueur.

Marius resumed,

"Who are we to comment?" He repeated the question. "I hold saints or sinners have a right to be heard!"

"Mmm…deep matters…but, come with me, Marius, we must visit the cathedral. Since I closed the other churches in town there are now five priests conducting the daily rituals. How they manage is nothing short of a miracle." The young man took leave of his wife, saying,

"I do not know –"

"– when you will be home," she interrupted, completing his sentence, "and why should it not surprise me? Do not worry about me and Fabien, we will cope without you." The bitterness in her tone was unmistakable. As the Audience disgorged its miserable, humble petitioners into the Place du Palais square they exchanged few words, eager to return to the relative safety of their dwellings. The shadowy twilight matched their darkness as they dispersed alone, in pairs, children in front but, to a man, united through suspicion of the fearsome unknown. Unaware of *when* the Grim Reaper would cross their threshold, they were certain he *would*, at his chosen convenience, call on them: an uninvited, unwelcome guest.

"Let us sit a moment," the Magistrate requested as they reached the lychgate. The emotion stirred by the deception of Clément's sermon had wearied him. He could not understand the missed, opportune occasion for the Pontiff to have encouraged, enthused, and reassured his faithful. But, back to reality, and the two men gasped since there were no morts laid out on the seats to be taken for last rites, as had been the case every previous day.

"I do not believe my eyes! This cannot be, or the buriers have not yet begun –"

"Marius! They work through the night. We will soon have to give up our seats here to those more in need than you or I!" He regained his breath, "Something has changed in Clément. He is not the same man. Before coming to Avignon, he was Bishop of Arras and through that position I understand he was appointed a royal councillor of King Philip V1. Well, the king does not fill his court with bad men, least not generally…"

"That is so."

"When he became Archbishop of Rouen, they called him a Peer of France! Much happened – I'm not sure of my history – but he was given the cardinal's red hat and entered the Curia in Avignon. I do remember he preached the requiem for the deceased Cardinal Orsini, a fine man…so, Clément is well-accustomed to important ceremonies, like today. Afterwards, his luck benefitted him since when old Pope Bénédict died, the Conclave consisted fourteen out of nineteen who were French. May 7th, 1342…a Tuesday if I'm not mistaken…they reached agreement and Clément was elected the next Holy Father."

"Anybody deserves good fortune."

"I do not dispute it. But I know nothing of his life as a child, only he was born in Limoges. Does your own family not hail from that place?"

"It does."

"If a man displays a certain nature, it is, in my opinion, often due to events occurring many years before, as a boy. I wonder, did your father know Clément – or Pierre Roger as he was then – from childhood? Coincidences do happen…"

"I have no answer, Magistrate. My father said little, until his tongue came loose with drink. But, the stories he told were as rambling as Clément's sermon this morning. It is possible they met but, I can't say."

"I see," the old man muttered, mulling over what might have befallen the pope, now the dispassionate, arrogant, and, at times, incoherent figure in the pulpit that day.

Dominique felt a gentle tap on her shoulder. Alice had picked her out of the crowd.

"Good morning, Dominique." Surprised to see her neighbour, she smiled, but without genuine sincerity,

"Oh…hello, Alice."

"So, you too were in the Audience?"

"Yes, I was, but what is that to do with you?" Her brusque voice expressed annoyance. She felt in no frame of mind to banter, especially with Alice.

"I meant no offence –"

"None taken. Please forgive my rudeness, our life is not easy, although we are all affected the same."

"We are, and you must worry about Marius. He is closer to the horror than most – his efforts with the buriers, sextons, watchmen…but, he is much respected for it."

"I am sure he is but, I fear each day, he will bring the scourge into our house."

"That is quite understandable. I wager it has put a strain on your... er... relationship as man and wife?" Dominique stared hard into the woman's eyes, challenging her to reveal how she knew her marriage was in upheaval. '*Alice has a nerve to ask such intimate questions! She should mind her own business.*'

"There are surely days when you do not see him, such is his devotion to serving our town. His deeds are legend and you should be proud of the man," Alice said in a provocative tone.

"I am, of course. Now, will it be all? Fabien is hungry and –"

"Why, sot that I am! Come, I will walk home with you." She linked arms with Dominique who had a shiver of revulsion pass through her body. From their first meeting, she had mistrusted Alice, though she knew not why. '*She has appeared kind, on the surface, helping me at the market, the occasional basket of flowers or produce but...*'

Alice remained indoors for the rest of the day. A wind howled and raged through the squares and streets and, even without the plague, everyone would be sheltering in their homes. Those foolhardy souls at large who braved the elements, leaned into the wind's force to keep upright, their clothing held tight, heads lowered. Residents of Avignon took little real notice of a gale blowing: the Mistral was embedded in the folklore of the place. But, today, it felt as if the Lord himself spoke to them, given its ferocity. In such a state of fear, they read a message in everything around them. The early blooming of a lilac tree meant a time of beauty and relief; a rainstorm signified God's desire to wash away evil; the icy blast stood for the power of the saints, their effigies carved in stone atop the Pope's Palace. Like the rest, Alice had her shutters kept closed to the outside world. After a few hours, the ominous passage of the tumbrils seemed to cease, if the respite was temporary. The basic need for human contact suppressed even the probability of contracting the disease and, in this respect she was the same as her neighbours. She brushed her hair to a sheen, rinsed her face in scented water and donned a clean tunic to leave her house,

soon, for the inn. She doubted Marius would be there, having witnessed the urgent manner in which the Magistrate had escorted him
away from his wife and child. Though her body yearned for him, she
saw the arduous position in which he found himself.

The tavern was alive with customers, present, like Alice, to share a
common plight, seeking the warmth only proximity to another human
being could bring. As she entered, nobody paid her the slightest heed.
Animated, earnest conversations absorbed them. A man rose from his
table to go to the latrine in the back yard and Alice seized the opportunity to occupy his place. When he returned there was no argument
– he knew Alice and her feisty reputation. She made a gesture to Marcel, who deposited a bottle of her favourite eau de vie on the table. All
the men had, from time to time, admired her feminine charms as she
waited on at table. She no longer performed this role since all feasting
in public was proscribed. They exchanged no words. The glass filled
to the brim, she sipped the strong beverage. Her gaze went round the
crowded room: the men were worse for wear. The raucous laughter
and gross language she accepted as normal, but it struck her as incongruous since they were close to death. '*Joking, riddles, banter! Strange
how men change with drink inside them!' she mused.* A raised voice then
caught her attention: a swarthy, whiskered roughneck, well known
around the town, held court with a bevy of his undesirable friends.
She heard the name *Marius*.

"Yon Marius guy found me today. Said I was able-bodied and had to
join him to push the death carts! Well, I soon put him in his place –"

"Bet you did too!" One crony blurted in a fawning tone.

"I told him it wasn't the law so I didn't *have* to do anything, I informed him only the law *forces* you."

"Well said!" three of the men called in unison. "What did Marius
say to that?" asked one of the others.

"He grabbed me by the neck. I thought he was going to stran-
gle me on the spot, honest! And he ranted on at me something awful…screaming I was a coward, that I should do the *right thing* and
help…but, I've a wife and four kiddies to fend for. Well, I broke free

from his grasp and fair ran for my life! His parting words were 'It will soon *be* the law and you will have no choice.' Fancy, him calling me a coward –"

Alice listened to the hostile tirade, in silence, mortified by the pitiless onslaught against her lover, absent and unable to defend his actions. The oafish fellow drank, banged his tankard down, and resumed with yet greater venom,

"There are folk a-plenty to cart off stiffs and, anyway, I like keeping myself to myself..."

She could not contain her anger. Leaping to her feet, she flew at the man, overturning goblets and pushing his mates aside. With all her strength she punched him full in the face. So unexpected was the assault he recoiled barely a step. Seconds later, she sunk her nails into his flesh. Blood streamed down his cheek where she had gouged furrows – his loyal friends retreated out of harm's way leaving their leader facing the redoubtable woman. Like a dog preparing to attack a bear in a pit, she approached him. The unreal situation numbed the lout as she pulled her arm back then hit him in the eye. In pain and shock, he fell to his knees before her.

"Who's a coward? Speak, pray!" she bellowed, leaning over her defeated adversary, "Speak!" He said nothing. Only one of the group raised his voice, a hawker who roamed the streets, in a position to know everyone and their business,

"Let him be, woman, he's taken enough. What you say is true, we must each play our part, yet..." and he hesitated for a moment. "You seem to take offence at Marius' treatment. We might assume you are devilishly familiar with the fellow..."

The door opening rent the tense scene. Marius and Dominique entered.

CHAPTER NINETEEN

AVIGNON
late May/June 1348 AD

Marius and Dominique went to the counter to order their drinks, unaware of the drama that had just unfolded. The landlord, Marcel, greeted the two customers as if there was nothing out of the usual. The hawker lifted the bloodied brawler to his feet and, although Alice did not answer his question concerning her involvement, or not, with Marius, the matter was taken no further.

"Good evening, Marius and Dominique. How goes your work combatting the infernal outbreak?" He ensured he spoke loud enough for the entire inn to hear, knowing the roughneck would not have the courage to continue to insult Marius to his face. "Sit, Alice, please. Mine is ever a friendly house and, best we keep it so."

Puzzled, Marius wondered about possible events prior to his arrival.

"Alice," he began, "do I take it *you* inflicted damage to that ruffian's face? I know him...the other day I instructed him to help us with the carts but –"

"He told us that," she interrupted.

"So why did you fight with him?"

"He insulted my parents. I cannot allow such dishonour." She lied.

"You've done a good job on him, I'll say!"

"Thank you and, though a mere woman, I can hold my own. Anyway, he deserved it. Will you both take a drink? It would be churlish of me to sup this fine eau de vie on my own."

Marius, Dominique and Alice, sitting together, formed an ironic triangle of deception. The hawker passed their table and paused to stare at Alice, who dreaded what he might say. She needed not to have worried. He leaned over her and whispered, "Alice, you really should go about your business - let me describe it thus - with greater circumspection. An affair with Marius is one thing but, does not the Holy Father take a special interest in you?"

As he was leaving, he stopped in the doorway. Looking back over his shoulder, he smiled at her. *'He's right! She thought. 'My life is complicated. I often wish I'd not set eyes on either of them!'*

Marius was with his wife in the inn that night out of his sense of guilt. He saw her confined to the house through the day and knew she merited greater consideration. Organising the teams of men around the town consumed his time and energy. Dominique did not realise the significance of her husband and Alice, now deep in conversation. The bottle of liqueur emptied, Alice rose, and bade her neighbours goodnight.

"So, what did Alice have to say to you? I don't think she is wise about *any* subject...mind you, what do *I* know?"

"I was explaining to her how we seem to be losing the fight against the plague, so high is the death rate. She's well informed concerning town affairs."

Dominique grimaced, uncomfortable with her husband's assessment of the woman. Before Alice left, there were a number of fingers pointing in their direction from the other customers, voices tut-tutting – or, maybe she imagined it. The drink was strong and she was unaccustomed to its effect.

"Let's go home, Marius."

"Of course. Poor folk, are they not? Well might they consume ale - for all they know it could be their last."

The couple were about to retire when there came a knocking at the door. It was Luc, Marius' friend from the stonemason's yard.

"Why, Luc! What brings you here at this late hour?"

"I am sorry to disturb you, but... may I come in? I will not detain you long."

"Yes, do." With a respectful nod to Dominique, he strode into the room and began,

"I saw a light through your shutters... I have not seen you since the funeral of our son, Fabien, some months ago. Since the yard ceased its business through the pestilence... well... Marianne and I are recluses. We only set foot outside the house to purchase essential supplies. One can express grief in different ways and, we conducted ours in private. We shut ourselves away from the world."

"I understand, Luc," Marius said to his friend in a soft tone.

"When Fabien passed, we knew not the cause but, it is now clear, it was the pestilence."

"Most likely, I'm afraid to say."

"We talked at length and decided our mourning needed to end, or, at least, be put to a purpose. Otherwise, his death will have been in vain. In short, Marius, I am offering my services to you. The plague stole our baby son and, whereas fighting it will not bring him back, it will honour his name. What say you?" Marius considered the offer, moved by such generosity.

"The men I now supervise are, without doubt, fine, worthy, brave souls and we owe them a debt of gratitude. However, it requires fellows like yourself, intelligent minds, to translate brawn into benefit, if you follow. I accept your proposal. The Magistrate has summoned me to meet him, tomorrow, at his office. Be on the quayside at first light to join us. I'm sure he has matters of great importance to discuss."

"I will see you there Marius. May I wish you both a peaceful night."

Dominique listened to the exchange between the two men in silence. She knew when to hold her tongue. Marius slid the bolt in the door, poured a beaker of ale, and sat at the table.

"Luc's brave, is he not, Marius?"

"*Brave?* Do you believe any of us is courageous? Nothing of the sort! We recognise the evil contagion that smites our families and friends and, we adopt but one choice: to fight! That doesn't mean we are *brave*. I've not said it in so many words but, every day I leave the house, I am terrified I may return infected to pass it on to you and Fabien. However, I have no option. To surrender would, I swear, call for resolve I don't possess. Do you understand?"

"You've explained it well, my love, and you deserve an apology from me. I have not been the best wife of late. Whatever you choose, I promise to stand by you. Now, let's off to bed."

The next morning, Marius left the town gate and entered the quay. At intervals along the dockside, fires in braziers burned bright, lit by an old bargee who, many years before, had his skull shattered in a brawl: he remembered his name, nothing more.

Shadows cast by the flames danced macabre pirouettes, closing in, then retreating like a warrior thrusting and parrying. '*How they taunt and mock! Theirs is the power and each gloomy outline is a spirit that wields jurisdiction over who will live or die. Do your worst! Damn you! We will not succumb!*' Stepping through the floating phantoms, he showed defiance and determination. Faint yellow candlelight indicated the Magistrate awaited in his office. Marius knocked on the door.

"Come."

The desk groaned under piles of parchment - the only other items an inkpot and quill stand. The men were together only a few days earlier but, as Marius stared hard at the justice, he was aghast how the man appeared a score of years older. With a ragged grey beard that masked lips pinched tight, one might have said he was dwelling on difficult matters. Through the whiskers, his skin had a jaundiced hue. His gaze rose towards Marius, squinting, his eyesight fading, not only through the natural ageing process but, also, repeated reading and writing lists that grew longer by the day. The script needed to be more and more small and spidery to fit numbers and dates on each sheet.

"Ah, Marius, sit down, pray." He served ale into two cups from a barrel in the corner. "Drink, it's about the only friend I still have! Being the magistrate is not easy in these times. I make this decision, overrule that objection, say 'nay' when they want 'yea'...I will upset a wife, risk the wrath of a husband...no, it's not easy. But, a toast! To your good health, Marius!" Spluttering out a mouthful of ale, he then burst into laughter realising the irony of his words. "Did I say *good health*?"

"You did, sire."

"Old fool that I am! They should throw me into the dungeon for raising false hope! Health! That is the last thing I can offer...but, sickness, I guarantee! In every household and on every street corner, there is illness. It's sending them mad, don't you know? I've heard them singing for salvation, seen them dancing weird jigs on the bridge as if they're celebrating a wedding or, I know not what. Their faces distorted, eyes looking to the heavens for deliverance! 'Sur le pont, d'Avignon' – that's their anthem, their own, personal ballad. 'On the bridge of Avignon' – whatever are they thinking, Marius?"

"I have no answer but, we both see the same: death by infection, by starvation and, yes, by madness. The other day, we carried a wealthy glove-maker out of his home. The wife dropped to her knees before me, held out her purse, and cried,

"Take it! Gold coin, take it! You will know how to –"

"Woman! Put away your money," I shouted back, "All the treasure of Solomon will not make him live." She fell to the ground, rolling, screaming in tongues I did not understand. Which way should they turn? To the left or right? Either way, leads to death!"

The Magistrate listened, head down, tugging at his beard with distraction.

"Let it be known, we do our best to comfort bereaved relatives."

"Your work is lauded by all, Marius. The Holy Father himself instructed me to pass on his appreciation 'in the Lord', as he put it."

"I am, verily, humbled, and we are blessed with a fine man for our spiritual leader." He reflected a moment. "Do you know what is harder than fetching the dead out of a building? A soul fallen in an alley or side street too narrow to take the cart. By the time we find them, the death rattle has long since silenced and the carcass is stiff through *rigor mortis*...it is more skeleton than body. Some are already without a tunic or good leather belt. Everything has a price if you can believe it...?"

"I will talk of that soon, pray continue."

"We drag them out of the alley to the cart and, I wager it's true, I shed tears when no-one claims the cadaver...abandoned...unwanted...yet, they must surely belong somewhere? Is there a mother or father? Any family whosoever! But nobody recognises them as a member of the human race: mere carrion if we don't get to them before hungry vultures do! Yes, they sit in the street to die, alone."

The Magistrate nodded, sadness etched on his face. There came a knock.

"That will be Luc," said Marius, "I will explain shortly." Luc entered the office, shy and uncertain.

"Join us, Luc, sit here," bade the justice as he poured a cup of ale and placed it on the desk in front of the new arrival.

"Magistrate, my friend wishes to be one of our company. I vouch for his character and, I can well use his assistance to organise our efforts."

"So be it. Welcome, Luc. Yes...I recall you lost your baby son a while back...most regrettable."

"It is so, though I have reached the point where my grieving must cease. I will help others now, for selfishness was gnawing at my heart. Enough!"

"Well said, Luc," said Marius, slapping the boy on his back.

"Gentlemen, let us move to the business. Time is a gift we do not possess." He replenished their cups and prepared to deliver his instructions.

"To date, the town has suffered two thousand deaths...and who knows when it will end?"

Both men froze, eyes wide open in disbelief.

"In the ground between the cemetery and the woods, though you are aware, we have dug and filled three pits and, there is land available for more. The problem is in the numbers...I mean there are too many bodies awaiting burial while we dig a new trough. This being the case, the Holy Father issued a bull to enable our duties. Such a method of communication happens only on the most formal, solemn occasions. See, this is the document." He unrolled a sheet of fine vellum. "It came to me sealed with lead, as it should be, and I will make copies to be displayed around the town. It begins *Episcopus Servus Servorum Dei* – Bishop Servant of the Servants of God – then it goes on…in short, it decrees we may cast cadavers into the river, weighted, without proper consecration by the priest. This permission has not been given in our time. I will remind you, all the measures I explain to you today are *essential* if we are to prevail. Many will prove unpopular, but the plague is not our friend! Some, for their own reasons, may well choose to buck the regulations…be it on their heads! The Count of Provence agrees that you, as my appointed deputies, may wield the authority of the law. You may, therefore, arrest anyone who hinders our work or puts at risk the safety of their companions. There is a stone building to the north side of town and, few have any idea of its purpose. It is a gaol, though I have not needed to incarcerate any felon for…well, two score and ten years. Yesterday, I sent a boy with the key. It was his task to oil the hinges and the bolts on the iron doors and ensure each of the six cells has a straw mattress and a pail. Word will get around and I anticipate there will not be too many to lock up. Any questions thus far?"

Marius and Luc nodded, impressed by the Magistrate's planning.

"Corpses are to be taken, should the common grave of mankind be unready, to the bridge. There, they will be cast into the deep, central current and washed away downstream. It is a sorry state when we dispose of our dead in such a manner but, the evil facing us does not wish for dialogue - on the contrary! Our duty is to protect the living, as we can. We must prevent members of the public within sight of the pits. There are signs our society is falling apart at times and, we must avoid undue panic. The diggers now push the bodies into the pits using a pole. If a cadaver lies waiting for a day or longer – such is the number – a terrible gangrene eats the vital organs. I quite understand their reluctance to lay hands on them."

"Ay, Magistrate! The buriers wear brown hoods that cover their heads and gloves – they do whatever they think will defend them. Madness is never far from erupting, you are right. Folk leave it to the buriers at the lychgate to handle their dead and then, the priests show remarkable courage in performing their obligations, despite the ever-present risk of infection. Some fled the town and, who can blame them? They relate the saddest of accounts to me...a mother killed her own three children! Yes, blotches on the skin and coughing and, she wanted to save them the horror ahead, though it might not be the plague. She, herself, died of grief the next day." A noise outside distracted the justice. "One moment, gentlemen, there are buriers outside." Picking up a bundle of parchments, each covered with lists done in fine copperplate handwriting, he left the office to return a few minutes later.

"There are fifty-six dead during the night and, the number at the cathedral will be threefold. Heinous! But, Marius, you were saying –"

"True insanity reigns when a man throws himself, naked, into the pit, screaming 'My family is no more! I have no reason to live!' Fear and delirium! Some jump off tall buildings rather than face the plague!"

Luc listened without uttering a word '*Give me sufficient strength to confront such scenes? Marius is so confident and I will never be his equal,*' he thought.

"Worry not, Luc," Marius said, realising his friend's concern. "You will work alongside me to start."

"The taverns," the Magistrate continued, "are places where men – and women, come to that – congregate to drink but, also, to be together and share the calamity. We realise it is important they maintain human contact – without it, the Devil invades hearts and his wickedness triumphs. There must be no disorderly tippling else, the landlord will remove him and report his name to me: the stocks reward drunkenness! Furthermore, I forbid feasting and dining: germs spread with ease when men eat, chew or swallow."

"I cannot question this. It makes good sense," Marius confirmed.

"The streets are proving a breeding ground for the scourge, or so the healers tell me. Therefore, there are to be no children's games or the singing of ballads. Pet animals should not roam free but, if such are found, we will destroy them – this applies to cats, dogs, swine, tame pigeons or conies. Poisonous concoctions, in bowls put out, will tempt then see off rats and mice."

"I will see my men enforce these measures."

"Good! Again, I would remind any wrongdoers the dungeon awaits! What next…ah, yes, most burials take place at night. Torches around the edge must burn brightly. Healers, again, say flame weakens the ague."

"It will be done."

"And now…coins –"

"Coins, Magistrate?"

"Ay. For the meagre trading that still goes on, they exchange money, do they not? Passed from one person to another, and, so is the plague through dirty money. While we cannot prevent folk spending or buying whatsoever they choose, we can, at least, make them aware of the danger. Did you know, sous dipped in vinegar are cleaned bright, as if by magic?"

"I see what you are saying. It is simple but effective."

"For sure! And think on this, for it is my own idea: if the exact amount is given, there is no need for change. That means less handling and, you see, less chance of the disease spreading." Leaning back in his chair, he anticipated Marius' opinion.

"Ingenious! It reminds me of a story I heard the other day that suggests maybe our poor residents are one step ahead of you."

"How is that?"

"Somebody dropped a purse but no-one dared touch it until, one man - must have been a war veteran - laid down a trail of gunpowder then, from a distance, lit it. He snared the purse, well-heated, with a fishhook and line. Considering the money safe, he walked away, richer. Folk heard him mutter 'The plague does not bring misery to everyone.' Two days later, he died."

"A salutary tale but, let me return to the buriers. Removing deceased loved ones from their homes amid wailing is a thankless task. Our men deserve all praise, for they risk their lives day by day. However, it is sad to say there are some, like the man and the purse, who seek to turn disaster into gain. Once the cart is loaded, there is little sign of who is rich or poor – the plague does not discriminate. But, while they wrap carcasses in rags and some are even naked, they wind others in fine linen. It reaches me, on good authority, that, rather than burn all the cloths - as is the law - some have found a market for pure white damask."

Marius and Luc gulped, as one, unable to comprehend such despicable behaviour.

"This trade must cease!" The Magistrate pronounced.

Both men nodded their assent.

"Finally and, for the present, all must know begging on the streets is strictly illegal. Those guilty will be chained in the prison to consider their actions. We may not be aware of who they are or from where they hail…most likely not locals…but, they play on the good nature of our own people for long enough. Now is the time to drive them out or lock them away, should they choose to not depart."

"As the law demands, sire." Marius and Luc emptied their cups and left the office without further ado. The weak, rising sun cast shadows in front of them as they walked along the quayside. Grey outlines pointed to a future without prediction of either perdition or salvation.

CHAPTER TWENTY

AVIGNON
June/July, 1348 AD

Marius and Luc shared a pitcher of ale, in silence. The former looked at the patrons of the inn, all of whom he knew, all with a tale of misery to relate. Thinking back, only two months earlier, so many people of Avignon had attended the service in the Audience. The heady atmosphere in that place had enveloped them. With incense wafting, religious chanting from priests in robes, surroundings glorious and imposing, they were in awe of the Church with its orchestrated ceremony. Nonetheless, they remained hopeful, despite the number of deaths rising. Hope, optimism, dreams – a belief they would survive the horror of the plague – were present and, often, in households already struck down. To succumb was cowardice, and no-one wanted to be branded as fainthearted. But, on what was their faith founded? Inner strength is susceptible to human weakness. They needed an ally stronger than innate nature and, that was where the Church should have been a shining example. Instructions to pray, recitation of verses unknown, cajoling by loading the burden of guilt onto the poor congregation: this did not represent hope – on the contrary, the people were desperate and clutched at any ray of light, no matter how dim and distant. All they knew was death. Their cries for help went unheeded and the priests, besieged and inadequate, died. *What use the*

Church? – was a widespread and justifiable question. *Would Clément be next? If he is taken, what chance is there for us mere mortals?*

In the evening, the tavern would be full of drinkers, relaxing after a day's work, exchanging news, opinions, banter and jokes. Tonight, voices were muffled, heads bowed, handshakes avoided.

"I saw the Magistrate today. The death toll stunned me…" Marius began.

"How is that?"

"There are two thousand dead and, that out of the town's population of around six. In case your mathematical ability is low, Luc, that means one third…two thousand souls…can you believe that? If it doesn't come to a halt, we will be wiped from the face of the earth!"

"Marius, we devote our every waking hour to burying them. That means we are too close to the figures to appreciate them."

"Yes, I suppose you're right. But, what about the measures we've been supervising? Do they count for nothing? The Magistrate sat with me last night, in the place where you now sit. He admitted while the number of deaths is true, no-one is sure of the exact total of folk who reside here and call themselves *Avignonese*. The walls you and I worked on, until a few months ago, today enclose *bourgs* that, before, did not belong to the town. Those people once newcomers, risen to become our merchant nobility through hard toil, connections, advantageous marriages, and…how did he call it…sheer luck. It's thanks to this mixture of *bourgeois* that our fair Avignon is – or, rather, *was* – as we now know it. Luc, you've been burying them like me and, are they not all manner of persons? We include students, laity, priests, beggars, craftsmen, papal officials, and visitors. But, many of these are unaccounted for – they come and go – and, it's for this reason they may die alone in the streets: anonymous beings in our modern city that refuses to free its hold on the past. Does any of this make sense to you, Luc? I only relate what the Magistrate told me, but, that doesn't mean I understand it. All we can do is our best."

"I'm with you, Marius. Come, let's sup ale, for we will soon be back to our duties."

"Ay, right again! Thinking too hard is not good for us."

The following day, Marius felt more estranged from his wife than usual. She put it down to anguish caused by the deaths. So, she did not ask the cause. His liaison with Alice continued apace, undiscovered, except by Clément who had initiated it and one or two acquaintances, who suspected but did not know for sure. He lay in her arms, hiding away from the outside world, on the mattress in their secret refuge.

"I wonder how it will end…"

"Do you mean the plague?" Marius asked, stroking her bare shoulders.

"Yes, that, but also…"

"Go on."

"You and I. Since the first day you arrived in Avignon and I spoke to you in the street, outside your house, I felt an attraction, a fascination I do not experience with most men –"

"*Most men?* I could ask how many there are in your life! In fact, if I stop to consider our relationship, I know nothing about you. You are called Alice, you live next door to me, and you enjoy picking fights in public houses!" Giggling, she slapped his face, but in jest.

"Hey! Don't strike me, please!" He pleaded, feigning fear.

"So, what do you want to know?"

"Whatever you choose to reveal." '*This scene is a figment of my imagination, for sure*' she pondered. '*The man I love, but cannot have, gives me a chance to be honest. Yet, how much do I disclose?*'

"Tell me about your past, and what work you do." He replied. She took a deep breath, rose, and filled two cups with ale. Handing one to Marius, she sat on the edge of the mattress.

"There are women who are innkeepers, sell foodstuffs and goods, sew, make clothing…and, I…" '*I will speak of everything except my mission for Clement – he cannot know of that.*'

"I once had a husband. We wed when I was but seventeen years old. His family had a respected name in the region - more of that anon. Above all, he wanted a male heir, but, year after year, I did not conceive. Then came the beatings, yet, I could see no way to escape from his cruelty." Marius studied her face, absorbing every detail.

"Five years ago, he set out on the river, with his friends, on a flatboat... just for amusement. All drunk, they failed to see the strong current sending the vessel towards the centre of the bridge. It hit a pier, capsized and they all drowned."

"Awful!"

"Some might say so, but, for me it was salvation! I will explain. All love had fled our marriage, so, the need for mourning was spared me. I pray you and Dominique will never know such calamity. Avignon is forward-looking and, unlike many other backwaters of Provence, states that when a 'head of household' dies, and there is no male in line, the wife obtains rights of succession..."

Marius wrinkled his brow, showing incomprehension.

"... sorry, I mean she inherits the man's property, business, and land. I have seen women's status grow over recent time and, it's why I defended my name the other night."

"You are a freed woman... do continue."

"I came into money and owned a fine house to the south of town, near the Magnanen gate. It boasts a garden, a well, and an orchard."

"I know that house. Do they not call it *Marguerite's house*?"

"Yes. But, I do not live there – nobody does."

"Excuse me?"

"*Marguerite's house* is my... er... income. I provide girls who occupy the rooms and charge for their 'services'."

"Do you mean –"

"Yes, it's a brothel. Pleasure for the clients is guaranteed and I reap a percentage of the takings. I choose to rent the house next to yours to avoid people associating me with such a den of iniquity!" She smiled, relieved she had, at last, told him her secret. To finish her account, she went on,

"Running the house is a lucrative profession, nowadays, and I pay the Magistrate nine sous in tax every Michaelmas. Everything is proper."

"A brothel...do you –"

"Stop! No, I do *not* provide favours myself, I leave that to the girls, rest assured. Maybe you would like to frequent the place! What do you say? Are you shocked?"

"I have to admit, I'm surprised. You lead a double life and I'm amazed but all the more intrigued."

"Good! That's how we will keep it. But, back to my original question: how will it end between us?"

"If I could foresee the future, I would give you an answer." He kissed her on the lips.

"I must leave. Today, Luc and I are searching the alleys."

That same evening, Marius ordered a bottle of eau de vie in the tavern. It was less busy than usual.

"Where are your customers, Marcel?"

"That's a nice question. I hear they are lately afeard of their neighbour's company. Lord knows what will become of us. I just want to earn an honest living." He placed the bottle and glass on the table and left Marius to his thoughts. Those patrons present sat in huddles of two and three and he caught a different conversation emanating from each. The men were desperate to find hope in a situation where there was no reason to feel such an emotion.

"My wife forbids me to leave the house without a bunch of lavender tied around my neck..." He loosened his tunic to reveal the plant. "The pleasant fragrance kills the plague germs and protects me. Do you see?" He leaned forward for his friend to sniff the scent. "Hey! I'll tell my wife about this," said the friend, "although, she already closes the windows tight shut so the bad smells cannot get in."

From the next table,

"I take my wife and children to the cathedral twice every week. Mind, there's no normal services any longer. We just light a candle and kneel before the altar. Sometimes, the priest blesses us, other times he ignores us. But, I believe the scourge is a punishment from God. The Lord is testing us! Best thing we can do is pray for mercy."

Then,

"I paid the healer handsome money for molasses – black treacle – that was ten years old."

"Why?" asked his mate.

"He told me to spoon it into my wife's mouth when she could swallow solid food no more. The syrup has the efficacy to combat the terrible swellings on her body and, if she takes enough, he promised it would rid her of the disease once and for all."

"And, did it?"

"No. She died two days later, and I never did see the healer again."

Marius drank half a glass of his eau de vie in one draught. What he heard from these poor, vulnerable folk tormented him.

From another table,

"I don't hold with them that says foul air will bring us the contagion –"

"What are you saying?"

"The stench from the town's brook is so strong it destroys any clean breeze that is disease-ridden. I instruct my family to sit on the benches alongside the stream for one hour every day. They breathe in deeply and, let it be known, we are free of any marks of the plague!"

"You could be right…I think we will join you tomorrow."

"Yes, do! We will not be alone, either."

'Such abysmal times,' Marius thought. 'Whither shall we turn? What fate attends our smitten fellows? The Magistrate, Luc, Guillaume, Artois, Marc… we all toil, may the Good Lord be told, day and night! But, to what end? One death becomes ten, then twenty, then one hundred! Before the pestilence, the man in the slaughterhouse slaughtered beasts, and hung them from hooks to drain the blood. How skilful is his art, slicing off their hides for the tanner? The butcher dismembered the carcass, and the joints were prepared for sale at the market. Yet, is there any difference between the beast and the corpse? Both serve a purpose while alive, but, in death are reduced to food for worms! The fury of this visitation scorns our best efforts! The like of it has never been seen in Avignon – nor elsewhere in the world!'

"Potions and prayers be damned!" Came from another corner,

"The only way is to let the leeches do their business. A man in our street was afflicted with the early signs. His wife told me his humours were not in balance... said his blood, phlegm and black and yellow bile each fought the other – hence his illness. She sent for the blood-letter... fortunate for the family they had money to pay him. Anyway, he let out one cup of blood into a bowl..."

"Go on! Tell! Did he revive?"

"He did not die, that is all I know."

Marius felt a gentle touch on his arm. He looked up to see Alice, smiling.

"May I join you?" she asked, knowing he would not decline.

"Of course. Marcel! Another glass over here! What brings you tonight?"

"You might not believe me if I said I wanted your company, but I do so."

He filled her vessel and gazed into her eyes. She asked, "I sense you would like to tell me something? Tiredness is written on your face."

"Ay, I am tired, exhausted, frustrated, and angry! I have been listening to the crazy cures these people are resorting to – it's heart-breaking, truly, for there is no hope! Just listen for yourself." He became quiet.

"I've crushed an emerald – an heirloom from my grand-mother – into a powder and mixed it with ale... drunk it like a medicine... sometimes with bread... an old man gave me the recipe..."

"My baby son burned with fever... twisted in pain... we bathed him in urine... four times a day to relieve the ague..."

From a table behind them came the most pernicious of all the demented cures Marius had overheard,

"I met a sailor from Marseilles. He told me he stayed in our town because the plague down there was yet worse than here, if you can believe that! My aged mother lay in her bed and we knew her time was coming. We were at a loss, what could we do for her? The stranger said he would explain a very special remedy, one very few people from our region had encountered. But, he required payment if he was to share it with us. Five sous – a fortune! We had no choice if mother was to be saved, so we borrowed from friends and paid him the money."

"Sailors from that place are renowned for their ancient spells and elixirs. What did he prescribe?"

"We were to blend a paste of certain tree resins, flower roots and fresh cow-dung. Then, we had to push the concoction into the buboes, cut open. The wound would then be tightly bound to keep the salve secure and perform its magic."

"Did it succeed?"

"The smell was infernal! But, the next day, she came round, enough to sip a little broth. We thanked the Lord for her salvation! However, as we slept, she passed away. I am starting to wonder, after all, whether the plague itself is responsible for the deaths..."

"Marius!" Alice gripped his hand. "I have not listened to such mischief in my life!" her tone angry, "It is deceiving people who are in a most defenceless situation. Do you think they believe it? Surely not!"

"I fear they do, Alice. They throw whatever they can at the disease. With sad thoughts, they do not eat figs or meat. Neither do they run or walk outside or partake in any physical exercise. Bathing is ignored; there is no sleep during the day; there are no sexual relations – for that leaves them covered in dripping sores and, in the end, they die! And, all this, they believe!"

Alice's face turned ashen grey, but she said nothing. Marius replenished their glasses. The murmuring, from table to table, carried on, the plague the only topic of conversation. He continued,

"It is natural for a man to seek out the reason for any tragedy and that, in turn, breeds blame. They condemn their neighbours, visitors, traders, the sun and moon and, not least of all, the Lord in Heaven! If he cannot save them, who can? And, do you know who else are accused?"

"I do not."

"The Jews! It makes my blood boil! They only number two, maybe three hundred in the entire town. And, whilst they appear somewhat different to us in their dress and how they worship, why should they be guilty? What harm do they do to us?"

"I know little about the Jews," she answered.

"Trust me, Alice, they are a good breed. Pope Clément, himself, has published a bull – I have a copy here." He took some parchment sheets out of his tunic and laid one on the table.

"See…" He began to read the missive:

'*It cannot be true that the Jews, by such a heinous crime, are the cause or the occasion of the plague. Through many parts of the world, the same plague, by the hidden judgment of God, afflicted and afflicts the Jews themselves, and many other races who have never lived alongside them…*'

"So, you see, Alice, the Pontiff urges the clergy to take action to protect the Jews, as he has done in condemning any violence against them. Anyone who blames the plague on them is seduced by that liar, the Devil! I am saying in brief what the bull says. And Clément's most severe warning…he will excommunicate those persecuting the Jews! We are blessed to have a man of such high moral standing, to express his opinion in public. He is a beacon of light and love, is he not, Alice?"

She nodded. She knew the private face of Clément.

CHAPTER TWENTY-ONE

AVIGNON/lands to the west of the Rhône
August, 1348 AD

By August, 1348, the plague had dispatched half of the population of Avignon. Hot, dry weather provided ideal conditions for the epidemic to rage, uncontrolled. There was no indication of it abating. The survivors fell into three types. Some accepted Clément's condemnation that God had espied and was punishing their sinful behaviour. He commended the power of supplication as a weapon with which to confront evil in its myriad forms. They prayed in the cathedral – now the only place open to them. The second group remained indoors, either by choice or on account of their houses being closed up, the doors marked with the dreaded, red cross. The third, a minority, were the men and women who fought the disease, as best they could, without consideration for their own or even their family's safety. They were pragmatic in dealing with the deaths and subsequent burials. But, they possessed no means of arresting the scourge's progress. Neither medicine nor prayer existed as a cure, that which detached the people from their contentment and normality, back in January. They found themselves hurled into the abyss of pain and despair this August month.

The Magistrate summoned Marius and Luc to his office. On entering, seeing the justice slumped over his desk, surrounded by a confusion of parchment sheets, took them aback.

"Monsieur!" Marius announced their arrival in a raised tone, suspecting the man to be unconscious, or worse. He was relieved when the old man jerked upright.

"Ah, forgive me, gentlemen, I was dreaming...so many thoughts in my head."

"Indeed." It was not necessary to enquire as to their nature.

"How are you both? Not seen you for a few days."

"We carry on, as we can – there is no other way," Luc answered.

"If only everyone in this godforsaken place held a view like yours, but they do not!"

"You asked for us this morning, so what, pray is it about?" said Marius, expecting yet more bad news, if such was possible.

"Come, sit here. Luc, fill those cups with ale." He continued,

"After all the years doing my job, I find it hard to understand people. Why do they do *this* thing rather than *that*? Why choose the most difficult when the easier is an option and, when does fear become cowardice? Now, there's a question for you to think on! Do we say we're afraid as an excuse for something we should not be doing? I can't get it straight in my mind."

"I'm sure you are right," Marius added, although he did not follow the Magistrate's argument.

"Yes, I am. The wool merchants...Jean and Thomas Pagnol and their partner, Bruno Lapierre..."

"What of them?" asked Luc, not knowing what to expect.

"In March, Jean told me he and his brother were afeard of remaining in the town, so he had taken some chattels and his strongbox onto their barge. Its mooring is at the quay. At the time, I remember telling him if that was his attitude, he might just as well leave once and for all. I've known him from boyhood and his action was a surprise to me, I'll say. I'm a man of Avignon, and my family go back generations. I love the town, its beauty and history. Whatever is necessary to protect its name, I will do. Spiritless behaviour is unfitting. Imagine how saddened I was this morning, when their bargee, Mahi, came to inform me the three of them had fled – no other word for it. They wanted him to join them, but he refused, reminding them he had already departed a city, Marseilles, to the plague and he had no intention of deserting another. They have locked their homes and warehouse. Their boat has sailed from the port."

The Pagnol brothers and Bruno had cast off from the Avignon quay before sunrise. No-one, apart from Mahi and the justice, knew of their plan. They realised their leaving would not receive the approbation of the townsfolk left behind. Best they departed without a fuss. On the barge, they loaded sheets of sailcloth and Bruno's woodworking saws, axe, nails, ropes, and hammer. Tied with cord through the handles they had pots and pans. One sack was filled with tunics and nightshirts; another, smaller, contained purses, each with gold coin. The three men wore a belt that carried a long knife. A third bag had salted hams, beef, biscuits and other preserved foodstuffs they would need to sustain them.

Thomas hoisted a single headsail, Jean took the rudder. Bruno stared into the water of the Rhône, a river swollen by the summer temperatures. The boat tacked upstream and under the Bénézet bridge. Fifteen minutes later, and with care, they touched the west bank. A weeping willow, its branches and leaves overhanging the water, marked the place Jean had arranged to meet an acquaintance he had paid to provide a horse and cart. With the vessel tied securely to the tree, they waited in silence. Thomas gazed downstream to where the bridge and the town's ramparts stood out against the rising sun. The stonework reached up to the heavens, imploring salvation, sending long, dark shadows across the swirls and eddies of the river. This day, he watched the tenebrous, unpredictable current, wondering what lay ahead and whether they had made the right decision.

Shortly, the prime bell sounded in the distance and, on time, a voice attracted the men's attention.

"Pagnol, are you there?"

"Over here,"

A man approached, leading a horse by its bridle, pulling a rustic, two-wheeled, wicker-sided cart. Jean shook the man's hand and inspected it.

"You have done well. Take this for your trouble." He handed him a purse. Opening it, the stranger checked its contents, nodded, and made off. Bruno hauled off a sack and emptied a heap of feed in front of the horse. A pail of fresh river water completed the beast's breakfast and it was ready to work.

"Come, Thomas," Jean entreated, "help me load our things." Bruno attached a rope to the horse's bit. He headed the entourage with the men on foot since, with them on board, the rough track would have jolted the wheels to pieces. Following the river's course, their first destination was the small village of Les Angles, some two leagues north.

"Any distance we can put between ourselves and Avignon will increase our chances of safety," Jean said to his brother.

"Ay," replied Thomas, "I feel sorry for them we have deserted, but I see no reason to stay when we have the means to escape."

Bruno tapped the horse's hindquarters with a stick, urging it on. Conversation was muted as they made progress on the first stage of the journey. Jean's plan was to leave infected Avignon and pass the coming weeks or months in outlying villages or other places free from the plague. Once safe to return, they would resume their former lives and prosper again.

By late afternoon, Les Angles was ahead, wisps of white smoke spiralling skyward. A man and woman approached them, heads bowed, covered by brown hoods.

"Good day," greeted Bruno. There came no reply. The couple continued past them without looking back.

"What rude people! We will spend the night without the village."

A freshwater stream flowing into the river through a copse suited their needs. The horse, unhitched, drank and ate its feed. Thomas saw to lighting a fire with abundant deadwood. They supped on slices of ham and biscuits. Their wine was cool, clear water from the brook. Fed and tired by the travelling, they each made beds of scrub, pulled a sheet of sailcloth over themselves and fell asleep in the warmth of the fire's dying embers. The night was peaceful and unaffected by the pernicious scourge that the people of Avignon – notably Marius and his team of fighters – endured still.

The next day they rose at dawn. Faces dowsed with stream water, the cart loaded and the horse hitched, they set off once more, spirits raised. Guided inland, to the west, by the path of the sun, they felt at peace with the world, surrounded by God's bounty and beauty in nature'

"Within the day, we will make Villeneuve-lès-Avignon," Jean said to his companions. "I visited the place years ago. It's a fine, small place and virtuous people. I remember seeing monks...from their abbey. King Philippe Le Bel built a fortress to guard against enemies coming and going over the Bénézet bridge. The popes now spend their leisure time there, away from the noise and crowds of Avignon. We may find lodging for the night."

The track widened, as they approached Villeneuve, up to a crude, wooden barrier across their path. As if from nowhere, a fellow dressed in a serge tunic, tied tight at the waist. He stepped out in front of the horse, his face obscured by his hood. Holding a hatchet, as a warning, he bellowed,

"Halt!" A rag bound his mouth, as a further disguise. Bruno reined in the beast and Jean advanced towards the strange guard.

"Who are you? What do you want here?"

"Greetings to you," Jean started, "we are travellers who seek rest for the night and a meal –"

"Say no more! Whence do you come?"

"From Avignon."

"Do you! You will go no further! Be gone!"

"We have gold coin, see." Jean waved a purse, its contents clinking, at the man.

"Don't want your money. It cannot buy our preservation. If you are from Avignon, you could have the pestilence on your clothes, for all we know... even your horse might spit it on us. We trust no strangers.

Off with you!" He took a pace forward, hatchet in hand, and the three men needed no further bidding. They turned round the wagon and retraced the track.

Well away from the barrier, Bruno brought the horse to a stop.

"What do you make of that?" he asked the other two. No answer came, so surprised were they by the hostile reception. Bruno continued,

"We were not welcome, that's for sure."

"You're not wrong there," said Jean, stroking his chin in reflection. "So, Villeneuve is not visited by the malady."

"No, and they are keen to ensure it does not."

"I can understand that," Thomas, a taciturn man, agreed.

They followed the rough way that took them deep into a forest.

"We will cover as much ground as possible before nightfall," Jean decided.

As dusk neared, they pulled up in a glade that would be fine for the night.

"Thomas, make a fire. Bruno, with your axe, cut down some branches, and construct a shelter with sailcloth." The horse ate his feed and drank from a leather bucket. Huddled around the campfire to keep warm from the evening chill, they consumed salted ham and apples they had brought. None spoke, unaccustomed to sleeping under the stars, in the cold night, without proper food. Each questioned the wisdom of quitting Avignon.

Bruno hewed a tree and made a tent, of sorts. From the other side of the shrubs and undergrowth surrounding them rang strange, eerie sounds. The rustling of leaves could herald a wild boar hunting for a twilight meal. All were familiar with the damage a boar's tusks and sharp teeth could inflict. A different noise, on the ground, might be a slithering viper, prevalent in the warm, Provençal climate. Overhead, the timorous men heard frenetic squawking and mysterious hooting...perhaps a hungry, black, demonic raven or a harmless barn owl. They did not know which. Fatigued, little meaningful ensued.

The morning deepened their gloom as the heavens opened for torrential summer rain to lash them like the whipcords of a cat-o'-nine-tails. Clothing offered scant resistance to the downpour and they trudged through the forest soaked to the skin. The horse made heavy going of the thickets and sodden ground. The minor town of La Fontaine du Buis was next on Jean's itinerary, although it was still several leagues hence. Around midday, the trees thinned and, ahead, in a clearing, stood a stone-built farmhouse.

"Thomas, approach it and speak with the owner. Ask if he can offer us a roof for the night, and tell him we can pay," Jean instructed. Thomas obeyed his elder brother. A few minutes later, he returned.

"It's deserted. Doesn't look like anyone has lived there for ages, but it's not locked, nor has a big black dog snarled at me" – He had a morbid fear of dogs.

"Excellent!" enthused Jean, "we're here tonight, or maybe longer!"

The house had a thick, thatched roof so the inside was quite dry. An open fireplace on one wall would support a blazing fire. In the yard, a well with fresh water to drink, wash in and give to the horse raised their spirits. Apple and pear trees hung heavy with fruit in the orchard. Inspecting the yard, Bruno yelled with delight,

"Hey! Look what I've found!" In his hand he held an iron rabbit trap, its teeth jagged and free from rust, ready to set and catch any unsuspecting animal.

"Take it out to yon trees, in between bushes and, with luck, we will have a fine meal this evening! Thank the Lord!"

Bruno returned to the snare a while later and, as Jean had predicted, it had snapped closed on a fat buck rabbit. Prising open the jaws, he removed the dead creature. Entering the cottage, he waved it for the others to see.

"Well done, Bruno!" congratulated Thomas, who turned to Jean,

"Up to you now, brother. You are the one who knows how to skin and gut, so get to work! We're waiting for our supper!"

A poker, pushed through the prepared carcass, was supported by two andirons, as a spit, above a blazing fire in the hearth. The meal that night was a feast compared with the meagre rations of the last few days. In an outhouse, there was clean straw that served as beds. Sleep came easy.

For the coming weeks, the men enjoyed the comfort of the farmhouse. Bruno, the skilled woodworker, whittled straight branches into pointed spears. Hiding, in silence in the bushes, they awaited the appearance of a grazing deer. Leaping from their cover, they impaled it and wrestled it to the ground. Bruno drew his knife and, with one slash, cut open its throat. It took but a few minutes for the animal to become still. They dragged the deer back to the farm and Jean set to work removing the skin and cutting it into joints of fresh venison of a size for the spit. Tasty roast meat and delicious fruit from the orchard and berries foraged from the glade, meant they feasted like kings.

"We are blessed, my friends! Our Father has seen fit to endow us with these pleasures," and Jean waited, but there was no reaction. The other two were too busy eating. Again, he extolled, "Thanks be to the Lord, praise Him!" Such religious fervour was previously unknown in the merchant, whose only attendance at church was when funeral services obliged him.

Days passed by. Undisturbed by intruders, they strolled at leisure in the blooming forest, alive with midsummer growth, its canopy sheltering all manner of wildlife – birds, insects, flowers, boar, badger, squirrels, and fish in ponds. Pleasant banter and stories occupied their time. This comfortable, bucolic existence was in stark contrast to the horror of plague-ridden Avignon. However, living in isolation rendered them cocooned from the outside world. In their eyes, they had done nothing wrong, so there was no guilt. Every man is free to choose his path in life, Bruno reasoned one night after supper, sitting with his fellow runaways by the fire, still alight after cooking the meal. The choice to leave the town was made. With perverse logic, he justified there would be three fewer deaths to deal with, should they have remained and become infected.

The weather held fine. The tall trees around then afforded shade and an agreeable place to sit, sheltered from the powerful sun, but in the fresh air. One morning, Jean announced he was taking the horse and cart some six leagues farther inland, to the place called La Fontaine du Buis. There, he would purchase biscuits, salt fish and wine skins. Although the pure well water they drank was satisfactory, he missed the wine cellar in his warehouse, as he did the business. It should have been a minor inconvenience, faced with the catastrophic plague, but was not so. Man's desire for trading survived.

Jean untethered the horse and set off. He arrived at the town before midday. Thatched cottages lined the track leading to where he hoped to find a market for his purchases. Luck was in. Ahead, in a wide open area, stalls displayed all sorts of goods. Villagers inspected the merchandise and conversed to pass the time of day. He hitched the horse by a stone water trough and tied the feed sack around its neck. The beast ate and drank, snorting after its exertions. As he walked towards the market, he felt a hand on his shoulder, bringing him to a halt. Turning, a giant of a man with an unkempt, black beard, flowing locks and brawny biceps faced him. His sleeveless tunic exposed arms with hands as strong as a smithy's vice. The wool trader started to speak,

"Good –" But he was cut short,

"Who be you? Talk!" The local ordered in a menacing tone.

"My name is Jean Pagnol. I am a merchant."

"Don't care what you are… what brings you to these parts?"

"I come to buy wine and provisions –" Again, the huge man interrupted,

"Where is your home?"

"Avignon."

"Did you say *Avignon,* across the river?"

"For a fact." The hand moved from his shoulder in an instant.

"Take your horse and cart and leave! I'll not give ye a second warning… *fuck off!*"

Jean did not recognise this instruction as his own tongue, but the message was clear as clear.

"We don't have the plague in our town, and that's how we intend to keep it. The likes of you are not welcome… plague-bearers… all them from Avignon bear the disease." He removed a wooden cudgel from his waistband and raised it as if to strike. Jean retreated, unhitched the horse and left La Fontaine du Buis without further exchange.

'*We've been turned away from Villeneuve-lès-Avignon and now La Fontaine du Buis. What is happening? It's not as if we are black-skinned, wear blue-dyed turbans or boast mysterious, pagan tattoos on our arms, with the appearance of foreigners... but, how do we prove to them we do not carry the scourge? And, will it be thus wherever we go?'*

Night was falling as he returned to the cottage and fed and watered the horse. Thomas stood in the doorway and asked, with anticipation,

"What good things have you brought back for us, brother?"

"None."

"What did you say?"

"I said none. I was seen off – fled for my life – refused entry if you like."

"How is that?"

"They thought I might infect them, but how could I persuade them I would not?"

"Ah, that's serious for us," Thomas decided, "will we meet such hostility elsewhere in the country?"

That evening, sat around the fire with only water to drink, the mood was sombre, though not through the absence of strong beverage. Was their judgment in deserting Avignon flawed? Was there a way to redeem the situation?

Suddenly, the door burst open. Three men, faces hidden by the cowls of their tunics pulled down, took a menacing stance in the middle of the room. Each held a cosh and smacked his palm to show, whatever the reason, they would stand no nonsense. The tallest stepped forward.

"This is not your house!" He bellowed. The merchants were off guard and, in any case, their knives lay on the table in the other side of the room. The stranger continued,

"It belongs to an old man who asked us to care for it should he die, which he has. You have no right to be here!" The two henchmen behind him again struck his palm, impatient to put the cosh to the purpose it was intended. The leader half-turned and gestured them to wait.

"We have word you are from the plague town. Is this true?" Bruno, showing naivety, admitted without thinking of the consequences.

"Yes, we are."

"Then we don't want your kind anywhere near." He moved forward to Bruno, dealt a hard blow to the arm, then inflicted the same on Jean and Thomas.

"If you are not gone by first light tomorrow, you will be in for worse than that. Understand?" He put the question to each, in turn. "So be it!" With that, they left the cottage without the politeness of closing the door. Jean sat on the bench near the fire, head lowered in reflection, rubbing his sore arm. Looking at the others, he said,

"We have no choice but to quit this humble abode and return to Avignon."

Next day, they loaded the belongings on the cart, hitched the horse, and set off for the river. Seeing Les Angles to the north, it was not much further ahead. The barge was still safely moored where they had left it by the willow tree. Jean hailed a fisherman, rod in hand, on the riverbank.

"Hey, fellow! Would you like to earn a few easy sous?"

"Willingly, sire."

"Lead this horse to Les Angles. Inform the man at the gate that Pagnol requests him to see it is returned to the owner." The fisherman, pleased with his windfall, took the money and carried out the instructions. Some three hours later, with a following wind, the barge sailed into the home port of Avignon. Jean and Thomas gripped the handle on either side of their beloved strongbox and, Bruno walking behind, they approached the Saint-Roch gate to enter the old town. But the guard, a man known to them, leapt from his stool to bar their way. "Stop!" he barked, "you may not pass!"

"Richard, my friend, what are you saying?"

"Do you not understand plain speaking? The Magistrate has decreed any man or woman who abandons our town will not be accepted, should they attempt to return. If I was you, I'd further worry because the Pontiff has threatened *excommunication* from the Church." The simple fellow had no appreciation of what the word entailed but, as far as he was concerned, his master said that's how it was. That was good enough for him.

"But our homes are within the walls –"

"No matter, the law's the law!" the guard resumed, "and since you left, the justice has requisitioned your houses for corpses to be delivered before the buriers collect them. So, you see, you have done some good for *us* in *our* time of need."

Behind the sentry emerged the unmistakable figure of Carel Rostand, the beggar.

"So, you think you can sail back to port and regain the town as if nothing untoward had happened? You are mistaken, my friends. Before the plague came you sneered at me, mocked my lowly position, did you not?"

The men said nothing.

"I may only be a beggar, but – and you can ask anyone here – I am no coward, nor am I banished from our Mother Church!"

Jean Pagnol, his brother and Bruno Lapierre, had no option but to live on the barge, moored at the furthermost quay from the gate as they did before leaving. Three refugees, denied access to their birth-right but, few sympathised with their plight: no-one had compelled them to flee. Ostracised, excluded from prayer, rejected by the residents - many of them friends and colleagues – who had stayed, brave souls! *They* had not turned their backs on the challenge.

CHAPTER TWENTY-TWO

AVIGNON
September, 1348 AD

Marius sat in his usual corner of the tavern, alone and deep in thought. The tragedy of the plague overwhelmed his senses. Faced with the daily horror and depravity of the pestilence, he felt its toll on his body as on his spirit. But, if his role as the Magistrate's deputy was to be honoured, there was no place for emotion. Citizens died, so the safety of those living demanded a swift, efficient burial procedure. The summer had reached its most intense, blazing heat: flowers wilted, streams ran dry, and tempers became frayed. People showed signs not only of weariness but also sad resignation. They saw no end to their ordeal and the will to fight was descending into fatal surrender.

Dominique did her best to maintain marital harmony but, the strain of caring for a young son and her husband's protracted absence from their home, distracted the couple. They were married in name only - strangers under the same roof. Marius thought of his next meeting with Alice and, although this relationship ran no clear course, he knew in his heart that the future somehow rested with her.

"I wonder what thoughts occupy your mind, Marius?" Standing beside the table was Rostand, who continued,

"Forgive my impudence, but may I join you?"

"Why... of course. Another tankard, Marcel, and more ale," he called to the landlord.

"I am pleased to find you here. I would talk with you."

"We are not well acquainted... I recognise you... Rostand... but of no matter, sit, do." The men drank their beer, neither wanting to be the first to speak. Their first meeting, some six months earlier, came into sharp focus: Marius, indeed, recalled their conversation,

'It's my business to know who people are and what they do' Rostand had said, *'you could say it's an aptitude... when I keep company... I like to present myself in a favourable light... I am no fool. Yet, word brands me as such. This gives me the advantage... my superior intelligence... my mind over theirs... people feel sorry for me... sometimes, what's wrong is right and we make perverse, capricious choices...'* Rostand continued,

"I am a beggar – though I am not forced to be so. I –" Marius interrupted,

"I remember. You are related to the Count of Provence, from Fort Saint-Martin... you are a man of means, if unknown to the folk who drop a coin into your bowl!"

"Yes, my father was that count, who ensured I was not in need. He gave me a small vineyard near to Les Angles. I have heard news from that place concerning the wool merchants – but, more of that anon. When my father passed away, my elder brother assumed the title of count, but we argued and he disowned me. I had to work hard at the vineyard, but an awful mildew struck. The grapes rotted and died on the espaliers, I could do nothing. I quit, crossed the river, and bought a cottage here in Avignon. No-one knew who I was and that suited me. I started to play the game of my mind over the rich peoples', who can easily afford to part with their money. Well, you see, I do not need their charity but, there is an injustice when the wealthy live next door to the poor family who strive to provide for their children. What do you think, Marius?"

"I agree, Rostand."

"Last week, I witnessed those two wool traders along with the man, Bruno. They believed it would be possible to wander back into our town when they discovered life without was not as pleasant as they had hoped, having deserted us." His tone rose. Marius studied the beggar's countenance. Dark, piercing eyes met his own, and his lips tightened as anger and resentment were clear for all to see. At that moment, a third person joined them. The Magistrate sat down at their table, without any formality.

"Gentlemen."

"Good evening," Marius acknowledged, gesturing to Marcel for a tankard.

"Ah, Rostand, how are you?" the justice enquired.

"Well, and I am not yet afflicted by the plague, unlike so many others who —"

"It has come to my notice" the official cut in "that you are performing acts of kindness, visiting our townsfolk in their homes. You console them in their loss, sympathise with their plight. You are unheralded and carry out this unpaid labour in a modest manner. Is this not true?" Rostand looked down, embarrassed.

"...and so, you deserve our thanks."

"All you say is correct, but anything I do pales when compared with Marius, Luc and their colleagues who collect and bury corpses. I do not seek praise, but I believe our community will die if there is no hope, no glimmer of a better future. We *will* survive this ravaging evil, I am certain, and, thus, I sought Marius tonight to offer myself in the struggle." He lapsed into silence. The Magistrate resumed,

"Given your intimate familiarity with the town's populace, Rostand, I accept, on Marius' behalf." The latter nodded his agreement. "Herewith, I invest you as a deputy to my office. Do you consent?"

"I do, justice."

The three men consumed several pitchers of ale, reminiscing about days gone by when life was better.

"I find it hard to understand why you live the life you do, *by choice*." Marius said to the beggar. "You possess money, your own house and — how many wish *they* had such — and you are, the Lord forbid, not tormented by the infection..."

"When we first met," Rostand explained, "I told you how we each choose this or that path in life…you work for the good Magistrate, but you could shut yourself indoors and never run the risk that you do. Is that not so?" The Magistrate signified it was. "…you see, we control our own destinies to –" "That's as maybe, Rostand, but we hold no sway over the plague."

"Sad to say, we do not." The companions – for now, they were – fell into silence, pondering over the ubiquitous curse. The officer then said,

"Anyway, idle talk will get us nowhere. Listen, if you will. There is a particular…um…issue abroad in the town. I had intended charging it to Marius alone but now, with Rostand on our side, my boy has an assistant."

Both men put down their tankards and the alcoholic haze lifted a little as they anticipated further serious details.

"Yes, he does." He turned to Rostand, "Your expert knowledge of the streets and houses is, to my surprise, going to prove invaluable in tracking down a lunatic in our midst."

"Lunatic?" the men asked, in unison.

"Yes, for that is what he be, a madman, deranged and dangerous…since we do not know his name, we will now call him that…*lunatic*! Let me explain. You may or may not know that a certain person roams at large, not poisoned except in the head. He goes around, passing fearsome judgment upon anyone he finds, and in a shocking manner. Lurking in corners and behind trees, he is quite naked apart from a loincloth to hide his private parts…to protect his modesty, should we say. He screams '*Repent! Repent!*' at whosoever crosses his path or, unawares, opens the door to him. Picture this monster! I heard he wears a chafing dish of burning charcoal and brimstone upon his head – a blazing symbol of dementia, a perversion of the Scriptures! On sound authority, I have it he has set fire to parchments bearing plain chants and choral songs as if to distance himself from church music he holds is sinful. Such sacrilege! Foul perfidy!" He raised his tankard and took a deep draught of ale. His friends remained speechless.

"If I was a father," he resumed, "to children, would I wish they were dispatched by the plague or condemned through the twisted words of this lunatic? I know not, but he disobeys the law, of that I am sure. There is a regulation stating no person to be on the streets after night, is there not? There is, indeed! And when is he about? After dusk! I rest my case, gentlemen." He spoke in magisterial tones, for one moment, as if pronouncing at his assizes. "What is to be dreaded is the full moon that will show this very week. It lasts but four days before it is lost until the next month. The lunatic has announced such a lunar phase induces fever, rheumatism, and many other diseases – as if we do not have enough to worry about! Do you see…he threatens us with his cry of '*Repent!*' as if he is a messenger from above. Be told, he wanders our squares, avenues, alleys, and streets – he must be apprehended, without delay. He drives our residents to distraction and any understanding of '*Repent!*' in any case is beyond their world. I doubt the Holy Father himself can explain it, in simple words. Now, are there any questions?" There came no reply. "I wish you success. We must stop him!" With that, he left. Marius and Rostand stared at each other, exchanging expressions of trepidation and excitement for the trial ahead.

"He said *without delay*, did he not?"

"He did," confirmed Marius, "but wait, let's ask the customers here, for they may give us an idea where to begin searching."

The drinkers related this or that rumour, but nobody knew for certain where to find the lunatic.

"We will need to walk the streets in the hope of catching him performing his diabolical deeds," said Rostand in a resigned tone.

"No other way," Marius agreed, "and we will run him down, God willing, tomorrow, for a clear head is needed. Tonight there is a more pressing matter. Marcel! Bring ale over here!"

Consumption of alcoholic tipple rose to an excessive level for the duration of the plague. Without its numbing capacity, those making up the 'sanitisation forces' – the Magistrate's description of his buriers, searchers, sextons, and the rest – would fail in their efforts. Marius and Rostand, that evening, established a mutual respect. Their tongues loosened by drink, they discussed and shared personal stories and experiences in their lives.

"...have you not considered an end to begging...take a worthy woman for a wife?" Marius asked, curious.

"I have not! There was a certain lady, a long time ago, but...no...not to be trusted...women, I mean. I value my freedom too much! What about you, Marius, how are your women?"

"Why are you saying, *women?*"

"Remember, my friend, I am no fool. There is little happens here that escapes my notice. Mistress Alice."

"What of her?"

"She lies with you when she is not too busy studying verses from the Bible with the Holy Father. Also, she runs a lucrative business from a house on the Avenue – but we need talk no more of that." Marius lowered his head, realising there was nothing to be gained in denying the liaison. Rostand continued,

"I have observed Clément since he was invested. He is a fascinating man and, with a private life of which the good and great are unaware. He cannot conduct a ceremony in public unless he has consumed a quantity of wine and laudanum." Marius' gaze showed incomprehension. 'Laudinum...theriac...no matter, it is a strong liqueur that stops the hands from shaking. Only one merchant in the town can supply it, at a price, too. His appreciation of all fine things extends to the ladies, or, currently, but *one*, I should say to be precise. Have you suspected there might be a reason that Alice is your mistress as she is Clément's, as you now know? She is a spy for him. He uses her to be informed...to, how shall I put it...to keep an eye on people."

"There is no cause to pry into my life."

"I can say neither yea nor nay, Marius, but I advise you to tread carefully."

The following night, Marius and Rostand met again in the tavern. They drank only one tankard of ale and left to execute the mission ordered by the Magistrate.

"I have given our task some thought, Rostand. We go, first, down to the docks. From there we will follow the ramparts round to the east side, then up to the woods. We will have a decent view of the streets as we go. I don't know what to expect, though."

"Nor I."

To begin, they saw nothing out of place. Everyone obeyed the dusk curfew and the town was silent. Only a solitary owl, high in a tree, hooted a mournful noise: pity the poor souls who yearned for his wisdom, would that he shared with them the answer to their sins but, if he knew, he would not divulge it. The darkness of the night struggled with the penetrating shafts of light from the full moon and, except in the farthest corners, the pale yellow triumphed to guide their way.

"Halt!" Rostand hissed, holding Marius' arm. "That sound...do you hear it?"

"Yes. Turn right, here." Down the street, a high-pitched wailing drifted towards them. '*Repent! Repent! Again, I say, repent!*'

"It's him! Come, but quiet."

They were not mistaken. Ahead, a blaze of orange moved one way then the other. How it resembled the perfume censer swinging in the Grand Audience - an irony that was not lost on Marius. The madman knocked with abandon on one door then the next. No householder was brave or foolhardy enough to respond.

As they approached, the maniac went off. They could not discern any human form behind the glare that, of a sudden, turned into a lane on the right. Reaching the corner, Marius saw the radiance and heard the demonic cry again, but at a distance.

"He is running away!"

"Ay! Let us give chase." But, as it seemed their prey would come to rest, it was playing its evil game, shooting like a nocturnal firefly skimming across the waters of the Rhône.

"Damn!" exclaimed Rostand, "he's laughing at us!"

"He is, too. But, we must obey the Magistrate and capture the cretin, whatever it takes."

"Will you stop, in the name of the law!" Marius bawled, but too late, he disappeared. "Is this insane creature human?" Thus, the chase continued, avenue after avenue, street after street. The lunatic confounded them at every turn.

"He knows passages and shortcuts that I do not," Rostand blurted out, catching his breath, "but he cannot escape us."

Following the glow and deranged screams, the lane opened onto a small square. They advanced close enough to see, for the first time, the face in full view. The countenance was anathema. Long, black hair fell on either side, and central features covered in a powder, as white as swan down, the likes of which only noble ladies knew how to apply. The mouth, open as he yelled, revealed incisor teeth, pointed like those of a wild boar. Eyes, black, deep as the night, beamed insanity at them: a loathsome monstrosity! However, their luck had changed, for he ran into an alley wide enough for only one person. As unexpected as it was welcome, a voice – not the lunatic's – rang out: it was, for sure, that of a woman.

"Stop there, you cannot pass!" Alice appeared, some way behind the fiend who was now trapped. She held aloft a dagger, prepared to put it to good use should the possessed man decide to push by her. Marius and Rostand ran forward. The former knocked the torch to the ground, the latter pinned him to the building, undid a pair of dungeon cuffs hanging from his waistband that he clasped tight around their quarry's wrists. At last, they could breathe in and regain their senses, so swift had the end come. Yet, though he was done for, the insane man ranted and raged anew,

"Repent! I command you, repent!"

Marius leaned back, clenched his fist, and hit him square in his blanched, wench's face so he fell, unconscious. Alice walked up to the scene, the dagger lowered at her side. Marius gazed at her. He could never have foreseen this happening.

"Alice, you arrived at a seemly time, and we owe you a debt. If you had not been there to block the alley, this monster might still be on the loose, terrorising our people. But –" and he paused, "how did you know we were about the town, and for so dangerous a task? As well, why were you out, breaking the curfew?"

"A mutual friend, one who cares for our well-being, spoke with me." She had revealed enough.

"You mean...Rostand?"

"The same. So, you see, he is a good man, despite what ignorant folk believe."

"He is, for sure." Marius concurred. Throughout their exchange, Rostand remained silent, his head lowered. .

"Come, Carel, let us take him, when he revives enough to stand, to the gaol where he belongs!"

"Hey! Gaoler! Open, it is Marius."

The heavy, iron-hinged door clanked back. They dragged the prisoner inside to a vacant cell, threw him in and hauled the door shut.

"Do not remove the cuffs. See there is water in the pail and give him whatever stale crust you can find."

"Understood, master Marius."

The two men, from being strangers were now friends. Each appreciated the qualities of the other. They entered the tavern, pleased with the evening's work, and partook of several pitchers of foaming ale. Soon after, Alice arrived and sat down with them. No-one in the place suspected her involvement in the dramatic event that evening.

CHAPTER TWENTY-THREE

AVIGNON
early October, 1348 AD

Marius and Alice embraced outside their secret cabin in the Dom du Rocher woods. He left her and walked away in the direction of his house where Dominique and baby Fabien awaited his return after dealing with the daily death toll. Earlier, he reported to the Magistrate that the number of deceased had, of late, fallen a slight degree. Alice took the path that led to the Pope's private quarters. Following Rostand's disclosure, Marius was now aware of her relationship with the cleric. He chose, however, to not confront her – was it his business, he asked himself? Seeing her, a few nights before, showing such bravery, endeared her to him all the more. Without her presence he would not have captured the lunatic who roamed the streets, terrorising the people. The aged Clément did not pose a threat to her affections for him, although he questioned the future of the romance.

Sitting on his bed, he invited her, "Come, my dear, beside me." It was past terce but Clément remained in his shirt and floppy cap he wore for the night. Anyone observing the scene would feel pity for this comical figure, not befitting the head of a Church. She declined the invitation, instead choosing to sit at the table on the other side of the room. Her paramour came, with an unsteady gait, to replenish his glass from the familiar bottle of laudanum. He had, without doubt, already partaken of the liqueur before she arrived.

"Would you care to join me?"

"I would not, Clément. It is too early in the day to drink that magic potion like you do."

He did not answer. The lack of respect in her address went unnoticed, as did her description of his adored tipple. His mind was, day-by-day, confused through a triumvirate of powers, each raging with its own agenda. His Curia's counsel was for prayer and yet more prayer. He tired of these officials with their monotonous petitions: men who now kept to their rooms, in isolation. They were afraid of the contagion as much as their leader. Since his time as a novice in the Bénédictine abbey at Saint-Martial, evangelism and worship formed the bedrock of his faith. His God spoke to him, in his most private moments and he listened, as best he could: this became a second distraction. Third, came the voice and demands of the vulgar herd beyond the massive stone walls of the palace. Here, the Magistrate was the intermediary to whom he was duly mindful. Thus rose his confusion. Whose advice should he pursue? The Curia, his belief, the people? None satisfied his scrutiny. As folk had confined themselves to their houses, afraid of any contact with their neighbours, he kept to his rooms. No longer did the clergy conduct services in his fortress and he trusted only two cardinal-priests to bring food and, thus, penetrate the inner sanctum. Outside his office, on a wooden stand, rested a silver altar chalice filled with a mixture of vinegar and rose water. Before entering they were instructed to wash their hands and face with the solution. At the onset of the plague, the papal physician assured him this practice worked as an efficacious antiseptic. That medical man died one week later, but Clément continued with the measure. He placed a smaller chalice, containing the same ingredients, in front of the door to the hidden passageway, for Alice's use.

His glass filled to the brim, he sat next to her on the bench and made to pull her towards him. In an instant, she recoiled.

"Leave me alone, Sire! I do not desire your attention today."

"Why... what ails you?" He took a long draught of laudanum.

"Nothing *ails* me and, father, you are influenced by drink. Maybe I will agree to your advances on another occasion when you are sober – maybe I will not."

He did not recognise Alice was about to end their illicit dalliance.

"Yes... of course... another time," he muttered, thoughts racing. She could predict, with certainty, what his next question would be.

"So, what of our friend, Marius? He works all hours with infected and dead people... it would come as no surprise if you informed me of his sad demise."

"Sire, he is alive and, despite the danger he faces, day after day, he thrives on doing right. I am sure the saints protect him – if you follow my words."

"Ah... yes, certainly he is a good man..."

"Without question, he is so - courageous, generous and worthy."

'I have not heard her talk about Marius in such a manner. The more time passes, the less do I see cause to expose Edmond Nerval's son. He performs only laudable deeds, so are the years of anger and resentment for nothing?' he asked himself.

"I visit you today, Clément, out of choice and not because you sent for me. It will be my last visit."

His jaw dropped and he focused on the woman whose words were sobering.

"I will use your name, *Clément*, because I am your equal. You may bear the title of Pontiff, but the plague knows no distinction between king or pauper – it will strike you or me without warning, you must realise that."

He gulped his drink and poured out more, his mood sombre. Never, in his papacy, had anyone insulted him in such an outrageous, direct fashion, calling him by his name. She paused, then continued, her tone steady and menacing,

"From Marius' arrival in Avignon, with his wife and child, you employed me to spy on him and relate it to you, for I know not what purpose. To begin, I did not question your motives – you are, after all, Pope Clément and I, an ordinary common citizen. I satisfied the needs of your body. You see, you are no different from Marius, except he is the man I love, not you. I will betray him no longer." Resting, she wrung her hands, of a sudden aware of her audacious challenge. *'Fear not, Alice,' she told herself, 'he will not dare to even raise his voice lest the guards come running and discover this loose woman.'*

"Is there any eau de vie? I would welcome a strong drink." Opening the wall cupboard, he withdrew a bottle and filled a glass.

"Thank you." She sipped a little then carried on,

"People observe but know little about me, and that is what I prefer. Some call me a witch, and I suppose my black gown encourages that belief. Others say I come from a tribe of pagans – not so! The truth is I am the niece of the Duke of Provence, whose seat is in Arles. My late father, his brother, managed the estate. I led a privileged life and wanted for nothing. Both my father and mother placed great value on education and their hearts were set on my becoming a nun. With this in mind, they sent me to the nunnery, not far from our house, for tuition in reading and writing. Also, I studied arithmetic, science and natural history. I adored music. They had the means to pay for my lessons. When I was nine years old, all the girls I mixed with aspired only to running a house, getting married and producing children – no learning necessary for that! In my studies, I excelled at reading and writing, so much so that by my twelfth birthday I could under-stand manuscripts of the Scriptures from the Bible, in Latin. I loved all the stories about our Lord Jesus, his followers, his miracles, the times when he lived and – in particular – how he met his lamentable end." She leaned back to draw breath and drink. Clément supped theriac throughout her eloquent discourse, his gaze not leaving her for a mo-ment. He was enthralled yet uneasy about where this was leading and its implications for him.

"I trust my facts are accurate, but if not, you will correct me, for sure. I ask your patience, but all will be clear, I hope." She, in her turn, drank some more eau de vie.

"Jesus was imprisoned by the Roman authorities, for he refused to deny he was King of the Jews. He said he would not honour the Emperor, Tiberius Caesar. Now, the priests were envious of him, accusing him of many crimes. After his death sentence, they stirred up the crowd to demand the release of Barabbas. This man was a revolutionary who had committed murder. The governor, Pontius Pilate, however, found no fault in him." She rested for a minute. "That Roman governor had the power, if there was a popular demand, to commute a death sentence at the Jewish Passover. He addressed the people, asking them to choose between Jesus and the criminal. Although they wanted Jesus for his healing and other miracles, they cried '*Crucify him! Crucify him!*' Pilate ordered the Lord to be flogged in public with a lead-tipped whip then gave him to the soldiers, the innocent to be crucified. They freed the other prisoner. Is my recollection of events faithful to the Scriptures?" she asked Clément.

"It is." '*I do not understand why she relates this account. Is she proving she has an education…that makes her feel superior to other women?*' he mused.

"From the start, I try to bring reason to bear on the plague, on you, on Marius – to no avail. But, this episode remains in my memory since I was a girl and now, at last, everything is clear! Do you not see it, Clément?" He did not. Of course, he had memorised that passage from the Bible - it would be at the heart of his sermons at Easter time.

"Let me explain," she began. The Pontiff stood and paced the room several times. His head bowed and hands clasped behind his back – you would have said a monk of silent orders walking the cloisters of his abbey.

"Please sit. I must finish what I came for today." He sat like an obedient child, under the woman's spell.

"You, master, are Pilate. You possess authority over Marius who, like Jesus, devoted his life to doing good deeds. The plague is represented by the one in gaol with him. The wonderful spirit of God, vested in yourself, can *defeat* the pestilence! So, as Pilate held power over Barabbas and Jesus, *you, you Clément,* are in that same position of strength. You must decide. Will you reverse the Scriptures and put both the wrongdoer and the plague to death, and release Jesus which means you will cease your persecution of Marius. Do you dare, Clément? Surely, you must! Listen! Do you hear? The crowd in Jerusalem is the people of Avignon! Instead of letting Barabbas and the plague triumph, they beseech you to free Jesus and join saintly Marius in the Armageddon, where good destroys evil and the scourge is no more. Step up, Clément! Your people cannot be kept waiting!"

The Pontiff, always silent, made a slow movement with his arm, inviting Alice to leave him. She obeyed.

That afternoon, to her surprise, she received a message brought by a boy runner: Clément requested she attend him, within the hour.

After she had left him earlier, he drank more laudanum that served to focus his mind on their outrageous, emotional encounter. The prodigious Bible story, and the remarkable analogy drawn by his erstwhile lover, scythed through his consciousness like a thunderbolt from the heavens. The quest for revenge that lived in him for so many years, he now realised was futile and unacceptable in the eyes of God. Alice's passionate rhetoric convinced him that Barabbas should perish and goodness prevail.

She opened the door to the secret passage and entered the Pope's chamber. He sat, straight-backed, at his table. Parchments and scrolls he had out in an untidy fashion were now stacked neatly. He was shaved and wore a crisp grey cassock. The bottle of theriac and the glasses were replaced in the cupboard.

"Thank you for coming, Alice. Sit, please."

She was wary and hesitated. He repeated, in a soft tone,

"Please." She sat down without speaking.

"I would express my gratitude."

'Gratitude? These are certainly not the words of the leader of our beloved Church – he who is not known to ever humble himself thus,' she thought, perplexed.

"Your likening of the Lord's adversity, *in extremis,* to the dire world we share today moved me such that I now see there is hope!" His voice rose. "Together – my priests, my scholars, dukes, traders, sextons, magistrates, men and women, children, and beggars – will overcome this foul blight! The way forward cannot be to tolerate ourselves behind locked doors. Marius Nerval is a figure for us all to admire. He acts while too many of us prevaricate. My personal reasons for not trusting him are, from this day hence, over and done. I have issued a bull to be posted throughout the town. My churches will, again, open doors. If our townsfolk are in danger, we, in the clerical order, must expose ourselves the same. My clerics will leave their citadels and welcome my people through the hallowed portals that we battened out of fear and ignorance. Marius, Luc and the others are to be afforded our cooperation *sine qua non*. There, Alice, I have said my piece."

Hanging on his every word, she concluded, exhilarated,

"You want to express your gratitude? I implore your permission for me to call you *Holy Father*, once more."

"I grant your wish, Alice."

CHAPTER TWENTY-FOUR

AVIGNON
late October, 1348 AD

It was nearing the end of October, 1348. The temperature had fallen by several degrees to remind the people of Avignon that autumn had run its course and winter approached. The Magistrate sent for Marius and Luc to his office on the quayside.

"Come in, boys, come in." His tone was less dark than their last meeting, some two weeks earlier, which Marius found strange. He filled tankards with ale, pushed them towards his deputies, and paused while they each took a draught.

"It's a chilly morning, don't you think? As I walked here from my house the cobbles glistened and twinkled in the morning half-light, the frost only just lifting. Quite pretty...it's a pleasant time of year..." and his voice trailed off, abstraction and weariness moving his thoughts from worldly matters. The two young men drank their beer in silence, with respect for the Magistrate's standing. Working alongside him for these several months, they had come to admire his calm, authoritative, dignified demeanour. Without him, Avignon may not have survived.

"Is there a particular reason you want to see us today, Magistrate? We have duties to perform," Marius asked.

"Ah, forgive me, of course there is. I would not presume to waste your precious time otherwise. I come from an audience with the Holy

Father who has, to repeat his words, a 'grateful heart' for your efforts. He wishes me to leave you in no doubt regarding his appreciation, and he referred to you, Marius and Luc, by name – which surprised me. The responsibility of his office is a heavy burden, so, it is praise, indeed, that he is aware of your service. The town acknowledges your selfless devotion." They nodded their response. "It is a suitable moment for reflection. Our struggle against the horrendous plague continues and we cannot lower our guard. However, my lists show the daily figure for deaths is decreasing. Marius, what is your assessment?"

"My teams carry out their functions but we are not in a position to count bodies. What passes in one quarter may well be different from another. At the start, it seemed fewer people died in the east part - Rue Thiers, Rue Buffon. When folk moved there into any available houses, it became infected, as with the rest of the town."

"I understand, but take my word, the pestilence is waning. I do not know the reason, although I spoke with Maurice, a learned man, the other day, who informs me that all plagues in history died as the weather cooled. No room for complacency, mind you." His deputies listened, hanging on his every word. "Allow me to summarise. You treat our people with compassion – men, women, children benefit from your kindness, and in the most trying of times. The task is far from easy. They resent their houses shut up, and that is natural but, essential lest the bacillus spreads faster. We have enforced the curfew at dusk and we prohibit beggars and animals on the streets. The bridge is barred to prevent insalubrious foreigners entering Avignon. Any citizens deciding to leave will not be accepted back: we are privy to the wool merchants' cowardly departure, are we not? They wanted to return - should have thought about that to begin with! Marius, you are my deputy who has seen to collecting bodies, carrying them to the cathedral for burial with the shortest possible delay. An onerous undertaking, but one you have executed with genuine care for the families left behind. And you, Luc, my friend, have ensured all contaminated clothing and windings be burned – an extremely valuable contribution to our battle. You both toil, on our behalves, ignoring the risk to your persons. I am humbled in the presence of indefatigable warriors! To tell you, I am overcome!" The old man fought back tears, such was his emotion. "But, drink! Let me fill your vessels." He did so, and resumed, "I could go on and on, much have you given to us. However, I must not fail to mention our priests. With all the churches closed, they still perform their ministry – most of them – at the cathedral, conducting burial rites and hearing confessions. We cannot imagine the spiritual stress they have endured, yet they prevail! A papal bull issued this week is an indication that Clément and his clergy do not hide but join us by opening the church doors once more. We will now be able to worship, or just meditate, in our own favoured place. We are proud of them, as we are of you." The men still remained silent.

"Do you know, I am ashamed that I experience a kind of bizarre pleasure – perhaps that is the wrong word – when I examine the lists. I have maintained them from the beginning, the names, families, addresses, ages, dates, and they are a chronicle for future generations. They may be laid to rest in a communal grave but, their spirits will live on in the records I have compiled. Would that they were not needed."

Sad eyes flashed from one man to the other. They were involved at the heart of historical events to be written in the annals. Spoken words were unnecessary. They had witnessed scenes that celebrated the kindest, bravest, greatest qualities in mankind. But, to their eternal chagrin, timidity, selfishness and absence of morale had, at times, overtaken goodness. To face and manage death was possible, but to anticipate and affect human nature exceeded all capability. They drank and the Magistrate sighed,

"All the poor, despairing creatures struck by the distemper, fever, sickness – its name changes by the street, but it is the plague nonetheless – pray for divine intervention! They grow stupid or melancholy in their misery. I hear say that some wander away into the fields and woods, into secret, uncouth places – almost anywhere… creep into the bush or hedge and die." Luc, the more reserved of the two, coughed to clear his throat then, in a soft tone, said,

"I, too, have known of such happenings, and it is beyond understanding, for certain. We have lost so many children. Now, I am not learned, I cannot read nor write, and the Bible is a mystery to me. But, we are told the Good Lord is kind and loving. Indeed! I have seen precious little evidence of this! The town used to boast three midwives, gifted women in assisting births but, today, there are none. All smitten, so only unskilled handmaids are left. When they are too frightened to attend, the mother has to deliver alone. Picture that, if you can! Babes die in their mother's arms. Those that survive may drink the handmaid's milk that is tainted. I have carted off countless stillborn and the journey to the death pit breaks my heart. If the woman dies and there is no nurse, what becomes of the infant? It passes. What harm has that poor soul ever caused? A father, raving and distraught, killed his own new-born girl so she would not have to endure the same as his young son had suffered. She had not lived long enough to be sensible of any sin, much less to be punished for it! Is this not so, Magistrate?"

The justice and Marius had tears in their eyes, so powerful was Luc's testimony.

"She was innocent, Luc, no-one can deny it. The way of the Lord is, truly, a mystery that I cannot explain: if I could, then I would reside in the grand palace! However, let me come to the purpose you are here." He raised his tankard and drank more ale. "The Holy Father, this morning, has spoken of a grave matter - you may be familiar - concerning a group of persons who go under the title of *flagellants*." Blank expressions on the men's faces told him they knew nothing of this, certainly not by the word the Magistrate had used. "The reason given to me, and quite right, why this ungodly lot be driven from our town, is they break the law. Any bull delivered by the Pontiff is an edict we must enforce and, the townsfolk being good Catholics, must respect it. Anyone performing as flagellants do, in public, is a heretic, and if he does not cease his unholy practice, we are to arrest him. His Holiness finds himself in a delicate position. Shortly after his coronation he pronounced the '*act of flagellation*' to be allowed, but only within homes by those who sought atonement of their sins. In the meantime, he is cognisant that the Church has no authority over the custom, hence his now forbidding it if not done in secret. He wishes to protect his flock from unnecessary distress, for that is how onlookers would feel."

"Tell us more, do," requested Marius.

"They are religious fanatics abroad who demonstrate their extreme belief and seek forgiveness by whipping themselves, with insane force. They are known to resort to violence against those who oppose them."

"Sounds like madness to me," Luc commented.

"Ay, you put it well! The Pontiff informs me that large groups, through hunger, drought or plague, employ this flagellation for their relief. They existed in other lands, and not in Provence, until these last two months. So, you will summon a goodly number of your men – let us say one dozen – to prevent their ghastly ritual. My spies tell me they plan to occupy the Place du Palais tonight, before dusk, to avoid the curfew."

"Right under the Pope's nose then!" Luc jested.

"Hey! Not a laughing matter! But yes, it is an affront to the Holy Father if ever I saw one."

Marius, Luc and twelve of their strongest men assembled in one corner of the Palace Square. He had instructed them to come armed with a stave or cudgel in case persuasion more forceful than words was required. As the vespers bell rang, daylight was fading and the buildings around the palace grew indistinct but, evident by whispering and murmurs, groups of threes and fours already waited.

"Hold back here," Marius ordered his men, "let's see their mischief before we move in."

Muffled voices increased to become expressions of fear and amazement. From a side street a procession entered the square, but slowly, led by a tall, swarthy man. The others followed in single file, a line of some sixteen flagellants. Each wore cloths from the waist to the ankles, but otherwise, were stripped naked and went barefooted. They had on black, conical hats marked with a red cross – apart from the leader whose hat was white. In the right hand, they held a scourge with three tails. Every tail had a knot and through the middle were fixed sharp nails. As they walked forward they whipped themselves on their bare bodies, every lash cutting a bleeding furrow. They let out no sound of pain. The swarthy man chanted in his native tongue, a patois of an African land. The next four called out a litany in response, the ensuing four and so on, until the whole party of sixteen reached the middle of the square.

"Never in my life have I witnessed self-inflicted harm or weird reciting," Marius blurted through clenched teeth, shocked by such horror.

Then, they lay on the ground, stretching out their hands like the arms of a cross. The singing went on continuously as the onlookers gasped in disbelief at the bizarre spectacle unfolding before them. The last in the line stood, stepped over the nearest prostrate one under him and gave a hard stroke with his whip. This went on from the first to last until each one had observed the purification and bled from his wounds. At a sign from the leader, they rose. The chanting resumed as they began to repeat the penance anew. Marius had seen enough,

"Men, surround them, now! Raise your staves but do not strike them." His men obeyed, pushing the crowd back and facing the penitents. Marius moved forward,

"Hear me!" he bellowed, "I am the deputy magistrate in this town. My master, in turn, receives his authority from The Holy Father, Pope Clément. Your vile acts, in a public place, contravene the papal bull that is our law. This heretical flogging of your own person is punishable by internment or, worse, burning at the stake, should a curial jury so decide. Speak with your leader. You have fifteen minutes to consider. Men! Lower your staves!"

The heretics huddled under the gaze of Marius, Luc and his gang; the citizens lining the square hissed and spat at the hideous intruders. No more discussion was necessary: the flagellants stood, one behind the other, and filed out into a side street that would take them under the Porte du Rocher to the river. Seeing the weals on their backs oozing blood, heads bowed, still repeating their pitiful litany, Marius felt deep pity. That such madness to seek redemption in this manner had driven them to these extreme, penitential deeds astounded him.

"If any one of you remains come the compline bell," Marius roared, "be in no doubt, the retribution I have threatened will befall you. Be off!"

CHAPTER TWENTY-FIVE

AVIGNON
November, 1348 AD

As the tragic story of Avignon progressed to the winter month of November, the people had reason for a degree of optimism.

"Are you sure, Magistrate?" Marius asked.

"My lists tell no lies and I record every death, as you know. Monday, this week, seven were reported. Tuesday it was five, Wednesday two and today, none. I am no betting man but, if I were, I would not risk my money on the plague ceasing. We have seen rises and falls in the numbers, many times so, we need several weeks like this to be certain."

"You are right, Magistrate."

"Ay, and when there be no corpses for burial, I want you, Marius and Luc, to visit every house marked with the red cross. You will not be in danger since these houses were shut up after their family member was removed. Inspect each to confirm the residents are decent - I mean clean. There should be no winding sheet or infected bedding if we have performed our duties well. Inform me of those places you consider...mmm...wholesome. Yes, that's the word. It will not surprise you that I will compile a list. We may scrub off the infernal stain at some time in the future."

"Understood."

The men left his office looking at each other but not speaking. Was this a turning point for them, they wondered?

The Magistrate poured ale into a cup and leaned back in his chair. He was a short man, but strong and broad-shouldered. A calm, fair manner earned him the respect of the town. Unmarried, his responsibilities as a justice were his *raison d'être*. In good times, he served, helped, and punished the people. During the plague, he organised buriers, carters, grave-diggers, and spoke with confidence to pope and pauper alike. The vigour with which he ensured the preventative and remedial measures were observed belied his advancing years. His sense of duty remained steadfast. He loathed acts of cowardice, such as those of the wool merchants fleeing, and felt no compunction decreeing they be denied their return.

"When I am gone, if folk who know me say, with an honest voice, *'He attended upon us well'*, then I will sleep I peace. If those who know me not say the same, I will be, equally, satisfied."

The first three doors that Rostand knocked on brought no response. *'Perhaps the houses are untenanted or, those within are afraid to open to anybody. They bear red crosses, so it is likely the residents are dead.'*

Carel Rostand, was recognised by all Avignon as a beggar. Dressed in threadbare clothes yet, sporting an incongruous, floppy, velour hat, he accepted coins from passers-by he deemed to have the wherewithal. With the poor, he merely exchanged a 'good morning'. Marius mistrusted him at the start, perturbed by his begging on the occasion of a funeral wake in the tavern.

Tall and thin, dark eyes flashed from one person to the next, observant and skilful at the game he played. His nose and chin were slender, pinched lips revealing even, white teeth. This contradictory man was no fool, nor did he beg out of poverty: his family came from the line of the Counts of Provence. He was, although he kept it secret, wealthy. The sights he now witnessed tormented him, but he saw rays of light and hope, acts of kindness and unselfish behaviour that fuelled his optimism. The Magistrate had invested him as a deputy justice, and his pride was beyond reckoning. After some deliberation, he decided on an unusual benefit he could provide for the people – *his people* as he now called them – who came under his magisterial appointment.

The door of the fourth house, in Rue Saint-Joseph, was not marked in red, but his knock, at first, suggested it was empty. Then, but faint, he heard a whispered,

"Who is it? What do you want of us?"

"You know me not but, open up, I wish to speak with you and it will be in your interest." From the time begging, he had come across the poor as well as the rich, and society all too often ignored the former.

"You may carry the plague and, thus far, my family are not infected," the voice within said, in a quiet and tremulous tone. After a second knock, the entrance opened, but not wide enough to make out the householder.

"Sire," Rostand urged, "I have coins for you." That was sufficient persuasion for the man inside to show himself. Rostand saw three children wrestling, in fun, on the only bed in the room; a woman remained obscured in the half-light. He reached into his sack and pulled out a small purse that he held towards the man.

"What is this? Again, I say I do not know you."

The beggar found this hard to believe, but continued,

"See for yourself," Rostand invited.

Undoing the leather thong around its neck, his hand felt not one but ten gold écus! Unable to contain his joy, he gasped,

"What! Ten écus! This is surely stolen money bringing Satan's curse with it – something I can do without! Nobody...in my entire life...has given me coins...nobody! Ten écus!" he repeated, moving aside in the doorway so the woman could gape, in turn, at this unexpected, bizarre gesture. Catching his breath, he went on,

"I have no employ since the plague came, so this will save us. Now I can buy bread...the bakery still works and I know where to get vegetables...my wife makes a stew to be savoured! But, how can I repay you?"

"You will not. It's a gift."

Nodding farewell, Rostand moved on to the next house in the street, to repeat his act of benevolence to whosoever opened their door. This deed he performed for several weeks.

'I possess more money than I will ever need, and these impoverished people have little or nothing,' he decided. 'Will I continue to beg once this scourge is over? My answer is yes! There is no justification for the rich leading an easy, debt-free life while our poor souls struggle to provide basic commodities for their family. All my wealth will not be spent in a lifetime.'

Alice placed her arm around a slightly-built, weeping woman's shoulders.

"Come, let us sit a while." They were the only citizens in the grand Place du Palais, under the Pope's paternal vigilance. The secret *madam*, the owner of *Marguerite's House*, smooth skin and silky, braided hair, looked softly into the other woman's countenance. Her alluring smile and eyes that darkened almost black when angered had, however, the desired effect of calming her acquaintance. Alice was, without doubt, a beautiful creature.

Following Clément's request, she had succeeded in lying with Marius in the hideaway hut in the woods north of the cathedral. It was a frequent liaison. *'At first, I did not question the Holy Father's reason for me to seduce Marius. When the most powerful man in the Church orders you to do something, then you do it, without a second thought. But now, I've told him it has to end, enough is enough. What I mean, of course, me running to him with titbits of information. Nor will my sexual services to him continue. However, I'm too in love with Marius for our friendship to stop. Marius loves me too – even if he hasn't said it in so many words... oh, how can it end well?'* She turned her attention to the distressed lady sitting beside her.

"How does your household fare? You have lost your daughter. That much I know."

"She was a wonderful baby – her father's pride and joy, and he takes it bad, Alice. I expect a beating every time he comes home drunk.

He doesn't mean to harm me, but...it's just that...he can't believe she's gone. He thinks it's an unpleasant dream and one day he will walk in and find her still sleeping peacefully in the cot. I wonder if he blames me...like I've not cared for her as a good mother should...it's so hard..."

"I can hardly imagine your pain, but I would help if I can. With your permission, I will take your son out for the afternoon. We will play games in the forest. It's the only thing I can offer, but it will give you some respite."

"Alice, I accept, and with gratitude."

"So, I will come to your house within the hour."

She often met Marius at the hut – nay, daily. *'Would that Dominique was no longer around, she thought, but that is not the case and I am resigned to never have him for mine own.'*

Later, on her way to the woman's abode, she called in at *Marguerite's House,* to ensure all was well and her girls were plying their trade as they should. *'It's strange, but as the plague rages, so my takings rise. Business thrives yet, now, I find I am comforting the same wretched women whose husbands purchase the services my ladies provide. Nothing is simple in these times.'*

Best friends, Edmond Nerval, had beaten Clément – or Pierre Roger as he was then - cruelly, when he was thirteen. Humiliated and incensed, he carried the event in his heart over the years. He resented the absence of any punishment for Edmond inflicting such violence on him. The desire for vengeance accompanied him always – from novice monk to head of the Holy Roman Catholic Church. When he heard the name *Nerval,* as if from out of nowhere, he realised at once it had to be the same family and, if not Edmond himself, an offspring. Contriving a meeting with Marius to confirm his suspicion, he wove a scheme to slake his thirst for revenge, using his mistress, Alice, as bait. The plan was to destroy Marius' marriage.

He was a good pope. Intellectual, well-read and artistic – his private papal library was the most extensive of its kind. He loved music and fine wine. But, thanks to Edmond, his broken body pained him still and he drank the potent laudanum, initially for relief, but it soon became an addiction. Over-indulgence led to depression, rapture, paranoia and hallucinations. By nature a shy man, and sermons challenged him: laudanum gave confidence to face a congregation.

'If not for Alice showing me my weakness, I would yet be despising Marius and blurring my mind through drink. When I poured the contents of the bottle into the commode, I pledged never to sup again. I have forgiven Edmond, through his son, and I will spend my remaining days, if granted by the Supreme Being, preaching the message of hope and love. The Lord has pardoned my sins, my dark quest for retribution. Laudate Dominum.'

Luc Charron, a decent, young man with a strong handshake and ready smile, understood the pain of family bereavement. His baby son, Fabien, died at the onset of the plague. This sad event, rather than plunging him into a downward spiral of mourning, moved him to serve alongside Marius. He said to his wife, Marianne, after the boy's funeral,

"We were not prepared for our lives to be affected in this way. Well, stricken we may be, but broken, not! I will fight this scourge to honour Fabien's name." This he did with distinction and courage. Under an apprenticeship mentored by the stone-yard foreman, Christian, he became a master stonemason.

Marcel Duval, the short, rotund innkeeper, repulsed Marius when he touted for custom on the occasion of a burial. He made unwanted advances towards Alice one day when they were alone in the tavern. But, as with so many other characters, the evil of the plague brought out the best in them. Marcel refused to accept payment from his customers for ale. A barrel of his renowned cider rested on a wooden cradle on the bar top for anyone to serve themselves, and for free. He considered,

'I have made enough money from my trade. The pestilence has spared my own family thus far, but it is not so for many of my patrons. If drinking my ale or cider distracts them from their worries, just for one evening, I am satisfied.'

The wool merchants and partner – Jean, Thomas and Bruno – were refused entry back to the town after they had fled in cowardly disgrace. They had to live on their barge, moored at the far end of the quay. Their bull-necked, muscular bargee, Mahi, on a daily basis, pushed a cart, laden with baskets of fruit, vegetables, eggs, hams and salt-beef, up and down the streets. The produce was left on the doorsteps for people who dared not or were forbidden to set foot outside. The three traders headed off boats on the river and asked for donations of food supplies *'for the miserable folk of Avignon.'* They assembled them into piles on the quayside, much as they did with bales of wool. Mahi filled the baskets and distributed them on the men's behalves. Maybe, one day, they would be allowed to return and resume trading.

The debt of gratitude, owed to Marius Nerval by the citizens of Avignon, was immeasurable. This generous, hard-working, loving man exposed himself to the bacillus of the contagion day by day, week by week, month by month. He touched, wrapped, lifted, carted and buried corpses, all innocent victims in his eyes, executing the office conferred on him by the Magistrate. It was not his fault to have fallen in love with Alice. On the last day of November, two priests sat on the bench inside the lychgate, capes and cowls pulled tight against the bitterly icy early morning. They waited, every day, to receive bodies for interment. The number was dwindling.

"Nobody today, then," one priest observed, his teeth chattering from the cold.

"No, and it seems that's the way it's going, thank the Lord," replied the other.

"Amen to that. But say, we have not seen Marius for these last two days, have we?"

"Now you mention it, we have not."

They fell silent for a few minutes, deep in prayer. The sound of someone approaching ended their meditation. It was the young Nerval, cradling a body in his arms.

"Ah, good morning, just the one?"

He did not reply. He gently laid the figure, wound in shining white damask, on the bench opposite the priests.

"Do you know the name? The Magistrate likes to include a name in his lists." The priest stopped short when he saw Marius' eyes well up with tears that streamed down his face. He gathered himself, to explain,

"The name is Nerval, Dominique Nerval, my wife."

The priest's jaw dropped, confused, barely able to take in what he had just heard, and he regretted speaking in so casual a manner.

"She became ill two days ago and I stayed indoors to nurse her, but there was no doubt the illness was...it was only a matter of time. The end came quickly, during the night, and she did not seem to be in great distress, but who can say? I will bear her into the cathedral where I beseech you to pray for her soul. Then, I will accompany her to the grave."

That day, news of Dominique's demise soon spread around the town. Alice visited the Nerval house, without delay.

EPILOGUE

January, 1349 AD

By the fourth consecutive week of January, 1349, no deaths were reported to the Magistrate. A declaration, issued and signed jointly by Pope Clément V1 and the Justice, declared the plague had expired. The original version of the document, together with the Magistrate's extensive, methodical lists of the deceased, was deposited, for posterity, in the papal library of the Pope's Palace. Guards posted copies in every square, street corner and public building. Gradually, the town regained the prosperity and contentedness it had enjoyed before the disease visited it. Householders scrubbed their doors clean of the red cross, leaving no indication of the horror that had unfolded within. However, they were nervous: the thought that it might return, without warning, just as it had arrived, was not far from their minds. The plague deprived Avignon of two thousand men, women and children: nearly one half of its population.

The authorities proclaimed a day of great rejoicing and thanksgiving, culminating in singing, dancing and unbridled merriment on the Saint Bénézet bridge. Marcel set out tapped barrels of ale, cider, and cups for people to drink their fill. A hog roasted on a spit over white-hot coals. Troubadours sang songs and ballads about love and valour in battle. There were jugglers and magicians, musicians playing the lute, drums, bells and cymbals. Joyous sounds rang out over the river Rhône to the north, to the south. Boats passing under the arches heard and broadcast the good news to all greater France! The jubilant citizens, wearing their best clothes - since they could not remember when - cavorted and jigged about with gay abandon. They performed country dances, caroles, rounds and saltarellos, with steps, kicks and jumps, either measured or out of time due to an excess of ale.

Following a service of praise in the cathedral, the good and great of Avignon, with a liking of the spiritual, entered the bridge to join their brothers and sisters already celebrating. Clément led the procession, a brass cross held aloft, with pride. His purple, velvet mozzetta, edged in gold braid, covered his shoulders and cassock. The Magistrate, next in line, wore his black tunic and green floppy hat - signs of his office. Alice was hardly noticed among the lower orders, in her best white embroidered gown and rich silk scarf. She walked hand in hand with Marius, young Fabien toddling, doing his best to keep up. The couple would live happily in *Marguerite's House* – no longer a brothel and soon to lose its infamous name – as one family.

Dusk neared, and Marius leaned on the parapet, gazing over the waters of the Rhône, considering the glowing silhouette of old Avignon town, a cup of ale in his hand. A soft noise caused him to turn round. It was Clément. He spoke first,

"It is truly a wonderful day, do you not think, Marius?"

"Eminence, it is."

"I have sought you out to say…" and he hesitated, "I once knew your father, but…I forgive *you* your sins."

"How so?"

"Do not be concerned, my son, I grant absolution to all. Did you not know that?"

"I thank the Holy Father." Marius did not comprehend why he had been chosen thus, in person. Clément's conscience was now clear: he was at peace with Edmond.

Festivities continued into the night. Flaming torches illuminated the revellers, rendering their joy yet more intense despite the January cold.

The troubadours sang, the musicians played and, for certain, the inhabitants of Avignon danced on the bridge.

The office of Justice came to Marius upon the death of the Magistrate, in 1351, at the ripe age of seventy-nine. Alice learned the skills of midwifery and delivered countless babies: for her, every new birth was cause to be joyous and thankful for her calling and domestic bliss.

Pope Clément V1 passed away, after a short illness, in December, 1352, the eleventh year of his reign, aged sixty-one. Someone heard Marius say,

"He had the reputation of a fine gentleman, a prime munificent, a patron of the arts and learning, but no saint."

On the occasion of his passing, Avignon's people congregated once more, to praise his life. And, as forty-five years before, **they danced on the bridge.**

THE END
John Bentley
Heckington, March 2018.

Dear reader,

We hope you enjoyed reading *And They Danced Under The Bridge*. Please take a moment to leave a review in Amazon, even if it's a short one. Your opinion is important to us.

Discover more books by John Bentley at https://www.nextchapter.pub/authors/john-bentley

Want to know when one of our books is free or discounted for Kindle? Join the newsletter at http://eepurl.com/bqqB3H

Best regards,
John Bentley and the Next Chapter Team

You might also like:

In The Name Of The Mother by John Broughton

To read first chapter for free, head to:
https://www.nextchapter.pub/books/in-the-name-of-the-mother

Made in the USA
Monee, IL
28 April 2021